Goldsmiths University lecturers and tutors, especially Senior Lecturer in Creative Writing Maura Dooley who accepted me on the Masters program without any formal qualifications.

Rick Copeman and Hannah Ferguson (fellow Goldsmiths students), for their clever and sensible feedback.

Jose Catalan for so much.

Greg Jones, Editorial Director at Running Press, for always answering my emails.

Patrick Merla, for his eternal support.

Don Weise, who edited this book, my autobiography, and my previous novel, for being a joy to work with and never giving up on me.

"*Our culture has lent dark powers to narratives of drug use, more than to drug use itself, and I am taking advantage of them, like a painter using the severity of northern light.*"
—Ann Marlowe, How to Stop Time

1

"Had enough?" said David.

Ryan slid a rucksack half his size off his shoulder and onto the front porch. "Very enough!"

"*Very* enough. Is that how the kids are talking now?"

"For over a decade."

"You're looking . . ." David paused. The chaotic colour from the flowers in the garden framed Ryan's airbrushed looking features. " . . . Pretty as a picture."

"And you look like a Ken doll. All you need is a pie in your hands and you could upgrade to a Stepford husband."

"If you're referring to my baby blue gingham shirt, yeah it's a bit too quaint, but it's my favorite, a present from my Man."

"Oh! Speaking of heavenly He-Men how is Joe?"

"He's . . ." David tried to find the right word and drifted off for a moment. " . . . *Joe.*"

"Wow! Could you be any more in love?"

"I try, but I think I've peaked. Anyway, what happened exactly?"

"When?"

"At home."

"Mum found some pot in my jacket."

"And?"

"Big deal, right?" Bothered by the memory of this Ryan shifted his weight from one leg to the other and sighed. "Are you going you make me stand out here all day?"

"I'm sorry and *you're* cheeky!"

"You love it."

"Well, I love you," said David. "So I guess I love it."

"That's why I'm here."

David took Ryan by the hand and said, "Come in. And give me that rucksack. It looks heavy."

"It is. I didn't know how long I'd be away."

"Well, we'll talk about all that later. I'll stick this here for now" David said putting the rucksack at the bottom of the stairs. "And you can take it up later." He kept on talking as he guided Ryan into a huge living room. "It's a generational thing, I think . . . With your mum, I mean."

"She's only a year older than you." Then acknowledging the décor, "And wow! This room's crazier than ever."

"Yeah," said David both responding to Ryan's comment about his mum and the way the room, looked. "But she's a different species."

"She's your sister. Same blood."

"More important though she's a parent,"

"And we know they're from *Planet Freaky*. I like this

paving on the floor, it's like outside in."

"Right!" David tried to relate to Ryan as a youngster talking about his mother, and at the same time not feel offended as he listened to somebody straight talking about the decor. "But!"

"Does there have to be a *but*?"

"Hold that tongue Young Man. Don't be blasphemous! The butt is sacred. What would we gays do without them?"

"I don't know." Ryan rubbed his chin in a comical way, yet still considered the question seriously. "Stand up?"

"Anyway, back to the less important thing I was going to say. *But* . . . I don't need to tell you how much she loves you, do I?"

"No, so don't. It's not what I want to hear right now. Just humor me."

"Okay. Well you're fine here until this blows over."

Ryan took hold of David's arm. "Listen, I appreciate this."

"Shut up, you soft bugger. I couldn't have you sleeping on the street."

The living room smelled of fresh paint. It had, as long as Ryan could remember. "Some things don't change", said Ryan looking around the room. "And by that I mean this house looks completely different, but just as mental every time."

"That's Joe for you," said David. He noticed that Ryan still held onto his arm, but he didn't mind. "Anyway, are you going to give me a hug?"

"Of course, I'm sorry. Come here."

They pulled together. Anybody watching would have

thought them lovers, not friends, and definitely not rel-
atives.

"Do you hug all your male friends like this?" David
asked.

"If they're as cute as you are. I don't do un-models."

"Oh shit! I haven't modelled for a while now. Am I
still good enough?"

"Once a model, always a model. Just because you
went from London, New York, Paris and Milan to
Hampstead house-husband, you can't just shake off your
heritage."

"Oh great!" said David with sarcasm in his voice.
Then his tone changed to one of concern, "Look, come
sit here." He led Ryan to large emerald green velvet sofa.
Directly opposite was another sofa that looked just the
same.

"Why so much seating?" said Ryan, flopping down.
"Jesus Christ Almighty!" he added. "Comfy!"

"It's goose down."

"You're kidding."

Embarrassed by the decadence David nodded his
head apologetically. On the floor beside the other sofa
Ryan noticed several beer cans and what looked like a
couple of discarded paper wraps from some drug.
Knowing David and Joe, he guessed it was cocaine.

"I see you like your beer," said Ryan.

"I'm afraid so."

"Me too."

"You drink?"

"Yes!" said Ryan intending to prove that he was adult
enough, but only showing that he was still young
enough to think it made him seem older.

"Whoa! A proper person."

"Not *so* proper." At this, Ryan laid back in a cocky way. He put one hand behind his head and hooked the thumb of his other hand into the waistband of his worn out jeans.

This sequence of actions made David feel weird, and he took a moment to understand what was happening to him. When he realised that he felt aroused, it came as a question, an answer, and a surprise. With seamless timing, he managed to mask his reaction by raising one eyebrow and saying with a patronising tone, "Well, I'll get you a beer from the kitchen and when I get back you can shock me rigid with an anecdote or two." Slightly taken aback Ryan turned away with a huff. David's eyes automatically skimmed over his nephew's body, noticing a thread bare t-shirt that had risen up just enough to reveal a toned tummy and the tip of some golden pubic hair. Full of conflicted thoughts and feelings, suddenly David stood up and said, "So, beer it is!" Then he headed towards the kitchen while his confusion developed into anxiety. "Make yourself comfortable," he added to distract himself from his own thoughts and feelings.

"That's not difficult on this sparrow down sofa." Ryan settled into its welcome and rubbed his cheek against the soft fabric. After enjoying the physical sensation of the texture, he turned his attention to the decor. At the far left of the room was a huge window with a chemical blue wooden frame with purple and black striped shutters. Directly under the window was an old iron bench. This was all set against a faecal-brown wall that Ryan assumed must have been some kind of decor irony.

To the right hand corner of this wall was a solid looking wooden chair with a seat covered in some kind of reptile skin. He thought it looked twisted, moody, and masculine, despite the obsessive attention to fuck with colour. At the opposite end of the room, hundreds of typed sheets of paper covered the entire wall. Between these, and directly in front of Ryan was a pale green expanse, in the centre of which, outlined by a two inch glossy red line was an enormous flat screen TV. To the right of this, was the sofa that faced Ryan. He tilted his head back to check out the wall directly behind him, and saw inch wide vertical stripes, a combination of all the other colours in the room.

When David returned, Ryan picked up the conversation where they'd left it, "Yeah, sixteen, so don't mess with me."

"I wouldn't. Child Services would take you away from me. And that would break my heart."

"Hey, less of the *child*, if you don't mind."

"Oh that's right, you're sixteen." David handed Ryan a can of beer.

"Nice one!"

David got onto the sofa, layback and put his feet up on Ryan's lap. "Cheers Kid. Oops sorry . . . It's just an expression."

"I know. Don't get all paranoid."

Ryan opened his can, tipped it to toast David, and drank. Since Ryan was eight years old, David had seen him nearly every year. Still, it surprised him that his nephew was turning into a man. Not just any man, but one with a slim waist, smooth hairless suntanned skin, and striking hazel eyes. His hair was about four inches long, and because the sun had lightened it, he looked like a surfer. With a slight erotic charge, David watched Ryan's Adam's apple move up and down as he swallowed.

"Do you feel different now you're a man?" David wondered if he'd voiced the word *man* in a creepy way. He hoped to obscure his apparent attraction, and so after taking several large gulps of beer he forced a burp, but this made him feel more self-conscious because he knew it was so out of character.

Oblivious to David's concern about what shade he might have laid on the word *man*, Ryan began to massage one of David's feet.

"Please don't patronise me," said Ryan acting as though he'd said it thousands of times before.

"Sorry, puppy."

"There you go again."

"I didn't, did I?"

"You said *Puppy*."

"It's a term of affection. You've got to let me call you that."

"Oh okay," said Ryan "Anyway, where's Joe?"

"He's gone to the West End with some kid."

"Bitter?"

"No. I just don't know his name."

"I saw the Levi's ad he did. That was so cool."

"Yeah, Joe's cool all right," David said with a note of irony.

"There's that tone in your voice again."

"I'm just a bit down. I could do with a holiday."

"So why don't you have one?" Ryan seemed genuinely sincere, which touched David.

"When'd you get *so* adorable?"

Ryan responded with an expression he knew was cute. "Who me?" he said, feigning surprise and humility.

"Yes *you*! Getting back to what you were asking. The main reason I don't go away is work." David paused, as he thought about what he'd said. "But I'm sure somebody would be happy enough to pick up my shifts." This thought made him rub his feet together.

Ryan understood rubbing feet as happy thoughts. "So go," he said as encouragement.

"And you won't have a party when I'm away?"

"Of course not."

"Of course *you would*. You act as if I was never young."

"You were young?"

"In the Eighties. Or Seventies."

"Keep going."

"The Sixties?"

"Try Fifties."

"Give me a break," said David, prodding Ryan's ribs with his feet.

"Ow! Stop! Stop! Please!"

"Well you stop being so cheeky." He climbed on top of Ryan. "I didn't know you were so ticklish. "Prepare to die, or say you're sorry."

"Okay. Okay." Ryan pleaded. "I'm sorry."

"Really though. How old did you think I was?"

Ryan squinted, and then his face shone with a smile. "What really?"

"Don't you dare," said David.

"You know I dare."

"That's what I hate about you," he said, acting angry.

Then he paused and his voice softened. "And love."
David stood up again, walked over, and closed over the
shutters on the window. "I'm hot," he said. Then to clar-
ify. "The sun's a bit intense this time of day." On his
return, he knelt between Ryan's legs. Then he rested his
elbows on his Ryan's knees, and for a moment couldn't
help wondering how much, if anything, Ryan was aware
of David's underlying feelings for him. "How was your
journey? Did you have any problems with the tube?"

"No, but it took ages."

"That's the Northern Line for you."

"You think there'd be a special service for their
Hampstead clientele. A high-speed train."

"Get recent. London underground, spend money?"

"Sorry," said Ryan, and was amused that David said
get recent. "I'm not up with your big city ways."

"You country kids are so cute."

"I hardly think Manchester's classed as country."

"Where is that place, anyway?" David asked playfully. With this, he hooked his arms under Ryan's knees
and lifted his legs in the air.

"What place?" Ryan laughed. "You going to fuck me
now?"

David played along. "Maybe . . . I meant that
Manfester place you mentioned. I *have* heard of it, I
think. "You must take me sometime. While I'm there I'll
visit Judy."

Ryan set down his beer. "It's odd hearing her called
that."

"What should I call her?"

"Mum."

"It would be a bit twisted calling my sister mum.

Don't you think?"

"That would suit you."

"Enough," said David using Ryan's legs to lean on as he stood up. "You're too quick for your own good."

"That's what my girlfriend says. Too quick!"

"*Girlfriend*?"

"Yeah! Not everyone's gay."

David sat down on the sofa and put his arm around Ryan's shoulders.

"You're very touchy feely," said Ryan without a trace of humour.

"What, too much?"

Ryan thought for a moment, "No." Then he grinned. "Aren't you getting enough?"

"I've no idea. Got no benchmark."

"Arh! Sweet Man." Ryan cuddled into David's chest, and then to comfort him further, he stroked David's tummy like a pet. This simple action created a more complex reaction, which ignited in David's brain, fluttered while moving from his chest to his gut, then rushed down to his groin where it pulsed. Spooked a bit, David withdrew and reached for a cushion to cover his crotch. "Here put your head on this Puppy. You must be tired."

"Thanks Dad." Ryan paused thoughtfully. "You know sometimes I wish you really were my dad."

"*Your boyfriend*, thought David. "Me too," he said instead.

"I love you."

"Me you too. Anyway, what's she called? The girlfriend."

"Her name's Leila, but she answers to Baby, Foxy, or

Slut, depending on her mood."

"You mean *your* mood."

"Oh no, not with Leila." Now Ryan stared off into space. His gaze wasn't dreamy like David's but looked more intense and exhilarated. "She's a model," he continued distracted by the picture in his head.

"Shit! You weren't kidding about not doing un-models."

Ryan looked serious. "I wouldn't kid about such an important thing."

Leila had been brought up Jewish, although she was Persian in origin. She was extremely intelligent, and beautiful, a tentative combination in itself, but added to this she had an at-times-childlike-but-always-rebellious nature and a changeful personality. Ryan liked the blend he knew as Leila, finding her enigmatic and so intriguing. The thing that attracted him most was that she was kooky.

Once, when modelling for Vivienne Westwood, she went on the catwalk drinking whiskey from a bottle. Then when she stopped in front of the photographers, she lifted her skirt to show them she wasn't wearing underwear. Somebody must have intervened, because she never came back on.

Leila was six feet tall; hardly the tallest model working but she had a distinctive quality about her. She held and carried herself in a unique way that was compelling to watch. Her lips, eyes and face shape all verged on average, but this generally worked to her advantage, because make-up artists could make her look any way they chose. Still it was her manner that set her apart from her pears, and so despite her behaviour in

Westwood's show, she was still booked season after season. Bookers and designers alike never seemed to get tired of her.

The coolest of people usually wanted to be near, with, or preferably in Leila, but her interests lay mainly with one person; Ryan. Generally, she couldn't get enough of his time, and attention but most of all his affection. She mothered the boyish, sweet, and unaffected him. While at the same time respected and looked up to him, especially when he protected and guided her. They had a tight relationship; both intimate, and sure. When Ryan died his hair green, Leila did too, and when he shaved his head, so did she. Invariably they looked stunning as a couple. They had been seeing each other a little over a year. Leila often tried and succeeded in impressing Ryan. She knew he liked unusual behaviour, so played up to this. One of her favourite tricks was to shock strangers. When entering a busy café, she would stand in the middle of it and lift her skirt over her head. Usually nobody complained. Women tended to pull a sympathetic expression, or look away. Men simply stared, embarrassed, confused, and excited.

Another of her favourites acts might follow immediately afterwards. She'd sit next to somebody, sometimes at a table full of people. Putting her head in her hand, and resting on one elbow, she'd stare at the food they were eating. She'd lick her lips, not taking her eyes off the plate in front of them. After a short time, the people who were eating would usually offer her their food. Other times, she'd wait until they were finished eating, then ask if she could have their leftovers. If they said yes, she'd slide the plate in front of her, and using their fork, would finish their meal. Predictably, several cafés banned her. Still, Ryan encouraged her behaviour, thinking it was funny.

When Leila had her head shaved, she took to wearing a long red curly wig. On close inspection, it was obviously not real hair, but from a few feet away it was surprisingly deceptive. When stopped at a red light, other drivers would always look to see who was driving. This is when Ryan took hold of the wig, from the bottom, out of sight. Slowly, he'd pull at the wig so it slid back, off Leila's head. Sometimes, she would pretend nothing had happened, simply turn towards those watching and smile. Other times, she would face the other drivers, put both her hands to her head and scream.

Leila had a scar in the middle of her chest, two inches under the base of her neck. She liked to wear *V-necks*, so it showed clearly. No matter how glamorous a dress she was wearing. It was never covered. The way it was displayed felt as though she was saying, 'so what!' She lived off a large allowance given her by her parents, so had enough money to have it removed, but preferred to keep it.

"I like her," said Ryan.

"Sounds serious."

"I didn't use the L word."

"Everyone knows," David added as he leaned forward and whispered into Ryan's ear. "*Like* is a euphemism."

"Give me a break."

"Sorry! Don't straight guys *do* love?"

Ryan smirked. "No, it's so Victorian. Why? Do gays?"

"Of course not," said David and put his hands behind his head. We're famous for our fickle relationships and proud of them too."

"Oh, yeah! I saw the movie *Cruising.*"

"It's all we do, you know."

Ryan gave the room a swift once over with his eyes. "*That*, and decorate."

"Yeah, but you have to admit, we do it well."

"What, decorate or cruise?"

Now David looked around at the décor, but gestured more subtly with his eyes. "Cruise, of course."

"Hey Buddy! You're not being very comfortable."

How do you know how I *feel*? thought David. However, he opted to voice a different question, "So? What's going to happen with Leila now?"

"She said she'd move down here as well. Manfester's too small for her, anyway."

"We'll have to meet her first, but she could always stay here until you both get settled."

"Cool!"

"Don't mention anything to her yet. First, let me have a word with Joe."

"God that would be so great."

"*Room*, we've got," said David, using a caricature of a Jewish accent.

"What rooms they are." With his beer still in his hand, Ryan got up and walked over to the wall with the writing on it.

"What is this?"

"A fairytale." David looked suddenly nervous.

"I won't make the obvious joke."

"You'd be the first not to."

Inspecting the paper more closely Ryan asked, "Who wrote it?"

"Joe. You might recognise it. I read it to you when you were a kid."

"No, I don't remember," said Ryan, and paused. He read a little. "Nice idea."

"Thanks. It was Christmas, the first time you visited. I read it to you in bed."

"Aah Stop! You're making me feel all fuzzy."

"You loved it at the time."

"No doubt," said Ryan with his back to David. "It looks sweet, but I *really* can't remember."

"Really?" David smiled, but this betrayed how he felt inside.

Sorry I'll read it sometime, and see if it jolts my memory," Ryan said with a sip on his beer." But, why on the wall?"

"I haven't a clue. It was Joe's idea." David paused, seemingly distracted. "He likes how it looks, I guess."

"Now *he's* a funny one."

"Yeah, creative," said David...

"That sounds like you're referring to his sexuality, or what he likes to do in bed."

"Well, I guess it covers all bases."

"Spare me the details," Ryan said with a wave of his hand.

"You're the one who brought it up."

"Actually, I'd love to know what you get up to."

"Really?" David folded his arms, but only for a moment before. He needed a prop again and so reached once more for his beer.

"It's interesting for me," said Ryan with his attention still on the writing. "I haven't a clue, you know. What's the weirdest thing you guys have done?"

"Joe's not weird," said David. Then, almost wistfully, "He's quite vanilla actually."

Ryan turned, and joined David again on the sofa. "Ah, come on! Give me something juicier than that."

"Well, it would have to be somebody else then."

"So download," said Ryan clearly prepared to focus. "I'm ready."

"I used to see this man called Rob."

"Rob . . . Good. We have a name . . . And?" said Ryan joking, but a little impatient too.

"He used to like to take *Rohypnol*, that's a sleeping tablet."

"I know. Do you think I was born yesterday?"

"No. The day before. Anyway, it's hard to get hold of now."

"You've just got to know the right people."

"And do you?" asked David sceptically.

"My man can get me any shit I want," said Ryan with an admirable Brooklyn accent. David was a little surprised. Ryan dropped it seamlessly and continued, "Anyway, what about Rob?"

"Oh yeah. Rob." David paused and wondered if he should censor the anecdote, he was about to tell for his nephew. He didn't. "We'd take enough to knock us out. It usually took three or four to do the trick properly."

"So what's so fun about sleeping?"

"Only one of us would sleep. The other would do whatever he wanted."

"I get you."

"I mean whatever."

"Did you do it to him?"

"Oh yes."

"What did you do?"

"Are you sure you want to hear this?"

"Why wouldn't I?"

"Sorry, I mean, am I sure you want to hear this?"

"You should be. You know what a culture dog I am. If I haven't done it, or can't do it myself, I sure as hell want to hear all about it, especially the inside story."

"Exactly how inside do you want to get?"

"Does it involve poo?"

"No!" said David covering his mouth and holding his stomach as though about to vomit.

"Bum holes?"

"Of course there'll be bum holes," said David. "Do you think we'd sketch each other then clean house until the other woke?"

"Phew!" As long as there are bum holes it's bound to be good."

The fact that Ryan was so bold in joking about sex turned David off, as it made him feel freakish and side-show. Also, it was too upfront, not innuendo enough.

"So give me the scoop."

"Uh, graphic visual." The more they spoke, the less attractive David felt, but Ryan looked so enthusiastic and he obviously wasn't going to let up, so David did as Ryan asked, but in a matter of fact way, and without his usual sparkle he said, "Well, I'd play with him, then fuck him."

"Jesus!"

"Now, it all seems a bit dull and pointless."

"Did you let him do it to you?"

"Probably," said David, hoping that by sounding jaded it would bore Ryan, but Ryan was intent on milking David and knelt beside him as though begging for scraps.

"He could have done anything though."

"Uhm. I thought it was sexy at the time."

"You'd think," said Ryan, and sat back down into the sofa.

"Funny. . ." David turned to look at Ryan who seemed to be lost in thought. " . . . I had thought that the idea still turned me on."

"It does me."

"Really?" said David with curiosity.

Ryan didn't notice. "Yeah, I'll have to try it some-time."

"When?" David's heart raced.

"Dunno," said Ryan, turning and looking David in the eye. "I'll have to see if she's into the idea first."

"Right, of course."

2

"My place," said Flora and paused to check her watch. "Eight o'clock."

"Sure."

"Okay. See you later."

"Flora?"

"Yes?" she said doodling on a scrap of paper beside the phone.

"I'm really looking forward to seeing you."

"Good," she said and smiled at his earnest declaration, then put the receiver down. For a moment, she stared at her reflection in the computer screen, lost in thoughts of sex and summer. Then she licked her thumb and wiped at some dirty fingerprints.

The phone rang again.

"Flora?" It was the same voice as before.

"This better be good," she said, half teasing.

"Do you like me?"

"I'll show you tonight, eight o'clock. Bye." They both hung up.

Finished for today Flora switched off her computer, and left her studio. On her way home she stopped off at the gym, and then popped round to see her drug dealer. By the time she arrived home, it was seven o'clock, so she just had time to eat quickly, and get ready.

The doorbell rang. Flora walked to the door, while at the same time she reached back under her blouse to fasten her bra. She was having trouble.

"Fuck!" she said, gave up, reached for the door handle, and pulled it open aggressively.

"Madame," said a man, with an exaggerated French accent. He stood leaning against the door surround, and filled most of the space within it, in both height and width. In one hand, he had a large bottle of vanilla vodka and in the other a bottle of champagne. His head was facing down, yet he looked up. This gave him the appearance of a classic screen hunk, complete with thick black wavy hair and dense stubble, the kind that is still visible even after shaving.

"Hey cutie," said Flora as though he were a little boy. She paused and ran a hand absent-mindedly through her short brown hair. "You clean-up well." Then spotting the labels on the bottles, "Absolut and Dom Perignon. Classy!" Despite her approval, still she frowned reaching for her bra clasp again.

"Have I caught you at a bad time?"

"No, it's just this fucking bra."

"Let me help," he said stepping inside her home.

Flora continued with the clasp. "I want to do it up, not take it off."

"Would I?"

"Err. Yes!" she said with a laugh. "If you're the stud I invited. I hope so."

The man was flattered. "No really! Let me help."

She paused and looked him straight in the eye. "Seriously though, is there any point? It'll be coming off soon."

"Now, that's the kind of talk I like," he said with a smile, and set the bottles down on the marble coffee table.

"That's if you're horny." Flora paused for a reaction, and she got one. It was positive. She pulled him towards her, wanting to toy with him rather than offer real affection. "Would you like that?" She held him close, but somehow her embrace lacked authenticity.

"Sir yes sir!"

Flora looked amused and said, "I think I like that."

"Sir yes sir!"

"Yes, let's keep it."

"Sir . . ."

Flora cut him off and pushed her lover away. "*Okay*! I'm over it already."

The man didn't reply, only put his head down and looked hurt. Seeing this, Flora softened, "Oh, come on, Cutie," she said. "Do you want a coffee, a drink, a line of crystal?"

"Ugh! I don't know how you can drink that coffee shit. It keeps me up all night. Just some crystal, please."

"That's my boy."

Flora went to a near-by table. There was a mirror on it, with two big lines already prepared.

"After you," said Flora. "Go for the burn."

The man picked up a gold tube beside the mirror, bent down, and snorted hard. Flora stood behind, looking at his butt.

"Nice view," she said, and got hold of his hips.

He turned round and pulled her close. "This way's okay, as well. I hope."

"I rather like the other, but I've got plans for that later."

"What plans?"

"You'll see."

"What are you up to?"

With her gold tube in hand; Flora bent her knees to one side in a ladylike way. "I said, you'll see." As she came up, she held a finger against each nostril. "Ouch!"

"You're telling me," said the man, hovering behind her.

"Would you like some bubbly?"

"*Oui*, Madame." He took off his jacket.

Flora poured a drink, knocked back the first, and then immediately poured another. She handed one to the man, then took hold of his hand and led him across the room. She pushed him onto the sofa, knelt over him, and unbuttoned her blouse. Her bra was sheer blue and still unfastened.

"Jesus! You look fuck . . ."

Flora cut the man off in mid-sentence. "You can stop there.

"Okay you look fuck."

Flora leaned forward so her breasts touched his lips. "You're so sweet."

Muffled and excited the man looked up and said, "Can I add *able* to the end of that *fuck*?"

"It's not necessary. *Fuck's* fine. I think I get your gist."

Beautifully choreographed, Flora took off her blouse and swung once around her head as though on a rodeo. Then she stood up off the man, put her wrists together, lowered her hands, and let her bra slide off. Next, she unzipped her skirt, let it drop, stepped out of it, and nudged it to one side. Now she stood in a pair of black high-heeled shoes, and a pair of seamless tights that were the same blue colour as the bra. The man stared at her without her clothes on, his eyes lingering, his dick swelling as he mesmerized by the view. He caught Flora's eye, and for a split second, he thought he saw indecision, even vulnerability. This wasn't something he expected to find. It made his dick hard.

"You're so goddamn fuck."

"Less talk," said Flora as she knelt back down over the man. "And more action." As though to instruct, she kissed him. Then she straightened up, took hold of one of her breasts, and aimed it towards his lips. "Nice," she said as his mouth closed around her nipple. She felt sensational and let the weight of her body press against him.

"Mm!"

"Suck on mama's nipple."

"Mm, mm, mm!"

"Yeah. There's a good boy."

Flora pulled away. "You're hungry for that nipple, hey? Crystal will make Baby so piggy." Flora held his face in between her hands and looked at him. Was there a boy in the hunk she saw before her? Or was he simply a horny man who knew what he wanted and how to work a woman like Flora to get it? She opted for the latter as it was much sexier to her, and driven on by this idea she squashed his cheeks together, making his lips pucker. Unable to resist them she leant forward and opened her mouth around them. This turned into a long and passionate kiss. Her tongue went deep into his mouth and she groaned. Then unexpectedly she pulled away and got off the man's lap.

"Let's do another line."

"Whatever mama wants."

"*That's my boy!*"

Again, she swigged back a glass of champagne and poured another. When the man bent over, Flora reached round from behind, undid the button, and unzipped his fly. She pulled his jeans down over his solid thighs and knelt, taking them to his ankles.

"Off with these," she said.

The man stepped out of his jeans. Flora came back up and did the same to his underpants. When she came up, she leant over his back and took hold of one of his arse cheeks. Then she straightened up, leant back, and looked down. The man's butt was tight, perfectly round and where his Speedos had covered him from the sun, his cheeks glowed white.

"Jesus! Your bum is good enough to eat."

"So eat it."

"*So*, bend over."

The man bent over the table again. He used the back of his hands to support his chin. Flora knelt down and kissed his butt.

"You're fucking hot," he said.

"You ain't seen nothing yet."

Flora ran her tongue down his crack.

"My God," the man gasped.

"Let's go into the bedroom," said Flora, and passed him his glass.

"Actually," he said. "I fancy a vodka."

"Good idea!"

She poured and drank two large shots then headed towards the bedroom, taking the champagne with her. She pushed open the door with her hip, kicked off her shoes, and put the champagne on the bedside cabinet.

"Where do you want me?" said the man.

"On the bed. Face down."

The man pulled off his sweatshirt, revealing a well-defined looking torso despite the swirls of dark hair.

"So what's in store?"

"Do you trust me?" asked Flora.

"Sure."

"Okay. Lie down. Relax, and I'll be back in a second."

Flora left the room, and the man lying naked with his face in the pillow. She was gone a good five minutes.

"Flora!" the man shouted.

"I'm coming. Close your eyes."

She stood just outside the door. "Are they closed?"

"Yeah," said the man, wondering what was going on. Although he'd been with Flora a dozen times, she was just as mysterious to him as when they first met. He heard Flora come back into the room. She must have stood at the end of the bed. He felt her lift one of his legs, and move it away from the other. He now lay with his legs wide open.

"What are you up to?"

"You'll see."

She knelt on the bed in between his legs. The man felt Flora lift one his butt cheeks, and push something against the hole. It felt slippery.

"What's that?" he asked apprehensively.

"Patience!"

Flora massaged the man's butt-hole, until it began to relax. She started to prod it a little. He'd never felt anything like this before. Leave it to Flora to do the unexpected. He moaned and arched his back, and pushed towards her finger.

"Slow down, greedy," she laughed.

Flora took her hand away. Next, the man felt something hard, which poked his sphincter.

"What the fuck?"

Something spurted inside, warm, and tingling. He'd never felt anything like it. "What the hell's that?"

"It's a booty bump."

"I hate to sound naïve," he said sounding naïve, "but what's a *booty bump*?"

"Crystal."

"What?"

"Crystal in water."

The man tried to look around at Flora. "How?"

"With a pipette."

"Jesus. You're a crazy bitch," he laughed, impressed by her ingenuity.

"I'll take that as a compliment. It's how everyone does crystal these days. It's less hard on the sinuses and it's a smoother ride."

"Smoother ride?" There was a note of concern in his voice.

As if detecting his apprehension, she responded reassuringly. "The high kind of comes from within, and it feels less twitchy too."

"Since when have you been such an expert?"

"I first read about it on the Net."

"Hang on," said the man. Then he paused and

squirmed. "Ooh!"

"You feel it?"

The man didn't answer at first. Then he said, "Woo, woo, woo."

"You, feel it."

"Woo!" he burst out in excitement.

Flora glided her hand over his butt. "You're very eloquent all of a sudden."

"You can't complain. You did this to me."

"I'm not." With this, she rammed her face into his butt and pushed her tongue into his hole.

"Jesus!" he cried out. Then his voice got even louder. "*Woo*!"

Flora slapped his butt. "That's right cowboy. Fucking squirm."

"I *love* that."

"Of course you do. I've never met a man who didn't. You've never had it done before?"

"No."

"In that case, this night might be one you never forget." Flora reached over and picked up the champagne. "Let's drink to that."

He rolled over and half sat up. "But I don't now what I'm drinking *to*."

"Let's just say, new experiences." Flora took a swig and passed it on.

"To letting go," said the man twisting his torso just enough to take a swig.

"To bums," said Flora and swigged again.

"Hey, don't finish it." The man pulled it away from her mouth and Champagne ran down her throat. "To mama's juicy . . ."

Flora leant forward and pressed her breasts into the side of his face, muffling the end of his sentence.

"What, these? To baby's juicy dick." As she said this, she slid her hand under his abdomen and got hold of it. "Ooo. Rock hard!"

"Of course," he said with a profound sense of pride. "Surprising though, since you haven't given it much attention." He sounded almost ungrateful for his butt play.

"Steady on Boy Baby. I'll get round to that. I'm going to ask you again. Do you trust me?"

"Sure?"

Flora leaned in closer. "Will you let me do whatever I want?"

"Yeah," he answered with a nod.

"Can I tie you up?"

"I guess so." It's not that this man trusted Flora completely, but judging by what she'd done to him so far, he didn't mind. The Crystal was affecting his decision-making and so allowing him to be more open-minded. This was exactly what Flora had hoped would happen.

"Okay. Playtime!" Flora stared down at the man beneath her for a few seconds considering him as prey. She looked at his wrists resting above him next to the bedstead. His face was in the pillow, and so he couldn't see what was going on. He liked this, a lot, but the trouble was she was being too quiet. There wasn't enough going on, and it wasn't happening quickly enough, and so the man fidgeted. This reminded Flora to get on with the job at hand. She reached to the side of the bed, and felt under the mattress. "There!" she said.

The man was getting so high now that he was beginning to feel hungry' for what came next. He was impatient. Couldn't wait for it. If he'd had half a mind he'd have guessed what was coming, but the man was mindless now.

Flora clicked a pair of handcuffs around his wrists.

He looked up at them. "Hey! What's this shit?" He got up onto his elbows.

"Calm down, cowboy. Are you scared of little old me?"

"No." He tried to sound unconcerned but was unable to hide the hint of suspicion in his voice.

"So behave. Come on, be nice to mama." The man lay back down. "This is where the fun begins. Close your eyes baby."

He did as he she said, and heard shuffling, a cupboard door squeak on its hinge, a drawer open and close, then an odd sound. It was almost familiar. Flora's breathing seemed to change, held, released, and stammered. Possibly, it sounded like somebody was trying to put on something that didn't quite fit. "Here comes the good bit." Flora knelt on the bed again, between his legs. Once more, he felt the slippery sensation on his butt-hole, and a finger slipped inside. It eased in and then out, at the edge of his sphincter. Gradually, it went in deeper. She began to use two fingers. The man squirmed more than ever, thrusting his balls into the bed, and then pushing his butt back towards her hand. Each time her fingers went in deeper, he groaned a little more. His breathing became heavy, his grinding deeper.

"Fucking hell, Flora. That feels amazing."

"I've only just started."

"You do what the fuck you want."

"That's exactly what I was going to do."

"Please. Do what ever you want," said the man, his voice muffled by the pillow.

Flora needed no more encouragement, and definitely no more orders. She forged ahead, and in response, the sensation in his butt intensified even better than before. It felt like she was climbing inside. Nothing he'd experienced compared to this. Flora continued to prod his butt, but she no longer used her fingers. Something round and smooth, and thick prodded his hole. Well that's how it seemed to him. It didn't really make much sense to him, but this didn't matter. He wasn't going to begin questioning anything about what was happening, and so his tight yet eager little hole was stuffed. Flora packed a solid rubber shaft into the man, hesitantly at first, then deeper and deeper. Flora pulled back her hips and the shaft came with her. She pushed forward and it disappeared inside.

"Fucking hell. What are you doing?"

"I'm fucking you, baby."

"What?"

"I'm fucking your hard bum, Boy Baby." Again, she thrust forward.

He cried out, "Fucking hell!"

"This isn't hell, fucking you baby. It's me, and it's the nearest thing to heaven you'll ever feel."

Flora pounded the butt beneath her, giving him no time to react. With each thrust came a cry. Then before he had voiced it, another came. Simply pounding, and pounding, fucking and fucking.

"Do you like my dick up your bum?"

"I love it."

"Beg for it, baby."

"Please, please, please!"

"Beg me to fuck you with my big dick."

"Please fuck me. Please don't stop!"

Flora looked down and could see the shiny rod sliding in and out. Another went inside, into her cunt. In addition, a little nodule prodded her clitoris. So each time she thrust, it tickled her, making her wet. What a clever contraption, so handsome, and so useful. It never ceased to amaze her how powerful she felt when she penetrated somebody. No wonder men went crazy for it, the competence, control, and intrusion. Such a beautiful butt, to honour and defile. She wanted to bite it, but kept fucking it instead.

Flora fell forward onto the man's back. Her face was at the nape of his neck. She dragged her tongue over his shoulders, licked the sweat there, and bathed in the heat that rose from his waist and the muscles on his broad back.

"Fucking hell!" shouted the man. Flora's picked up the pace. Her dick hovered at the edge of his hole, and then plunged all the way in. The man's body seemed to spasm. "Oh God!" Flora did the same thing again. "You're going to have to stop!" His voice gravelled, and he barely used proper words. He couldn't. The sensation was too intense. He was all physicality now, with no logic, or reason, or clear strands of thoughts. "Jesus, fucking Jesus!" he cried. There was only sensation surging through his body. "I can't take it. Please, please, please!"

"Please, *more*?"

"No. Don't know." He started to sob. *"I don't know!"*

As though it were an afterthought, the man took hold of his dick. After just a couple of strokes, he said, "I'm going to cum."

Flora felt a stirring within. First, it was around the surface of her cunt. Then it began to grow from deep within. Her clitoris highlighted everything. "Fuck, *I'm* going to cum," she said. Something started to drive from within her, yet flicked and trickled over her clitoris too. It prickled, itched, ached, and thudded as it rushed around her cunt. It was painful, but good, a dull shifting of perception and physiology; it grew and stormed until all she could feel was hyper-sensational bliss. "I'm cummin!"

This sent the man over the edge. Sensation surged along his prostate. It churned around his balls, shot through the base of his dick, beat, pulsed and fired out.

"I'm cummin too. Fucking hell, fucking hell, fucking hell!"

She kept on pounding.

"*Jesus!*" was his final spoken word, his whole body trembling. His tears began to drown out his speech. Flora now saw things with a more physical self. It made her feel, rather than think.

"Baby!" she said.

There was now this thing beneath her. It was weak, fragile and needed babying, not *wanted*, but *needed*, holding, and loving, and kissing. Her dick was still deep inside him, which was exactly where she wanted it. She imagined it felt secure, reassuring, and very real, especially when things were making no sense at all.

Flora watched the sobbing, broken, soft man beneath her, the boy lost and confused. There was no point in trying to pretend there were options now. This was real. The only urge she had was to protect, be tender, look after, and hold. She had no choice but to care.

In answer to his question, *do you like me*? Flora hoped she'd shown him *yes*, despite the fact that she didn't really know the answer herself.

Again I covered the mouthpiece.

'We could get some more stuff,' Ace said in a whisper-like voice.

'How? We've got no money left.'

'We can pay for it tomorrow,' he said. 'With the money you earn.'

'Genius!' I said, and believed it too.

There was a coke dealer at the end of my street. Ace's plan was I run there, pick up the gear, free-base it before the customer got round and do him while still high. How bad could that be?

'Could you make it in an hour's time?'

'Splendid,' he said, as though tucking with greed into a delicious steak. I gave him the address. As Ace instructed, I picked up the coke. He produced the free-base activities. Then the others waited in the living room while I did the punter and even enjoyed it, I think. Although I couldn't remember what he looked like or what we did. Everything went to plan, and we even managed to time it so that we took some Rohypnol before hitting the pit of our comedown. Then we all slammed into sleep, hoping for the tranquil sleep of babies, only we weren't at peace, content, or happy.

3

Killing time, Joe flicked through CDs on the living room floor. He had a glamorized masculinity, which was less truck driver and more off-duty California Highway Patrol without the giveaway sexy uniform. Every item of Joe's clothing looked grateful to be snuggling against his body. Even first thing in the morning when unshaven with bed head Joe looked as though he'd spent hours 'off set' in wardrobe and makeup in an attempt to create this Hollywood version of just-woken-up.

"I bet you don't get morning breath," Ryan said, more out-loud than he'd planned.

Joe hadn't been allowed the luxury of the train of thought that preceded Ryan's odd remark, so his response was a baffled, "What?"

The doorbell rang.

"That'll be Leila," said Ryan, getting up, rushing towards the front door, and opening it. "Pony!" he said. Then, "Hair *do!*" This was his response to Leila having dyed her hair a Lilac colour. "It's grown so much."

"I did it last night. Sorry I'm so late. The train stopped just outside London for about an hour. Do you like it?

My hair."

"No doubt, they were checking passports at the north/south border. They probably knew you were trying to escape." Then he tousled her hair and stroked her face. "Of course I like it."

Leila stepped into the hall. "*Nice* place."

"It's just my summer pad, you know."

Ryan led her into the living room."

"Joe, this is Leila. Leila, Joe."

"Good to meet you, Leila. I've heard a lot about you."

David entered the room with a wooden spoon in his hand. "Hope you don't mind if I fast-forward past the formalities for a second," he said. "Dinner. Is pasta okay?"

"Sounds great," said Leila, taking his free hand.

"Fine. In that case. Hello! All we've been hearing is 'Leila this, Leila that.'"

"Vice versa," said Leila.

"I wouldn't worry what the food is," said Ryan. "He's a great cook."

"Stop," said David. "Now I've got to live up to it."

Ryan rolled his eyes. "That's why I said it, stupid."

"It looks like you've settled in okay," said Leila.

"Yeah. I just can't wait for these two gays to move out, though."

"We'll be gone as soon as we find somewhere proper," said Joe.

"This looks proper to me," Leila said admiring the room.

"That's Joe's doing," said David. "If it were left to me, it would be white walls throughout."

"Ryan told me it was cool, but it's something else."

"A paint showroom?" offered David.

"I was thinking, more an art gallery," said Leila.

David smiled. "People have said that. It must be what Joe finds comfortable these days."

"It's what I call home," said Joe.

"This bag's my home for a while," said Leila gesturing towards her suitcase.

"That's what youth's all about," said David wistfully

"You're only *thirty*," said Joe.

"I imagine these two think that's retiring age."

"Of course," said Ryan. Then, "Give us a break!"

"Yeah," said Leila. "I once knew somebody who was *thirty-two*."

"There you go," said David.

"Who was that?" Ryan asked.

"I don't know. Some woman I read about in the paper. She lived in Japan, or somewhere, and she lived off potatoes."

"Enough, already!" David wagged his finger. "I'm obviously going to have to watch you, young lady."

"That's my *job*," said Ryan. He looked at Leila, and she looked back. It lasted for seconds and neither seemed aware they were on display, but then they did, and both looked away a little embarrassed.

"How cute," said Joe.

"You used to look at me like that," David reminded.

"I don't think cute was ever in my vocabulary."

"You *used* to love me."

"I *still* love you, retard. But I hate you for making me say it." Now, it was their turn to look at each other.

"How cute," mimicked Ryan.

"Watch it," said David. "If you're hungry, that is. That

reminds me." He left the room, smiling.

Joe followed him with his eyes, but quickly turned his attention to Leila, "Take a seat." He motioned to a couch and paused for a moment for her to sit and get comfortable, and then crouching beside her, he said, "Can I get you anything?"

"Do you have any whiskey?"

"I think so. What would you like with it?"

She took a few seconds to decide. "Milk?"

"I've never heard of that," said Joe with a look of surprise.

"Me neither," she said.

Ryan burst out laughing.

"Leila, you're one hell of a crazy cow. Joe, can I have the same?"

"Sure. That's two whiskey and milks coming up. If you two get sick, *I'm* not cleaning up."

"It's a deal," said Ryan.

"That's if I can choose a CD," said Leila.

"Okay," said Joe, slightly amused. Ryan loved the effect she was having on them already. He'd put off introducing them for months, uncertain whether the time was exactly right. He wasn't taking any chances. Leila meant the world to Ryan and it was critically important to him that his uncle and his partner not just like Leila but adore her as much as he did.

When Joe left the room, Leila went over to the CD player, pulled a CD out of her bag, and put it on.

Ryan waited for the track to start. He knew Leila well enough to expect a surprise. It started. The music was strangely foreign, not songs per se but short little excerpts that lasted no more than twenty seconds

"What's this?" asked Ryan.

"TV jingles."

"From?"

"Hong Kong."

"Where did you find it?"

"A thrift store just off Sixth Avenue."

"That's *New York*, I presume."

"Aha."

Joe returned with drinks and hearing the noise, looked confused. "This wasn't in our collection."

"No," said Ryan. "Leila brought it."

"How," Joe paused trying to find the right word, 'resourceful," he said, puzzled. "Got anything else, Leila?"

"I do have one more. If you're sure you don't mind."

"No," said Joe. "Why would I?"

"You might once you hear it," added Ryan.

"Shut up, you," said Leila, and handed Joe another CD. "I like this one the best."

There was nothing on the outside cover, no clue as to what might be inside.

"Here goes," said Joe, putting the CD on.

He and Ryan both lifted their heads to listen carefully.

A dog started barking. And it continued to do so. A couple of minutes into the track, Joe said, "Does it do anything else?"

"No," said Leila. "Isn't it great?"

"Yeah," said Joe absentmindedly. "It's. . . ." He stopped. "Actually, it *is* great. It would be perfect for my exhibition."

"Fill us in," said Ryan, pleased that Joe and Leila had made this special connection

Ignoring Ryan, Joe said, "Can I borrow it?"

"Definitely," said Leila, touched that he shared her taste. "But you won't lose it?"

"It's too late," said Joe carefully putting the CD into its case. "I lost it years ago."

David walked into the room just in time to hear the tail end of laughter.

"What have I missed?"

"Us, I hope," said Ryan, leaning backwards and laying his head upside down off the sofa.

"You're getting too cute for your own good, sonny."

"I wish I was your son."

"It's a good thing your mother didn't hear you say that. She's already phoned."

"Like I care," said Ryan, pouting.

"Don't act so hard. It doesn't become you. I called her back."

Ryan sat up quickly. "You did what?"

"Did you think I wouldn't?"

"I don't believe *you*! I ran away."

"She *is* my sister," said David.

"That's not *my* problem." He wanted to sound independent in front of Leila.

"Be reasonable. I can't have her worrying about you. She was just glad you were okay. She wants to come and visit."

"*Jesus!*"

David came and sat down beside Ryan. "She only wants to *see* you. You don't have to go back with her." He could tell that he wasn't going to convince Ryan of anything at this time. "Anyway, dinner's ready. You lot must be starving. You sounded like a pack of dogs from the kitchen."

"That wasn't us," said Leila.

"I know," said David. "I was just kidding." He watched Leila's face for a couple of seconds as she caught up, surprised at how naive she seemed. She couldn't have been much more than a year older than Ryan. "If you'd all like to follow me."

David led the way into the kitchen. Here, fluorescent yellow squares covered all the walls. It had an Eighties/Fifties feel to it. Running the whole length was a grey wooden table set for dinner, and on it were fluorescent pink plastic placemats.

"Wow!" said Leila. "It's beautiful."

"Thank you," said David. "Well, thank Joe." He glanced around. "It's not too much, is it?"

"No," said Leila.

"Shit!" said Joe. "Sounds like we need to change it."

David went into auto-host and said, "Sit where you like." Then he proceeded to gesture where he wanted them.

"Are you interested in working?" asked David.

"Sure," said Ryan, making a face, both surprised and resigned.

"You can bill us by the hour. That way you can organize your time however you like."

Joe opened a bottle of wine that was on the table. "Anybody?"

Leila nodded. Ryan held up his glass enthusiastically, and David said, "It's red." As if this mattered. They were content with it simply being wine.

Ryan was all smiles. "Is that going to be cash in hand?"

"Of course," said David while he put on a pair of oven gloves. "I wouldn't miss a chance to screw the taxman."

"So . . ." said Ryan whose eyes were now waiting to see what came out of the oven. " . . . It's true. You would screw anything."

David lifted out a baking dish, and turned as though to a much bigger crowd.

"Yum! Yum!" Lasagne said Leila.

Although there was only three in the audience, he got the response he wanted. "And it's coming your way," he said. David focused on what he was doing but spoke addressed Ryan. "Anyway kid. When did you get so cheeky?"

"You leave my cheeks alone," said Ryan holding up an unthreatening butter knife.

"You wish I'd want your cheeks," said David. "Anyway, how's Monday sound?"

"I'll be there, cheeks and all."

"Can't wait," said David. Joe caught Leila's eye, and then rolled his own. In response she smiled and acting out of character looked down at her plate demurely. The other two continued their silly interaction, David wondering if he was in fact flirting and Ryan feeling proud, believing he'd been able to hold his own. They were both oblivious to the others joking about them.

Meanwhile the place mats were throwing a reflected glow up under each of their faces, and this gave a *Holy Manger* look to the meal. Joe served the lasagne, and at David's request helped themselves to vegetables.

Two bottles of wine later, they were all a bit drunk, and so laughed whilst talking around and over each other. Then without warning Leila stood up and lifted her skirt. David looked at Joe, who looked at Ryan, who simply shrugged and smiled.

"Leila," said David. At first, she didn't respond. "Leila."

Hesitantly, she lowered her skirt a little, enough for her head just to appear over the top. She looked puzzled. "Leila, be a dear and pass the pepper."

She did this, and to do so she had to put her skirt down. She handed David the pepper. "I can't eat spinach without it. How about you?"

"I like butter on spinach," she said. Then she sat down and continued, as though nothing had happened. "I'm having trouble believing the sauce on this pasta is low fat."

"You don't have to believe," said David. "As long as you eat it."

"Why do you care about fat?" she asked.

"You may not believe this, but I used to model."

"I believe it," said Leila. "You're fucking gorgeous."

"That's very sweet. The agency liked my stomach really ribbed, so I usually watched what I ate. Now, I guess, it's just habit really."

"Why did you stop modelling?" said Leila. She was genuinely interested. Joe frowned. Ryan winced.

"What?"

Joe raised his eyebrows.

"I guess I've said something wrong."

"Don't worry," said David. "It's okay."

"Somebody may as well tell me now."

All fun and silliness had gone now from David's face. "You may have noticed this scar on my forehead, and this one just under my nose."

"No," said Leila.

"You can bring her again," said David trying to mimic his own playful manner from earlier.

"You do know they're sexy, don't you?" she said with perfect seriousness.

"Anyway . . ." said David.

Joe stopped him. ""David, are you sure?"

"Let's skip it," said Leila, definitely feeling uneasy.

"No. It's okay." David assured her. Leila's head came forward, ear first, waiting to hear what he said. "I was attacked."

"You were almost killed," said Joe gravely.

Leila put her head down. "I'm sorry. It's so unfair."

"That's life," said David. "Anyway, it was a long time ago. I'm fine now."

"You're so lovely," said Leila. "I'd have killed the bastard."

"What?" asked Joe.

She took a large gulp of wine, wiped her mouth with her hand and said seriously, "I'd have blown his brains out."

"I wasn't carrying my gun," David joked, looking at Joe and Ryan.

"I always do. A woman has to. It's okay for you men, but we can be raped. I think it's possibly the worst thing that can happen to a woman." Again, Ryan winced.

"What have I said now?"

By this point, David was rubbing his forehead, with his eyes closed.

"What?" said Leila. Then suddenly understanding the situation, "Oh my God! No! David! You weren't?"

Tears began well in David's eyes. Joe sprung up from

his chair, and within seconds was holding David who'd begun to cry.

"Ryan," Leila whispered. "I wish you'd told me."

"It's not the kind of thing . . ." said Ryan.

David interrupted. "Leila, it's okay really."

"Still, I'm sorry for bringing it up."

Although polite conversation resumed, Leila was quiet for the rest of dinner. She and Ryan cleared away the dishes and prepared drinks for David and Joe who sat on one of the sofas in the living room and listened to music. Leila started yawning.

Leila attempted to stifle a yawn as she handed them glasses of port. "What time did you set off at?" asked David.

"I was up at nine. The train was at twelve."

"Don't let us keep you up," said Joe.

Ryan shook his head. "We're sweet at the moment. Maybe just one more drink."

Joe went onto the kitchen, brought back the drinks, and sat on a cushion on the floor in between David's legs.

In spite of the awkward moment during dinner, David was very fond of Leila. He hoped to see more of her and soon. "Are you going to stay in London?" he asked.

"I'd like to for now, at lest until Ryan knows what he's doing, but I have to find somewhere to live."

"You can stay here until you do," said Joe. He leant back and twisted his head so he could see David's response. "That's if you don't mind My Sweetmeat."

David felt as though Joe had just answered a question he'd been asking, "No, not at all."

Leila's face lit up. "Wow!"

"More than wow," said Ryan, excited that things were going so well.

"That's very kind of you," said Leila.

"I'm not here much," said Joe. "I should have discussed it with David, but in eight years, we've seldom disagreed."

"Because I'm always right," said David. "You'd be stupid to disagree."

"Yes honey," said Joe playing right along. "That must be why." They both made an exasperated expression.

"Anyway, we could do with some fresh . . ." David paused, and licked his lips. "I mean new blood around the place."

Leila felt moved by Joe's sudden offer, less the generosity of the invitation, as much as the sincere warmth behind it. Ryan had prepared her for this meeting by sharing his accounts of growing up under their watchful, loving eyes. As a rule Ryan wasn't the type to come right out and tell you his inner most feelings but in this case his admiration for his uncles needed no formal declaration. He practically gushed at the mere mention of David's name. The hospitality they now showed to Leila proved that all Ryan felt was well founded. She just hoped she could live up to all their expectations of her as well.

They discussed keys, tubes, and landmarks, all with Ryan lying flat out on the floor.

"Let's go to bed," said Leila.

"I'm coming," he said, not moving.

"Come on," she said.

Joe could see she needed help.

"I'll show you where the bedroom is. Come on, slug-boy. Your lettuce awaits you." Joe helped him stand and led the couple upstairs.

Once on the landing Joe swung open their bedroom door. On the walls were circles painted in the primary colours blue, red, and yellow. Where they overlapped, they created secondary colours of green orange and purple. Half spheres, in all of these colours covered the ceiling. In each corner, there was a light fixture. From these hung hundreds of tiny white lights. They looked as though they were falling to the ground.

On seeing the room Leila said, "Cool."

"Sorry," said Joe. "I'll turn the heat up." Leila gave him an expression showing she thought his comment was dry. "It *is* late," he offered as an excuse.

"I'll forgive you," said Leila. "But tomorrow I expect wit, wit, wit, and sharp."

"I'll see what I can do," said Joe in mock apology.

"Now be gone," she said with a flourish of her hands.

"Okay, Ma'am." Joe started to close the door.

"Hey, wait," said Ryan. Joe raised his eyebrows as if he couldn't guess why he'd want him to stick around any longer. "Give me a kiss."

"Sorry," said Joe. "I thought it too familiar."

"Shut up and get over here."

Joe went to Ryan, whom he tried to kiss on the cheek. Ryan turned his head to offer his lips. Joe followed Ryan's cheek, and so had to bend his neck to compensate. Now, Ryan turned back. Their faces hovered, neither sure which way to go, until Ryan got hold of Joe's face with his hands, and kissed him squarely on the mouth.

"Why, sir!" said Joe, pretending to hide his face out of

embarrassment behind a fan.

"Me! Me! Me!" squealed Leila.

This time Joe didn't bother being coy and just kissed Leila on the lips.

"That's better," said Ryan. "We'll train you yet."

Joe left, saluting at the door.

As soon as it closed, Leila said, "So fill me in."

"About?"

"David."

Ryan pulled off his t-shirt. "There's not much more to tell." With knee jerk response, Leila placed her hand on his smooth skin above his belly button. "He was raped, and beaten up badly."

"Poor thing!"

"Yeah. He's such a softly." Ryan lifted up Leila's arms. She grinned. He lifted her t-shirt to reveal her bare breasts. "At the time, he used to live with this woman called Flora."

"What, as a couple?"

"That's right. She was a bit dodgy though." Ryan pulled Leila in close, and for a moment was motionless, as he simply appreciated holding her. With his head now over her shoulder he continued. "He'd been living with her for years when he met Joe, but I think he began to realize he was gay."

"Poor cow."

"Yes and no. She did some weird stuff."

"Like what?"

Gently, Ryan pulled away and made a brushing teeth gesture. Then walked to his bag and crouched down to get his toothbrush. "She sent him some shit."

"What you mean drugs?"

"No," he said squatting and looking at her. "Actual shit."

"What!"

"Go figure." Ryan looked through his bag.

Leila stood perfectly still, completely absorbed by what Ryan told her. "Was she a psycho?"

"Well, yeah, kind of," he said, while rummaging. "I guess." Ryan found his toothbrush and stood up. "Anyway, Joe found out that she'd sent the shit, and confronted her."

"It's like a film," said Leila, and a little spooked by the story she held out her hand to Ryan, as she needed some comfort.

He was happy to oblige. "I know. Unreal, hey! But it gets worse." Ryan tucked his toothbrush into his back pocket and held Leila again. The skin of their tummies touched. "Flora actually managed to convince David that Joe sent the packages."

She let out a strange laugh, which expressed both amusement and disgust. "Wow! I'm beginning to like her."

"She must have noticed that David liked Joe. Apparently, Joe made it clear that he liked David. I guess she hoped it would ruin their friendship."

"Did it work?"

"Yeah, for a while. They didn't see each other for ages."

"But how . . ."

"Get this! They bumped into each other on the tube, completely by chance. David was living with this other guy called Rob by this point." Ryan paused, remembering. "He was nice."

"So," Leila said trying to get Ryan back on track. "David and Joe lived happily ever after?"

"Well, kind of. It's quite romantic. You should get David to tell you. He loves to talk about it."

"So, what happened?"

"To cut a long story short, they started seeing each other."

"What happened to the bitch from hell?"

"I don't know. They don't speak to her."

"It's hardly surprising. *Esta loca*?"

Ryan walked to the bedroom door on his way to the bathroom. "Love does scary stuff sometimes."

Disturbed by the story Leila sat down slowly on the bed. "Please, don't ever love me like that."

"Okay," said Ryan standing at the door.

"Promise?"

"I promise," he said, now with just his head peeking through the door.

Leila had images in her head that she didn't want there. Also, she felt more alone than she should have. "Flora," she said aloud. Then she shuddered. "I'd kill that bitch if she ever hurt you!"

4

Cum squirted out my of pulsing dick. I'd only jerked off.
David and Joe were alone in their bedroom. Unlike the
rest of the house, this was much more sombre, even
relaxing, and had a slightly autumnal feel to it. Mustard,
salmon, turquoise, amber, and plum bands, about a
quarter of a metre thick, covered each wall, joining at the
corners to circle the whole room. A thin line painted
with black gloss helped define the bands. Joe started to
change the sheets on the bed, but David grabbed his arm
and said, "Shouldn't we dirty those first?"

"Okay, guv'ner," said Joe, sounding like a character
from *Oliver Twist*. David found it surprisingly sexy.
They kissed. As they did, Joe felt David's hand at the
side of his face. "What . . ." David cut him off by putting
something in his mouth."

"Acid," said David.

"No!"

"You'll believe me in about 20 minutes."

"Is it really?"

"Yes."

Joe thought for a moment. "I guess. I don't have anything planned tomorrow."

"I know," said David. "I checked your day planner first. Now you probably understand why all the inane questions at breakfast."

Joe thought back, and smiled. "Oh yeah. You sly bugger."

"Are you okay about it?"

"God yeah! Well, here goes."

"Let's have a joint in the bath and wait to come up."

"Nice," said Joe.

"Where was I?"

They kissed again, but more passionately, and longer. Pulling apart, David took off his T-shirt.

"Even nicer," said Joe.

David threw his T-shirt on the bed and headed towards the bathroom to run the taps.

"We should get Ryan to work on *this* room," said David, loud enough that Joe could hear him in the other room.

"Please! I'm sick of it," said Joe.

In the bathroom, Joe had painted each wall with a luscious purple gloss, and in contrast, the ceiling was fluorescent green. There was writing on both, in thick black marker. It gave the impression of graffiti, but on closer inspection, it wasn't so chaotic. Each line was evenly spaced and done very neatly. The bath was high up on a scaffolding platform, the drainpipe on show, curling around in a corkscrew underneath. The whole floor slanted toward a small grate, so overflow drained away. Access to the bath was from one end, by an aluminium ladder. David put the plug in, ran the taps, climbed down the ladder, and went back to the bedroom. By this time, Joe was bending over, peeling off his jeans.

"Jesus," said David. "Your bums look amazing."

"They feel even better."

David kissed Joe, and cupped his butt.

"You're right. They're so fucking hard."

"Told you."

"I love you," said David.

"I love you too."

"Which two?"

"Flora."

"Now, I know you're kidding."

"Get in the bath," said Joe. "I'll rub your back."

"It's a deal," said David, taking off his jeans. He walked towards the bathroom naked. For a moment, Joe watched him. David's waist was still slim, his shoulders still broad, but his body had gotten more natural, since he'd stopped modelling.

"You look the best I've seen you." David turned around in the doorway and posed as though for a photo, but more extreme. "Ugh! I take that back." David relaxed and smiled. "That's better," said Joe. "God, you're beautiful."

"Must be all the cream cakes I eat," said David, and continued into the bathroom. Joe followed. Again, Joe watched as David climbed the stairs into the bath. When David's butt was at head height, Joe got hold of his thighs and buried his face into it. Resting on the side of the bath, David bent forward, arching his back.

"Jesus!" he said. "I love that."

Joe pulled his face away slightly, leaving his nose in the crack of David's butt, just far enough away to be able to focus on the tiny blond hairs, yet near enough to smell the skin.

"I know you love it. Why do you think I do it?"

"He licked right up David's crack, and said, "Um!" Then he pushed his tongue deep into the actual hole.

"Fucking hell!" said David.

"No. Fuck in the bath."

"Wherever! You know me."

"I do," said Joe. "That's why I can't wait."

David continued up the ladder, climbed into the bath, and turned both taps on full. He knelt and mixed the hot and cold with his hands. Joe sat on the floor, rolling a joint. Every now and then, he looked up. When the bath was full, David lay back and went right under the water, blowing bubbles out of his nose. Then he leant over the side with his chin resting on folded arms. "Come on, baby," he said, with an exaggerated moan in his voice. "Get in."

"Okay, one second!"

Joe lit the joint, and waited while David dried his hands. Then he passed it up.

"Lovely," said David, taking a long drag, and sliding back into the water.

With big solid legs, Joe climbed the steps three at a time. By the time he got to the top, he had a hard-on.

"Where do you want me, front or back?" said Joe, his dick bouncing in front of David's face.

"There *was* talk of a backrub."

"Okay. I guess that's behind."

He stepped in behind David and slid his legs around either side of his hips.

"That feels nice," said David. "But what's that lump?"

"Nothing."

"It doesn't *feel* like nothing."

"Okay it's not *nothing*." He started to rub David's

neck. "How's that, baby?"

"Incredible."

"So you like my lump?"

"You know I love your lump," said David. "But I was referring to the massage." He turned over to face Joe making the water overflow. It fell in a single sheet, and splashed onto the floor. He nuzzled into Joe's chest hair, and then he kissed down the ridges of his stomach to his abdomen. Joe pushed his pelvis towards David's face. The head of his dick rose out of the water. David opened his mouth around it, and took it as far in as he could. When he came up for air the front of his hair and eyelashes were wet.

"Do you know what you look like?"

"No," said David. "Tell me."

"The most beautiful thing on the planet. That's what."

David rested the side of his face on Joe's chest, feeling completely content. He closed his eyes and started to daydream. When he acknowledged his thoughts next, he realised the acid was taking effect. David opened his eyes. Slowly, he shifted his body, in an attempt to look at Joe. Again, water splashed out of the bath. For a moment, David's thoughts ran with this idea. He imagined the water hitting the ground. Only it was falling on top of him. He was under the bath and could hear them above, like giant sea creatures moving in the water. The squeaking of skin against the side of the bath became their cries. Tired, ancient, and sad they tried to communicate. Once more, he acknowledged his thoughts. He had been distracted for some time. The bath water was getting cold.

"Baby?" he said.

"Fuck!" said Joe. "That acid's strong."

"You're telling me."

"For a while, I thought I was still down-stairs, only the whole room was filled with mud."

"Err!"

"It was quite nice," said Joe. "Until the water started to go cold."

David watched as he spoke, and suddenly realised how similar Joe's lips were to Flora's. Joe broke David's train of thought.

"Let's get out, before we catch a cold."

"Okay. You first," said David. "Baby. Will you do me a favour?"

"Anything."

"Will you stay at the bottom of the ladder, in case I slip?"

"Sure. You must be pretty fucked up."

David made a face that meant *very* fucked up. Awkwardly, he managed to turn around in the bath so he faced Joe and could see him as he climbed out. As he did, David noticed the hairs under Joe's butt joining in little peaks of water. For a second he became engrossed in them, noticing how filled with light each drop was, as it formed, hesitated, and then dripped off the skin. He couldn't concentrate on anything for more than a few seconds at any one time. By concentrating, Joe made his way down the steps. As his head went below the side of the bath, David thought Joe was drowning, but then realised how ridiculous this idea was. He put his own head over the side and watched. Joe shook his head like a wet dog, causing him to lose balance, so leant against the washbasin until he finished drying off.

When he was done, he looked up, and said, "Come on baby."

"I can't be bothered moving. Do I have to?"

"No, but I'm not getting back in so if you want to have sex with me, you'll have to."

"You drive a hard bargain."

With incentive and great care, David made his way out of the bath and down the steps. As he got to the bottom, Joe took hold of him round the waist and, lifting him, carried him, still dripping, out of the bathroom.

"Put me down," said David.

"When I'm good and ready."

"And when might that be?"

"Now," said Joe, as he let David down onto the bed.

"Let me dry off."

"You'll dry soon enough on the sheets."

Joe pulled a blanket up over his head and lowered onto David, covering them both. They fell into each other, their faces becoming wet with sweat, and saliva, their bodies hot and slippery. They welded together, gasping, penetrating, and smearing into the bed.

Even though the sex lasted over two hours, their acid was still in full swing. Without the sex to focus on, the acid began to play with their minds. Joe understood this could happen, and tried to relax, whereas David began to get a little frightened.

"Joe. Will you give me a hug?"

"What's wrong?"

"I don't know. I feel scared."

"Come here," said Joe and held David. "What's going on in my baby's head?"

"Crazy stuff."

"That's acid for you."

"How come you don't?"

"I have crazy thoughts, but I check myself and try not to let them consume me."

"Easier said than done."

"It's actually something you can learn."

"If I keep talking, I don't get scared."

"This may sound obvious," said Joe. "But that's because you're concentrating on speaking."

"So, I should try to concentrate on something?"

"That's right, baby. Or, just carry on talking if you want. I'm happy to talk. If I get tired I'll just listen."

"Don't go to sleep," said David, slightly panicky.

"I won't, baby. In fact, I can promise I won't go to sleep before you."

"But what if you do?"

"Well, you could wake me, but like I said, I won't. You could take something to be extra sure."

"I don't have anything," said David.

"I have. How about a special Joe cocktail?"

"What, a long hard screw up against the wall?"

"I was thinking more a comfortable cuddle in this bed."

"What's that?"

"Some Valium and Rohypnol."

"That sounds nice."

"Hang on, I'll get them."

"No," said David. "Don't go."

"I'm only going to the bathroom."

"Please don't go."

"That's where the tablets are. Come with me."

David thought for a moment, a confused look on his face.

"Okay." He jumped to his feet like a kid.

"Get on my back," said Joe. David did, and instantly felt better, distracted and loved. Joe walked into the bathroom, making racing car noises. He got a bottle of Valium out of the cupboard and passed it over his shoulder.

"How many, doc?"

"Two should be enough. So take three."

"Four then?"

"Good boy. A man after my own heart."

David handed the bottle back to Joe, who put them back in the cupboard. Joe took the Rohypnol in his hand.

"Back to bed?" asked Joe.

"What about the Rohypnol?"

"You think I'd miss an opportunity to have you turn to putty in my hands."

"What was I thinking?"

"Stupid!"

They went back to bed. Joe must have kissed David more than fifty times before he gave him some Rohypnol, then more than a hundred before David began to breathe very heavily.

"Are you asleep?" said Joe.

David didn't answer.

Joe was still tripping, and without David to attend to, he began to have thoughts he didn't like. He felt it was a shame to waste the acid, so decided to go downstairs and watch TV until he was sleepy. Taking the duvet off the floor at the bottom the bed, he slipped on some boxer shorts and left David sleeping peacefully.

Joe put the duvet on the sofa opposite the TV and attached the headphones so as not to make too much noise. He got a six-pack of beers from the fridge and generally enjoyed his acid. For a while, he watched the movie Blade Runner. Then he turned off the TV and just lay with his eyes open. He began to notice what little light there was in the room. Headlights from cars going by outside darted into the room and across the walls. Yellow and red lights turned in the corners of the room, then chased towards the kitchen door. An ambulance went by outside, and instantly, the room was chaotic with white and blue shards of light. The room appeared to twist, deforming, then reforming, as the ambulance passed, only fading as it drove on down the street. For over thirty minutes, Joe watched the room, hallucinating, seeing shapes form out of previously unnoticed areas of light and shadow. Every now and then, he'd close his eyes and embark on a series of convoluted thoughts that would divide and meander off in different directions. At some point, during a visit inside his head, he fell asleep.

Joe dreamed vividly. Sexual images merged one to the other. Figures transformed, mutating from somebody in one period of his life to somebody he'd seen on TV just that night. The woman from the corner shop, flipped violently on the ground, becoming a teacher who'd taught him geography when at school. David reoccurred, often. He took many forms. Sometimes he was simply himself, but usually he was a combination of other people. Still, it was David, although only an aspect of him, his laugh, his concern, or his anger. Joe fused with another Joe, and then became a bull charging towards a toreador. Only he wanted to kiss this man. Joe knew if he did, it would kill him. He would bleed and die in shame. A crowd who watched this fight taunted Joe, so he charged and caught an arm. Then he turned and charged again, this time he caught a leg. Now he went for the kill, the lips he wanted to kiss. Joe felt a throbbing in his balls, and continued to run, but as he did, the toreador remained the same distance away. Still, this throbbing. Joe wanted to cum. There was golden stitching on the toreador's waistcoat, crammed with flowers, stars, and tiny motifs. The detail was intense. It had a smell, and a sound. It glistened in the Spanish sun. The light took shape, shooting above and dropping like broken glass. Then this shed, this cloth, this colour, texture, and skin. This young man stood naked in the arena, yet he hung like a carcass in an abattoir. This bacon, beef, barely animal now stood waiting to be speared. He was muscle and meat, turned on by the crowd, by the attack from the bull approaching. Although, still dreaming, Joe's attention switched to himself. He began to wake. His dick throbbed. Something prodded his butt. David must still be horny.

"Yeah," is all that Joe could think to say. For a moment, he thought of Ryan smiling. Licking and sucking. "I'm going to cum," he said, into the darkness.

"Cum, please . . ." said a voice, intending to say more, but eager to take Joe's cum, closed around his dick.

5

David sat waiting to see Sky his therapist. Each week, he'd buzz himself in, then would come upstairs and let himself into the actual therapy room. This week she must have been in another room, perhaps her office, possibly even the bathroom. David started to visualize her doing this, but then stopped himself, thinking it not right. Sky may not have been busy at all and this might just be a devise to show him that he shouldn't cross boundaries. Whatever the reason, he resigned himself to cleaning the nails of his left hand with the thumb of his right. *What do I want to talk about today*, he thought. Nothing came immediately to mind. He looked around the room, trying to discern anything more about his therapist than he had already worked out. No. There was nothing. It was a blank environment, not the wood-panelled executive style portrayed in Hollywood, or the rundown council type funded by the British government. The room was as nondescript as it could be with off-white walls and the carpet grey. The fixtures and fittings were nondescript. David heard some noise outside the room. Still, Sky didn't appear. The telephone rang. He assumed the answer machine got it, because he heard no talking.

At three o'clock, precisely the door to the room opened. "Hello," said Sky.

"Hello," said David.

Sky closed the door and stood smiling with her hands together. Her hair looked as though it was once a bob, which parted slightly to one side. This silhouette extended into both her face, and clothes. "I'm sorry I kept you waiting."

"No problem. I was early anyway."

"Really?" She looked at her watch. Then shaking her head said, "Not really."

"Maybe a bit."

She walked over to her chair, stood behind it, and again paused. This was something she always did. David presumed it served a necessary purpose, and although he didn't understand it, he trusted that it probably had an affect on him.

Sky took one side of her hair and rested it behind her ear. "It wouldn't matter, if you *were* early."

David looked at the floor. "Okay, I thought maybe . . ." His words petered out until there was silence.

"How are you today?"

It felt to David as though Sky always left plenty of space for a response.

"Okay."

Sky walked around to the front of her chair, sat down, and rocked side to side as she tucked her skirt underneath her. "Just okay?"

"Life's never more than okay. Is it?"

"Is that how you see it?"

"Most of the time."

"I remember you once told me how beautiful your walk over here was. I think you walked through the park."

"That's right."

"Is that a nice memory?"

David hesitated, seemingly reluctant to feel anything more than *okay*. "I guess so."

"You only guess it is?"

He thought for a moment, recalling the walk.

"No," he said and smiled. "It was nice."

"Is there something on your mind."

"Maybe."

"Tell me about your week."

"I've done nothing, really. Stayed at home a lot. Oh, I did some acid, after seeing you last Thursday. And, before you run with that thought, I don't think it had anything to do with therapy."

"Are you sure?"

"No."

"Last week you told me that Ryan was staying with you. How is that?" She gave him the usual space for his response. "You're smiling."

"Ryan makes me smile."

"Do you remember once telling me you were confused about your feelings for him?"

"Vaguely." David shifted in his chair.

"You're smiling again."

"He's such a great kid."

"You're no longer confused?"

"No."

"It's a long time since I did acid, but I remember it being confusing."

"That's an understatement."

"Do you think you wanted to be confused?"

"What do you mean?"

"About Ryan."

"No!"

"There *is* a certain comfort in confusion."

"Possibly." Then a little defensively, "You're usually right."

Outwardly, Sky didn't appear to react to this comment. "Maybe you miss how you used to feel about him."

"No." David paused, and looked confused. "Do you think?"

"I'm not certain."

"Maybe," said David lost in thought.

"What do *you* think?"

"It makes sense that I'd miss how he was. He was an incredibly sweet boy."

"How do you feel about him now?"

"He's an incredibly sweet teenager."

"More able to make up his own mind."

"I wouldn't have it any other way." David hesitated. "Don't you think?"

Sky smiled for the first time that day. "Yes. I believe you love Ryan."

"I do."

"I believe you wouldn't do anything to harm him."

"Never." David looked upset.

"You wouldn't want to hurt him like you were hurt."

David's features began to tremble. He lifted his hand

to cover his face, and bowed his head. Sky knew what this meant and reached for the tissues on the floor beside her chair. She stood up, walked over to David, and handed him the box. This was the closest Sky ever came to comforting him. It was enough. David imagined the gesture meant she wanted to help. Possibly, it even showed she cared, in a way appropriate within the boundaries of their relationship.

For a few minutes, David cried and Sky sat watching him with her fingers interlaced on her knees. Her head was at an angle and her eyes never left him. This David understood as concern, possibly even pity, definitely a learned therapy technique.

"I'd never hurt him." He cried with more force.

"But somebody hurt you."

David tried to say yes, but his tears wouldn't allow him. After a couple of minutes he said, "I'm sorry."

"There's no need to apologize. I understand. You nearly died."

David folded into himself, bent forward, and sobbed. He stayed this way for several minutes. It was a difficult position for breathing. Every few seconds, he gasped, drawing in chunks of air. Eventually, he lifted his head. The whole of his face was wet, and the whites of his eyes were red.

Sky sat waiting intently, almost listening for a cue. When none was given she said, "The attack changed your life."

"I couldn't model any more."

"I was referring to how it made you feel. How scared you were. You didn't like being outdoors or around other people."

"How could anybody do that?" David asked with a mix of anger and confusion.

"I don't think you're asking how, but why. And more specifically, you're asking why you?"

"I guess so."

"There's no reason. None that would make any sense."

He brought his hand to his face again. "It's such a horrible memory."

"Of course it is. Being attacked goes against the most fundamental human instinct to protect oneself. Being sexually abused is particularly traumatic. You might feel as though you weren't just violated physically, but emotionally also."

It helped David, having Sky talk about what happened to him. By doing so, she demystified the experience, took away an eerie element. David could never really know why it happened, but he could at least put it in some kind of perspective. Vile things happened. People could be cruel. This was sometimes random and often meaningless.

Sky continued to watch David.

"What are you hoping to see?" said David. Sky looked puzzled. "When you watch me."

"People don't just communicate with words," said Sky.

"What am I communicating now?"

"A certain amount of hostility."

"Does it frighten you?"

"No. Should it?"

"Of course not."

"Let's try and keep hold of this thought," said Sky. "But first I want to go back."

Sky pressed her lips with three fingers of her right

hand. The other she left palm up on her lap. She looked as though she was thinking. "You said that I was watching you. What do you think I see? Rather how do you see yourself now?"

"You mean after the attack?"

"Yes."

"I'm not as purdy as I used to be," said David, sounding like a character from an old cowboy film. It was an attempt at recollecting himself.

"Your features are the same. I'm sure you're aware of that."

"Well, yes, but I'm scarred."

"Some people think scars are attractive. What I'm getting at is that your image of yourself may be a fantasy to some extent. Do people say you look different?"

David thought for a moment. "I guess not."

"I think maybe we could look further at what the fantasy is." Now it was David's turn to watch Sky. He nodded to show he was listening, understanding, and even agreeing. "We can come back to this. You mentioned something else." Again she got into her thinking position. For a moment, she looked to her side, onto the floor trying to remember. "Oh, yes. That's it."

"Fire away."

"It's not clear to me yet. Something about you thinking, I might be afraid of you. Again, I can't help thinking this could be about Ryan." David looked caught off-guard. "Like I said it's not clear. I'm wondering if you don't still have feelings for Ryan, but you're sacred of hurting him, afraid of your own rage. These feelings could be linked to you being hurt. I'm sorry. This isn't well thought out. Does it mean anything to you?"

David shook his head, but recalled being in bed with Ryan. At that time, his nephew was only seven years old, but the feelings David had were adult and sexual. These thoughts took only a fraction of a second, but it was long enough to make blood rush into his dick. There was movement in his jeans, at his crotch. Sky seemed to notice. Quickly, she looked away. It wasn't quick enough. David noticed and blushed. Sky looked into his eyes. It was as though she knew what he was thinking. He felt uncomfortable, and looked to the window, focusing neither on the glass, nor on the tree outside. "Sky," he said. "If I liked him even when he was a kid," he paused, "was I a pedophile?"

6

Upon hearing a key in the front door, Ryan and Leila turned to see who it was.

"Blah, blah, blah," said David as he walked in acting the part of a lunatic.

"Well, are you fixed?" asked Ryan.

"No. Crazier."

"I could have done that for you," said Leila. "You could have paid me."

"That's true. Of all people," said David. "*You* definitely make me feel sane."

Leila was sitting on the floor painting her toenails. Ryan was finishing the surround of the door.

"Nice!" said David, referring to the paper on the walls. Ryan had used large photocopies. The image was a photograph Joe had taken of the road outside their house. "How long has it taken?"

"Including her distracting me, about four hours."

"Do you charge the same rate for distractions?"

"Sorry!" said Leila vaguely as she lifted a foot and blew at her toes.

"It's a great red," said David.

"Yeah," said Ryan. "But Hammorite's a bugger to use. It's kind of sticky and if you don't put enough on, it doesn't look hammered."

"I know all about Hammorite. It's a favorite of Joe's. Why do you think we got you to do it?"

"So you could see me without a shirt on."

Leila looked up to see David's eyes skim quickly over Ryan's torso. "I've never seen such smooth looking skin."

"It's beautiful, isn't it?" said Leila still watching David's eyes.

"Yes *it* and *he* are completely beautiful," said David. Leila smiled, seemingly satisfied, and then continued with her nails. Ryan blushed and blew his hair out of eyes.

"You may as well get used to the idea," said David. "I think you're perfect. I always have." Ryan looked him in the eye, but David's face showed no expression, gave nothing away. "Does it make you uncomfortable?"

"No" said Ryan. "But I suddenly feel very naked." He held a straight face for a moment then burst out laughing. "Come here you idiot. You sound like an old queer from the Fifties." He held out his arms to hug David. "Why should it bother me? Would it bother you if Leila fancied you?"

David pretended to think about it. "I guess not." He paused again. "Why, what are you trying to tell me?"

Ryan got hold of David. He put his arms around him and pulled him in. David couldn't help noticing the smell that came up from Ryan's armpits. He put his face into Ryan's neck and kissed him. Suddenly he thought of himself as lecherous, and this made him uneasy, but then a bossier sexual urge crushed these ideas. It made him even more aware of Ryan's sugary, pungent smell, but more than this, he felt skin, so soft. David even believed he could taste Ryan; the flavour of boyhood, boy mouth, boy attitude. Maybe this was just his imagination, a fantasy? David could feel heat rising off skin that had never been touched by a man, never been enjoyed by a mouth that said, "Let's fuck!" Images crammed into David's mind, Ryan's lower back as it stretched, trying to reach the top of the door, Ryan's slim waist, flat chest, and stomach, Ryan. Fuck. Within a few seconds, David's dick grew hard. When he had these feelings ordinarily, he'd gorge, let his sexual self charge forward. Desire. Kiss. He wanted to have sex with the thing in his arms. He wanted Ryan, must have something of him. Stop. Cool. This was inappropriate. At least, out of context. David pulled away.

Ryan noticed something strange about the way David let go of him. "What's wrong?"

"Nothing," said David, before even thinking. He knew this was the right thing to say, although he felt very different.

Ryan was concerned, which made him more attractive and only served to torment David. Within seconds, this twisted into resentment toward Ryan for causing these feelings and devolved further into contempt for Leila. David thought quickly and said, "It's probably a post-therapy thing." He turned to see Leila dip her nail polish brush in the Hammorite. She was applying it to her big toes.

"What do you think?" she said. "I like red and green together."

"Very doorway," said David, not sure what he really meant to say or what he meant by what he had actually said.

"When you guys were busy bonding. I had to entertain myself somehow."

"It's good camouflage," said Ryan and winked.

"My point exactly. You can never blend in too well."

Again, a key turned in the front door. They all looked round. Joe walked into the living room, headed towards David, and kissed him. "Baby, you're sweating." He looked around at Ryan and Leila. "I feel like I've interrupted something."

"Yeah, important interior design talk," said David.

"All interior design talk is important," said Joe. Taking in the room he added, "Nice job, Ryan. It looks great."

"It's your ideas."

"Ideas are easy. Making it happen is more difficult."

"I agree, but you also made it happen by asking me to do it."

"I suppose so. Can't I credit you for anything?"

"For looking amazing while doing it."

Joe looked at Leila who was also watching him. "Okay, she looks amazing while you're doing it."

Leila looked down at her toes, not sure if Joe was flirting with her or teasing her.

"Well," said Ryan. "A credit's a credit."

"Listen," Joe said to all in the room. Then he spoke just to David, "Do you fancy taking these two out on the town?"

"Where were you thinking of?" Ryan asked enthusiastically.

Joe shrugged, "Trade?"

"I've heard of that place," said Leila.

"Is it still cool?" said Ryan, acting as though he cared about such things.

"Cool's not a word I'd use for Trade," said David. "Hot is more appropriate."

"As in hawrt," said Leila, with a nonspecific American accent.

"No," said David, "As in, everybody's dripping with sweat."

"Sexsey," said Ryan sounding creepy and serpent-like.

"Well, are you all in or not?" There was silence. Joe pulled a bunch of things out of his pocket and threw them down on the floor in front of them. "I thought this might help persuade you." Leila's eyes widened.

"Jesus, what's all that?"

"It's party time," said Joe. "Are you in?"

Ryan looked at Leila who looked back and grinned. "We're in," she said.

"David?"

"We're in too," said David.

"Crazy cow," Joe laughed. "Oh yeah! I forgot it's therapy day."

"What's the plan?" said Ryan.

"Either sleep or not, and we'll go out about three."

"Cool," said Leila in an exaggerated way. "Sorry, I mean hot."

Ryan knelt down in awe next to the table. "So, what's in the stash?"

Joe picked up some wraps and casually gave them out. "Here's a little something to make sure you're ready to go."

"Coke?" said Leila, not hiding her excitement.

"You got it, sister," said Joe, counting out, picking up, and handing each of them three tablets. "This is to make sure you're in the right mood and make you like me."

"Ecstasy!" Leila squealed.

"You're good at this," Joe laughed. "Finally, just a little something in case we start flagging."

"Speed," said Ryan, before Leila had a chance to speak.

"Very good. You kids have obviously done this before."

"Joe!" said David with a stern look. "That's my nephew you're talking to." Then they all burst out laughing.

"Even more reason we should set a good example. Show them how to do it properly."

"Sounds good to me," said Leila.

David smiled in a wicked way. "Judy will kill me if she finds out," said David. "Promise you won't tell her."

"Okay," said Ryan. "Mum's the word."

"Ha ha. Well, your fathers here discussed this earlier and we feel that you're going to do this at some point anyway, so we'd rather be with you when you try it. Not so much to guide you or make sure you're okay, but more to take advantage of you when you're all fucked up. So, please promise, no word of this to Judy."

"I promise! What do you think I am?"

"Set your watches," said Joe. "We'll rendezvous here at two. I like to have a drink before I get there. I hate to arrive sober."

"Do you drink with ecstasy?" asked Leila.

"I'm afraid so."

"Hard-core," she said admiringly.

"Aren't I."

"Haven't people died from that?" said Ryan sounding like the sixteen-year-old he actually was.

"Exactly," said Joe.

"You can't not drink," said David. "How would you get drunk?"

"You don't have to on E," Leila reasoned.

"But it helps," said David. "It gives you something to do at least. I'm hardly just going to stand there and be high. It would be tedious."

"You could twitch and wiggle like everybody else," said Joe.

"Or act helpless like a first timer," said David.

"What's a first timer?" said Ryan.

"Somebody who's never taken ecstasy before. There's a routine." David explained. "They have to sit down when they're coming up, because they're rushing." With this, he held up one finger. "Then they get sick, somewhere close, like the floor beside the chair they're sitting on," he continued and held up another finger. Usually, somebody ends up being on duty. Often this person isn't a friend, or even care beyond what the ecstasy has induced. So let's just call this person Duty. They're happy enough. Now they have something to do and it's quite a good look because it makes them appear kind. Not that anybody gives a fuck about this at Trade." Finger number three slowly went up. "After about twenty minutes, the adorable, jaw-grinding, eye-rolling, fidgety first-timer has found a confidence they never knew they had." Consumed by his story David began to vibrate with enthusiasm and as he carried on, yet another finger shot up. "Now they can dance, sweat, and flirt with any man they like. Suddenly, there's nothing to hold them back. So they can be funny, sexy and clever, to men they ordinarily believed out of their reach."

"Enough!" screamed Leila, "We choose to witness this?"

"I haven't finished," protested David.

"Yeah, I want to hear what happened to the man on first-timer duty," said Ryan.

"Well," said David, taking a deep breath and smiling. "It goes something like this." With a certain amount of satisfaction, David had reached number five and stuck up his thumb. "Duty looks real pretty by now. He has vomit coating his trainers. His face is withdrawn and his body sinewy because he's so dehydrated. His eyes are bulging as though they no longer want to be a part of his face. He looks around the room and tries to focus but can't. The muscles in his face move so much, it appears to churn. He's almost pure drug now. Duty's become Ecstasy-man, an undulating, sweating, paranoid freak that would make you jump in fright if you saw him in day life." David took another deep breath. "Picture this," he said, holding all the fingers of the hand keeping count. "Duty's hair is sticking to his face, his jeans are soaked, and he's spent the last of his money on ecstasy, so he becomes predator now, amidst many others in varying states of . . ." he held two fingers of both hands to mean, quote, unquote, " . . . ecstasy. He doesn't want to leave, not yet. If only he was sexy again, sparkling and funny, but his high has faded."

"Anybody who can afford a cab home looks attractive.

If they're cute physically, it's a bonus. When so high, it doesn't really matter. He would have liked that guy showing his big dick at the urinal earlier but he was last seen smeared against some muscles in hot pants. Then he remembers the dealer who asked if he could take him home, with the chat-up line, 'I've everyfing at 'ome, even Viagra. And I love to fuck.' An offer Duty can't refuse.

"They leave with a bunch of other wet-faced, jaw-grinding monsters, presumably dropping en-route. Duty presumed wrong. Back in suburban-rainy-Sunday-day-light, they all pile out of the cab and into a small room that looks like it belongs to somebody's grandma, but with fluorescent lighting and techno music."

"Bleak," said Joe for emphasis.

"We're only just getting to the good bit," said David. "There's some knocking on the ceiling, so Dealer turns down the music. 'Old man,' he said. 'Just lost his wife.' That was more information than Duty needed. Now he pictures the man upstairs, lonely, sad, and he's wishing he hadn't left the club. It was warm and safe there, familiar, and full of mates who go every week."

"I'll have to take a toilet break," said Leila. "Or I might never touch another ecstasy again."

"God forbid!" laughed Ryan.

"Let me finish," said David.

"Sure, but I'm out of here," said Leila, and left the room.

"Lightweight," said Ryan. "Go on, Uncle."

"Across from Duty there's someone on a beanbag giving dirty looks, and whispering too loudly to his boyfriend. There's been a shitload of negative humour flying around since they arrived. Duty decides to make coffee, mainly to get out of the room, but also hoping it will stop him feeling so monged-out. The kitchen is cold and filthy. He fishes out cups from the fluid in the sink that actually stinks. He starts to make fifteen coffees, all with three or more sugars, but there aren't enough cups, so he makes some of them in bowls. Back in the living room, Dealer gives another tab to everybody, so it's not long before everybody's rushing again. As you all know, a rush this late on isn't like the first. It kind of staggers through your system, scratching along the way. It's less of a rush, more of an attack, with no euphoria, just the feeling that there are chemicals in your system."

"Please stop," said Leila as she re-entered the room.

"No. I want to know what happens to Dealer, Duty, Fidgety-first-timer, and all the Ecstasy at the chill-out."

"Yeah, please let me finish."

"You lot are bloody masochists," said Leila.

David barely hears what she has said. He's keen to carry on with his story. "There isn't even a whiff of sex for Duty. Dealer's in the middle of the floor, dancing to his favorite track. His feet are creating wads of fluff as his trainers scuff the carpet. He kicks over two coffees, but says it's not a problem. Dirty-look, and some more of the Ecstasies join him. Dealer hands out another tab and already it's time to leave for DTPM. Everybody thinks this is a great idea. Dealer knows the doorman, so the whole party is sorted."

"What's DTPM?" said Ryan.

"Another club, much the same, on Sunday."

"It's very different," said Joe, defensively.

"Okay, tell me how."

He thought for a moment. "Trade's on Saturday.

DTPM's on Sunday."

"Oh, I understand," said Leila. "What you actually mean is Trade's on Saturday, whereas DTPM's on Sunday. I get it. Will we end up at DTPM?"

"No!" said David. "It's crap. We're going to Trade."

"Cool," said Leila, with her American accent again.

"No, hot!" said David.

"Right!" said Leila. "That's what I meant."

David's story finally ended when Leila distracted him enough and they all went to bed.

At half-past two, David went in to Ryan's room, opened the curtains to darkness, and said, "Rise and shine. It's a beautiful . . ." He froze. "Oh, I think my clock might be wrong." Then he pounced onto the bed and began to roll around.

"David! You heavy thing," said Leila.

"I don't want you two falling asleep again. Your Uncle Joe's been up since the crack of dawn, chopping and mixing."

"You're kidding," said Leila, wide-eyed.

"No, he isn't," said Joe, walking in the room in pair of pajamas. He had a mirror in one hand and a glass jug in the other.

"Firstly," said Ryan. "What's in the jug? Secondly, you can leave that mirror with me."

"Long Island iced tea. And wait your turn."

"First things first," said Leila, and clicked her fingers sternly. "The mirror."

David handed it to her. "That's my kind of gal."

"I want to hear more about Duty, Dealer, Dirty-look, and the rest of the Ecstasies," said Ryan.

"Good memory!" said David.

"Hey, those guys are family."

"Don't worry. You'll see them all later. I'll make sure I introduce you."

"No thanks," said Leila.

"You'll like them I'm sure."

"I don't think so," said Leila.

"I do," said Joe. "You'll be one of them."

"Let's do a line first," offered Leila. "I don't think I can bear the reality of it all otherwise."

"Hear, hear," said Joe. They both stooped and banged heads.

David laughed, "Coke whores."

Leila took a seat. "Finish your story, granddad."

"I warn you, David," said Ryan. "She gives as good as she gets."

"I don't want to hear about your sex life," said David.

Ryan rolled his eyes. "Can we please cut the bawdy humour for one second," said Ryan. "There's an innuendo every other sentence in this house."

"It's part of our rich culture," said Joe.

"Which, gay?" Leila asked.

"No. British."

"You mean," said Leila. "The fact that we're repressed as fuck."

"Exactly," said Joe matter-of-factly. "So we find subtle ways of communicating those frustrations."

"Hardly subtle," said Ryan and Leila simultaneously before bursting out laughing.

Joe suddenly felt old, embarrassed, and separate.

7

At three-thirty, a cab pulled up outside Trade. Contorting faces stood in the rain, watching, grateful for the distraction from simply waiting. David and Joe got out either side, and Joe went to pay the cab.

Ryan put out a hand. "Is it still raining?" he asked.

"Come on, Nelly," said David, taking him by the hand.

Leila knew people were watching, so took her time. "Shit," she said, while still sitting in the cab. "Look at the line."

"Don't worry," said David. "Come on, I'm getting soaked. What are you waiting for?"

"Dramatic effect."

"It's working. I suspect people think you're in a wheel-chair."

Leila put on the finishing touches to her lipstick, closed her compact, and popped them in her bag. She stepped out as though to a ball. She'd made a special effort. Her hair was sticking up in twisted spikes, and she had a fine layer of gold shimmer all over her. She had on a silver metal-link dress and wore antique looking spectacles, which you could only pull off if you were an old lady or a supermodel. She looked magical.

"I can't stand in line," she said.

"I said, don't worry. Joe will sort it out."

Ryan stopped in his tracks. "Oh, my God, Joe's Dealer, isn't he?"

David ushered them towards the entrance. The line on the right was for regular punters, the one on the left for those on the guest list. Joe disregarded both, and approached the person with the guest list. Defensively, the bouncers pulled in tight creating a barrier.

"Josef 'Oltzmen!" called out a man squeezing through them.

"Lee!" said Joe with a hug that seemed to stick even when they let go.

Lee had hedgehog-like hair, pale skin, and ruddy cheeks that made him look like he'd just been snow balling. "Gird ta see ya," he said with warmth and familiarity. "Har meny av ya got wiv ya?"

"Just three."

"Let this lot frew," Lee instructed the bouncers. They lifted back the metal barriers. Lee gave Joe four tickets and giggled. "Let's have a drink later."

"Definitely!" Joe obviously liked Lee. "I'll save you a spot on my dance card."

"Thet word bey charming," said Lee, as near as he could to an old-fashioned, very proper accent. It was hopeless. His East-End accent shone through. Joe poked him playfully in the ribs. Again, Lee giggled, and shuffled his feet, looking about seven years old.

Inside the door, they heard muffled music. The air was

moist and warm. Two cashiers took the tickets Lee had given them, and gave attitude in return. Joe didn't recognize them. Another person stood to the right of the cashiers, with a rubber stamp.

"I feel like I'm on a conveyer belt," said Leila.

"Yeah, to hell," said David.

Finally, down just a few steps, at the first bend in the stairwell, yet another person checked the stamps.

"Joe Holtzman!" cried the stamp checker.

David turned to Leila. "You get used to this. I can tell when people don't really know him. They use his surname. That's how they think of him, the celebrity Joseph Holtzman."

"Is he that famous?" said Ryan.

"I hate to be cynical, but gays love it when someone is even remotely famous and gay as well."

Leila nodded. "It makes sense. It's validating."

"Yeah," said David. "Like what you said."

Joe led them further down the steps. They could feel the heat rise up their bodies as they descended, until it engulfed them completely. They stopped at the second bend in the stairwell. From here, they could see the whole of one room. Everybody had their shirts off, so there wasn't much colour, only varying flesh tones. There were a couple of neon wristbands. David sighed when he spotted them.

"Why do you pretend to be stupid, David?" said Leila. "It's obviously an act."

"It's cute isn't it?" He paused. "Marilyn did okay on it."

"Marilyn was working within a different world. In those days women . . . ."

"Okay!" David stopped her. "Enough serious talk.

We're meant to be mindless."

"When should we start?" Ryan asked.

David looked at his watch, "Twenty-two, twenty-three. Now!"

"In that case, I'm off to find my mates, First Timer and Duty." He scanned the crowd. Ryan pointed at somebody. "There's First Timer."

"That's not him. That's Look At Me I'm So Sexy."

"It can't be," said Leila.

"It is," said David.

"God, he's changed," said Leila.

Joe put his hand her shoulder. "Let's get a drink in the café upstairs. It's not so gym-like."

They turned around and headed back the way they came.

"Had enough already?" asked Lee as they passed the front door.

"I'll be back for you later," said Joe without stopping.

They entered a less chaotic room, with table and chairs.

"The café" said Joe with a wave of his hand. "Better?"

"I guess so," said Leila, clearly more impressed with the room they'd just left.

They claimed a table. Ryan and Joe sat down, Leila remained standing, and David went to the bar. Leila took hold of the hem of her dress.

"Here we go," said Ryan.

Leila lifted her dress, but instead of stopping at head height, she continued lifting it over her head. She took it off completely. Nobody took any notice. Leila rolled up the dress and stuck it in her bag.

"I wondered how long that would last," said Joe.

Underneath the dress, Leila wore a lilac bra and a pale green slip.

"You look amazing," said Ryan, a mix of lust and awe in his eyes.

"I'd have to agree," said Joe.

Leila seemed to respond more to Joe's compliment than she had to Ryan's. She pouted her lips and sighed. Ryan registered something slightly off-kilter about her response, but he wasn't being vigilant so let it pass. In Trade, with his uncle, was the last place on earth he'd feel it were necessary.

David came back with the drinks. "Somebody could have helped me."

"We were kind of busy," said Leila.

"Doing what?"

She put her finger to her chin thoughtfully, "I'm not sure," said Leila. "Oh yeah, changing."

A bunch of sweaty men came up to the table, shirtless, with shaved chests. They spoke to David but flirted randomly with each of them. After about five minutes, then moved en mass to the bar.

"They go to the gym where I work," said David, as if it were an explanation.

Ryan scrunched his nose in disgust, "They look like uncooked sausages."

"I don't understand," said Leila. "They all seem to be holding each other up."

Joe laughed, and David burst out laughing. "An amazing feat, considering they were all so wet and slippery."

Leila shuddered. "Ugh! They're grotesque."

"They're really popular," said David.

"You're joking. I'll never understand you boys," said

Leila with a sip of her drink.

"*Boys* is kind of patronizing," said David.

"It was meant to be. But I was only kidding."

"So was he," said Joe. "Let's take some more E."

"Yes," said Ryan, a bit too quick off the mark.

"You're keen," David smiled.

"Well, what are we waiting for? It's not going to take itself. And it's not as though we'll stand out."

"In that case," said Joe, taking an E out of his pocket and popping it in his mouth. "Here goes." He made a face, as though it tasted horrible and reached for his drink. "I wish somebody would sugarcoat these fuckers."

"Hear! Hear!" said David, doing almost the same set of actions exactly pop, grimace, and drink. "Ryan?"

"Why not?" he said, and followed suit.

"Leila?" offered Joe.

"I've already done mine."

"When?" Ryan looked upset.

"Back at the flat."

David raised his eyebrows, and shook his head in disbelief. "So, do you love me yet?"

"Probably," she said.

"Do you love everybody yet?" said Joe.

"I guess so."

"Do you love yourself yet?" asked Ryan.

"I only had *one*."

David and Joe laughed. Ryan was used to this type of answer, so he half expected it. For a while, the conversation carried on in much the same vein.

Lee came up to the table, and bought a round of drinks, insisting that nobody move to help him and darting back and forward through the crowd with surprising dexterity.

When done with his task he popped himself onto Joe's knee while he drank. Excited, he swung side to side, but because he was so little Joe could barely feel his weight.

A bedraggled-looking drag queen approached the table, and asked could she borrow Leila's lipstick. Although, a little disgusted, Leila was pleasant. The drag queen loved the colour so much, she insisted Leila write down the name and brand.

When she finally left, and was out of earshot, David said, "Your E. must be good."

Leila sat up straight. "I thought the poor bitch could do with some help."

"There's the Leila I know and love," David smiled.

A mischievous look came over Leila's face. "I'm glad I have you all together. I've been meaning to tell you this, and believe me, it's not the E talking." Leila burst out laughing. "But I'm quite fond of you three."

In time, they took another E. A different kind. It was more 'trippy" and 'mongy." This had the effect of making them speak less and stare into space more.

Bored, Leila said, "This is bollocks. Let's do some speed."

"I can't move," said David.

"Me neither," said Ryan.

"I'm up for it," said Joe. "If I can keep hold of you on the way." He stood up. "I feel as though I've never done this standing thing before."

"Come on," said Leila. "You'll get your E-legs in a minute."

Ryan giggled, "Good luck."

"Yeah, good fuck," David added. Leila and Joe were already too far away to hear. Ryan looked shocked. "Sorry.

I don't know where that came from."

"You're a weird mother-fucker, David." Ryan paused to think, but his train of thought went askew and wound up in mathematics. Not that he had the cognitive ability to do more than think how sound affects numbers. This went on for some time. Then he seemed to come round. "David. Can I put my head in your lap? I could do with less sitting up."

"Sure, puppy."

Ryan fell to one side, as though collapsing. David caught him, and lovingly stroked his head. "Ryan. Are you happy at our house?"

"God, yeah."

"I'm glad. I'm going to blame this on the E., but when you were a kid, I always hoped we'd be able to hang out."

"Shucks, grandpa," said Ryan. "I lurrrv you."

"I lurrrrrrrrv you too, Bobby."

"E.'s a wonderful thing isn't it?"

"Sure is."

As Leila and Joe passed the front door Lee stopped them. He gave them a bump of K, which made their journey that much harder. He also demanded a kiss, which lasted longer than Leila wanted it to. She twisted her hair, trying not to notice them. She eventually pulled at Joe's arm, which worked. They all laughed. Once more Leila and Joe headed towards the toilets. Lipstick drag queen stopped them to enthuse about the new colour of his lips. He now had only one heel and rambled on about how kind and beautiful Leila was. His makeup was barely on now, just stains, and smudges. He put his arms around Joe and Leila, spilling his drink down Joe's T-shirt. Joe unhooked himself, pulled the T-shirt off, and stuck it in his back pocket. It didn't actually go in his pocket, but fell into the black paste on the floor, unique to clubs all over the world. The drag queen made a fuss about Joe's hairy torso, and said what a lovely couple he and Leila made. Fortunately for them, he needed to go to the toilet to check his makeup, and had to go to the women's because the lighting was better. Naturally, this made Joe and Leila choose to go into the men's instead. Only two people were waiting, so it wasn't long before they were in a cubicle.

Vomit coated the toilet bowl.

"Delicious!" said Leila.

With his dick in his hand, Joe waited for piss to come out. Then when realising that all he was doing was staring at the pan, he said, "I forgot that I don't actually need to use the toilet."

"Right. It's quite pretty, really," said Leila as she closed the lid.

"I was thinking that."

Leila waited. "You've got the stuff?"

Joe snapped out of it. "Oh, yeah, sorry." He chopped the speed as efficiently as one would expect on so many drugs. Leila did her line first.

"It tastes sweet," said Leila.

"Maybe we'll get a rush from the sugar."

"I think we're beyond being affected by such things."

Leila got a little serious. "I find when I'm this high, sugar does affect me. I think it's when I haven't eaten for hours . . ."

Joe leaned forward and stuck his tongue into her mouth. He let the whole weight of his body press against her. She returned the kiss, and stuck her hand down the front of his jeans.

"Sorry, drug dick," Joe smiled.

This space gave Leila the time to think. Not so much think as react. Instead of continuing, she slid out of his embrace. Joe was so high he didn't think much of it.

"I'm sorry," said Leila.

"What for?" Joe wasn't being cool. His thoughts really had moved on to something else.

"I like you, Joe, and I think you're fucking gorgeous, but we've got to think about David and Ryan."

"Oh, yeah." Joe agreed because he was on E.

They finished the speed and forgot all about the kiss. They fumbled with the latch, got out of the cubicle, and made their way back to the others. They'd been gone about thirty minutes.

"That was quick," said David. "I thought you'd be ages."

"We were. I think," said Leila. "Oh, the adventures we've had."

"Lucky things! We've been melting into the chairs."

"As well as each other," said Ryan.

"And every plastic cup and cigarette end that got in our path."

"It's great here, isn't it," said Leila, and finally they all laughed as much as they could be bothered.

"I love you a lot," said Ryan.

"You've done that joke already," said Leila. "I think. Well, one of us did."

Joe rose from his seat suddenly. "You kids have fun," he said with a renewed speed-induced burst of energy. "I'm going to see who's here. Do you mind?"

"No," said Ryan.

"Are you going by yourself?" Leila asked.

"No," said David, getting up faster than he'd moved all night.

Ryan blew out a rush of air, closed his eyes and said, "We're cool here."

They both disappeared into the crowd.

"Thanks!" said Leila sarcastically.

"We're okay here, aren't we? Did I tell you how fantastic you look?"

"You said amazing last time."

"I'm not bugging you, am I?"

"No." Leila looked around as though what she was about to say was top secret. "Listen, I've an idea, but first you have to say whether you're in or out."

"Out. No, I mean in."

"In that case, follow me."

Leila led Ryan to the toilets. There were men and women in jumbled lines outside each. The only distinction between the male and female toilets at Trade was that one had urinals, and the other a couple more cubicles. Leila took Ryan by the hand and led him to the front of the queue in the women's. The people waiting were dazed and silent.

"What do you think you're doing?" said a women wet with sweat.

"Don't worry," said Leila. "We work here. We've got to get back to the door."

"You weren't there when I came in," said the girl.

"We've got to start now," said Leila. "Listen, do I have to get security?"

Like a slug in salt, the girl recoiled. She had visions of security dumping her outside on the street, and being high, by herself, in broad daylight.

Her eyes darted, eager to avoid contact. Eventually, she said, "Sorry, I didn't know you worked here."

Leila nodded and smiled in an overly patronizing way. She looked at her watch, as though conscious of being late. Feigning impatience, she sighed and knocked on a door. Just then, a door opened, and a man came out wafting the air in front of his face. Leila and Ryan stumbled in, closed the door, and only then realised what the wafting meant. She opened the door again and asked somebody for some matches. The man was still there, apologised, and gave her a box, telling her she could keep them. She lit four in one go, which pretty much dealt with the smell. Then they settled in. Ryan sat on the floor with his back against the door and Leila sat on the lid of the toilet. She opened her bag, and rummaged.

"There," said Leila.

"What. . ?" Ryan stopped as he realised what she was holding.

"Don't look so shocked. It's just a bit of coke."

"Just a bit of coke in syringes."

"Sssh!" she said quietly. "Give me your belt."

Ryan undid it, slid it out of his jeans, surprised at the casualness of it all.

"You've done this before."

"You know I have. Don't act so shocked. Inspecting his left arm, she said, "This one's got the best vein."

Matter-of-factly, she took hold of Ryan's arm and put the belt around it, tightened it, tapped on his vein and injected. For a second she watched him, as his eyes began to widen, and his back stiffened. She took the belt off his arm and immediately got on with her own. Again, she tightened the belt. The area where she was about to put the needle looked particularly dirty, so she licked it to clean it and took another quick glance at Ryan. He was staring ahead of him. He swallowed hard and said, "I love you."

"You mean you love the feeling," she said. "Intense, hey?"

There was no answer. Leila assumed he was enjoying it, so went to put the needle in her own arm, and then stopped. She looked up again.

"Ryan?"

By now his face looked like it was going to pop. He was sitting against the door. He started to bang his head backward.

"Baby, don't," she said, worried they'd be thrown out of the club. He banged harder.

"Baby!" Vomit spewed out of Ryan's mouth, splashing all over Leila's lap and legs. It was mainly alcohol, so just ran off her. In a state of shock, Leila watched Ryan as he closed his eyes and slid towards the wall.

"Ryan!" There was no answer.

Leila leant forward, undid the belt around her arm, and quickly did it up again around his waist. She didn't bother putting it through the belt loops. Next, she put the two needles in the sanitary towel bin, pulled open the door, and squeezed out.

"My boyfriend's passed out. Will somebody help?"

Outside the line had changed little, except the sausage men were splashing themselves with cold water.

"Let me deal with it," said one of them, sounding surprisingly sober.

He and Leila squeezed back into the cubicle.

Ryan already had his eyes open. "What's going on?" he asked.

"You passed out," said Leila.

"Let me take a look at you," said the man. He checked

Ryan's pulse. "What were you guys doing in here?"

"Just a bit of coke," said Leila.

There was a knock at the door. It was David. He squeezed in.

"It's nothing to worry about," said the sausage man. "They've just been overdoing it a bit."

"Thanks, George."

"No problem! Can you stand?"

"Sure," said Ryan. David and George helped him to his feet, but instantly Ryan slouched and fell into George, who caught him and laughed. Ryan looked very pale. Leila pulled the toilet roll out of its holder and dried the vomit on her legs.

"Let's get him some fresh air," George suggested. "David, you maybe should think about getting him home."

"That's probably not a bad idea," said David.

"But we've just got here," Ryan protested, barely using real words. Awkwardly, they all bundled out of the toilet.

Joe arrived. "What happened?"

Again, George spoke, assuming the voice of authority. "They've just been overdoing it a bit."

"Let's go home," said David. "Thanks again, George. I'm glad you were here."

They made their way to the front door. They might have been embarrassed they were in such a dishevelled state, but they were too high to care. There were many cab drivers touting for business. As they walked out onto the pavement, Joe spotted a black cab on its way toward them. He whistled. The cab stopped, and they all got in. Ryan lay with his head on David's lap, moaning dramatically.

"Had a rough night?" said the driver.

This ignited something in David, disgust, hatred, or

anger. He turned to look at the driver. For no apparent reason, David disliked him. Joe saw David's response, put a hand on his knee, and gave him a questioning look.

"You okay, baby?"

"I think so," said David. "I suddenly felt really scared."

"It's probably just the drugs."

"I know. But . . ." David's voice went quiet enough for only Joe to hear. "Don't you think he's creepy," he said gesturing towards the driver with his head.

"No! He's just some poor man trying to make a living."

"There's something about him. He gives me the creeps."

"Baby! My sweet-sweet-scared-kitten-thing. It's the drugs, trust me. He's probably the most normal man you'll ever meet."

David looked in the rear-view mirror, listening to the driver, watching his forehead suspended within the small rectangle. For a brief moment, eyes replaced forehead, then darted out of sight. David thought him familiar. His thoughts jumbled. Realizing he was fighting a losing battle with the drugs, he resigned himself to believing that he'd simply had the same driver some other time.

It wasn't long before the cab smelt of vomit, and the driver complained. To distract him, Ryan chatted. It was quite nonsensical, but the driver responded well, even seemed to like Ryan. Because of this, and opening the windows full, they managed to get home without the driver throwing them out. The cab dropped them right outside their house. As they got out David took a closer look at the driver, and didn't recognize him, so finally he let go of what he now believed to be drug-induced paranoia.

Ryan was left to pay, then run after them. "You must

have driven him mad," said Leila, as he approached. "The poor thing has to rest."

"What do you mean?" said Ryan.

"He hasn't gone yet."

"He's probably clocking off."

"Cashing up," said Joe, agreeing.

"With no lights on?" asked David.

8

Late into the next evening, they woke. Insecurity, irritability, and a closing off overwhelmed the loving, open sense of well-being from earlier. The most nutrition any of them could stomach came via the nuts and milk in a Snickers bar. By nighttime, David decided he would force down something more sensible and went to the kitchen with good intentions only to return with Sugar Puffs in warm milk with added maple syrup. Together they spent the rest of the evening in isolation, watching whatever flickered in front of them on cable TV. By three o' clock, it was the most anybody could do to get themselves upstairs and into bed.

The following day, David lay in bed, not wanting to get up. He tried snoozing, but his tiredness seemed to have run out. As a last resort, he attempted to count, but anxiety interrupted.

Leila tried a different method, although it wasn't so conscious. She got up early and cleaned. Neurotically, she dusted things. The usual cleaner did a good job, so it wasn't necessary. Still, Leila wiped the edges of things, vacuumed under things, and behind things. She emptied cupboards, wiped the contents, and put them neatly back again, often in exactly the same place, with everything facing the same way, the right way.

Ryan attempted to simply chill, relaxing in a hot bath, smoking a strong joint. The grass didn't calm him, only made him paranoid. After half an hour, he gave up.

Joe decided to work on his exhibition. His post-drug-contorted way of seeing things was an ideal time to root around in such ideas as desperation, suffering, and hopelessness, and, by default, safety, passion and kind-ness.

Reluctantly, David got up. He didn't want anything to challenge him, so had Valium for breakfast. Shortly after his second cup of coffee, he felt more able to deal with living. In case he'd missed anything important in the world, he put the TV on. In the living room, he found Leila bent over a pad, writing a letter to a friend.

"Are you sure *that's* a good idea?" asked David.

"She's used to it," said Leila, then paused a second. "Are you sure that's a good idea?" she said, pointing to the TV with her pen. "Apart from the cutesy-feel-good story they throw in at the end when they realize their viewers might commit suicide, so roll on the puppy story they keep in reserve and everything's okay. The world's not so bad."

Ryan came into the room, wearing a bathrobe. "Hello," he said loudly, feigning good spirits. In response, David turned off the TV and sighed just as Joe joined them. Everybody turned and looked annoyed. "Jesus!" he said. "What a sight. You lot remind me of those creatures from *The Time Machine*. Anyway, good news! I made some headway with my exhibition."

"What's this exhibition?" said Leila.

"It's just a little show I'm putting together. I was having a bit of trouble with some of the ideas, but it's all coming thick and fast now. Your CD is the cherry on the cake."

"CD?" she asked.

"The barking."

"Oh yeah! My party CD."

"And the TV jingles?" said David.

"That's my cultural CD."

David thought Leila was kooky. Leila thought David was obvious and a little flimsy. Leila pulled a smile at David. He did the same back.

"What are you doing today, Ryan?" said David, trying to change the focus of the conversation.

"Don't know. See a film. Buy a book."

"What about you?"

"I was thinking of the gym."

"You're not being serious!" said Ryan.

"It was just an idea," said David, a little embarrassed.

"We should all go," said Leila. "A family day out."

Joe crossed his arms with a doubtful expression. "At the gym?"

"It might be just what we need," said Leila.

"Yeah," said David. "We could just do bicycle. Anything to get the endorphins going."

Ryan lay flat-out on the sofa and had covered himself with cushions. "Dorphins. Isn't that what dolphins have?"

"Endorphins are what make you feel nice," said David.

"It's actually the body's response to pain." Joe paused, his mind clearly racing. "Fuck!" At this, he ran out of the room, leapt upstairs, and across the landing. After a couple of minutes, he came back into the living room panting and smiling.

Leila was curious. "Fill us in."

"Just an idea," said Joe.

"Tell!" said Leila.

"You'll see."

"We might be able to give you some useful feedback," offered Leila.

"I wouldn't bother," said David. "He won't budge."

"You can give me feedback at the exhibition."

"In that case I hope it's soon."

"A couple of weeks," said Joe.

"Fantastic!" said Leila.

Ryan saw something in her expression, and in a singsong voice, he said, "Leila's got a crush on Joe." Then he noticed that Joe was blushing. "My God. I've hit something."

"If you say enough stupid things," said Leila, "One day you might say something clever by mistake." She screwed her face up. "But not *this* time."

Now David realised it was true also. "If you don't shut up, Ryan, we'll go to the gym without you."

Leila looked at David feeling grateful for his interception. David looked at Leila and smiled with concern. She saw a kindness in his eyes she'd never seen in him before.

David threw a bit of rolled-up tissue at Ryan. "You're confused," he said. "It's me who has a crush on you." This embarrassed Ryan enough to shut him up. Having said what he had, David wasn't actually sure whether it was true. After having spoken to Sky about it all, he was beginning to believe it had more to do with himself than anybody else. Therefore, despite Ryan being lovable, adorable, and beautiful, David wondered if he'd been misinterpreting everything about his interaction and their relationship. Maybe Ryan was in fact a broken connection, a misunderstanding, a signpost, symbol, or just a clue.

After several more cups of coffee and lots of encouragement from David, they all got out of the house. They hopped on the tube and off it again in Covent Garden. The gym was only a five-minute walk from there. When they arrived, David was greeted with varying degrees of both resentment and lust. A man sitting having a coffee at the bar looked Joe up and down.

"*What!*" Joe said to the man, who looked into his coffee, swilled it around, finished it, and left.

"Was that necessary?" said David.

"I can't stand it when men do that. What the fuck does it mean?"

"It probably means he fancies you."

"So why can't he speak?"

"Because he's been oppressed all his life, because he's intimidated, he's not confident. Shall I go on?"

"Okay!"

A group of men came walking towards them, laughing and screeching.

"David!" said the one at the front. He nudged cheeks with David and made a kissing noise. Then he resumed his conversation with his friends

When they left Leila said, "Has he got hygiene issues?"

"Far from it," said Joe. "I've seen him on all fours in a leather club."

"Maybe he'd lost his keys," said Ryan.

"Lost his mind more like," said Joe. "His prissiness at least."

"*Please*, baby!" said David. "I've got to work here."

"Oh, that's why we've come," said Ryan. "I wondered why."

"So, we don't have to pay?"

"Exactly!" said Joe.

David went off to sort out passes, while the others waited all feeling self-conscious. Some men at a table a few feet away looked at them and spoke to each other conspiratorially.

Joe noticed and pointing towards the men with his head Joe said, "Watch out. I can smell gossip."

"How do you know?" asked Ryan.

"Well, which do you think it is? Take a guess."

"They might be talking about the weather," said Ryan.

"So why aren't they moving their lips?"

The men burst out laughing. Leila turned to look at them. One of them said something. The other pursed his lips then replied. The first looked shocked. Then they both took their coffee cups to the counter, made unfriendly smiles, and left.

David returned in surprisingly good spirits. "Sorted!" He quickly looked at each of them in turn and then pulled an expression of slight pain. "Shall we get started?"

Joe winced.

"What?" said David.

"Can I wait here?" said Joe. David scowled. "*Please*, Dad?"

"Really?" said David.

"I'm tired," said Joe in a whiny voice.

"Okay already," said David in his version of a New York Jewish accent.

Leila laughed. "Come on, then. That's if we're still doing it."

"I'll just sit and read."

"All right," said David. "See you when we're full of morphine."

"I wish," said Leila.

David directed Leila to the women's changing room and David and Ryan headed into the men's. Ryan undressed unselfconsciously. David couldn't do the same. He was aware that the men in the changing room all looked at each other. It seemed that because he worked there everybody stared even more. A yellow-looking man came back from having a shower and stood too close to David. He let his towel drop to the floor and stepped on it, keeping his feet dry. David had to back away from him, especially when he started spraying deodorant under his arms.

Leila was stretching by the time David and Ryan had finished changing. This impressed David. Firstly, that she'd got ready so quickly. Secondly, that she looked like she knew what she was doing.

"Get you!" said David leading them towards the step machines. "Let's start on these. It will help get the mor-phine circulating."

Once on them, they could see Joe sitting in the café.

"Joe!" shouted Ryan. Joe looked up. Leila stuck out her tongue and waved. Joe waved back. He watched them for a moment as they decided who was going to use what machine. He thought them comical but a treat to look at.

"Excuse me," said a deep voice.

Joe looked around. A man stood beside him. Because Joe

was sitting, he came up to the middle of the man's stomach. For a fraction of a second, Joe thought about leaning toward the man, unbuttoning his fly, and sucking his dick. "Do you mind if I sit here?"

Joe's response was little more than to look the man up and down quickly, then gesture with his hand to the chair in question. "Thanks. I'm fucked. I don't know how I'm going to get through this workout."

Again, Joe had sexual thoughts about the man. The word 'fucked' had set off a stream of images. "The name's Don," said the man and put his gym bag on the floor beside his chair.

"Mine's Joe."

"I'm just going to get some coffee," said Don and headed towards the bar area.

Joe tried to make out his body through his baggy T-shirt and jeans. Don turned to catch Joe looking at his butt. Joe blushed. Then he blushed more because he'd blushed in the first place. Suddenly, he felt teenaged, awkward.

Don came back to the table. "Why are you blushing?"

"I'm just hot," said Joe, and blushed again.

"I'll say. Are you okay?"

"I thought so."

"Until?"

"Until you came in. Do you always have this effect on men?"

"I don't know."

"You do know this is a gay gym."

"I know. I work just 'round the corner."

"Where?" said Joe, unsure if this was the only reason Don came to this gym.

"The fire station."

Every word Don said made Joe more attracted to him.

Joe folded the corner of his book and closed it. "You're a fireman."

"Yeah, what about you?"

"Good question," said Joe. "I guess I'm." He paused. "An artist?"

"Shit! I've never met an artist before."

Joe had a feeling in his stomach that was usually reserved for David. It made him uncomfortable. He looked through to the gym and could see David on a step machine. This sight reassured him, and he felt things he acknowledged as good. Relieved by this, he looked back to Don who'd begun to eat a sandwich. Fuck! His proportions made him look cartoon-like. He had curly black hair, wide hands, and the thickest fingers.

"Great forearms," said Joe. As soon as he'd said it, he felt too gay. *Great forearms, Jesus!*

Don gulped his coffee. "Cheers."

Joe imagined that all the men that came to the gym must coo over Don. A fireman!

"Do you not get sick of all the attention you get at this gym?"

"No."

Joe ran with a fantasy of Don not being straight. Then he felt pathetic for even having this thought. He imagined himself sitting talking to Don, and saw himself as corny and fawning. How could he not be seduced? Don spoke and his voice was sexy. He said nothing and his silence was sexy. The way he held his cup, his lips, his throat, his jaw. Joe watched. Aware of this, Don looked back as he drank. Then he put his cup down and laughed.

"Sorry," said Joe. "Was I staring?"

"I don't know. Were you?"

Silenced for a moment, Joe didn't know what to make of Don.

"Probably."

Don laughed again, but longer.

Leila appeared at the table. "What's so funny?"

"I don't know," said Joe.

"Who's this?" she said.

"Don. This is Leila, a friend of mine."

"Hello, Leila. Is that a Persian name?"

"It is actually." Charmed that he knew, she took hold of his hand and kissed it.

"Ladies don't kiss my hand any more," said Don.

"This one does," said Leila. "Anyway, I'll leave you in Joe's good hands. Then she kicked into the air dramatically.

"What's that? A Teenage Mutant Ninja Turtle?" said Joe, thinking he was being up-to-date.

"No. Turtles are out," said Leila. "It's kung-fu *this* week." She did another kick to near Don's head, but in slow motion. "Seee hyoo late ta," she said. Then she jumped and spun mid-air before running off.

"She's fun," said Don.

"Yeah," said Joe. "Leila and her boyfriend are staying with me."

"Cozy!"

"It's not like that. We're kind of related. *Her* boyfriend is *my* boyfriend's nephew." Joe felt odd saying the word 'boyfriend'. He pointed, "That's them over there."

"I understand," said Don. "I think."

Pointing again, Joe said, "The blond one's David, my

boyfriend, and the other one's Ryan."

"Leila's boyfriend," said Don. "And your boyfriend's nephew."

"You got it."

"Happy family."

"It is, actually." This was the first time Joe had paused to think of them that way and it warmed him.

"Listen, I'd better get started." He stood up. "But . . ."

"Spit it out."

"I'd love to see your work."

"I've an exhibition soon at Spitalfields." Joe paused. "Do you fancy seeing it? I'll be setting it up in a couple of weeks. You could see it before it opens."

"A preview?"

"Kind of. I could show you around it one evening. I had better warn you. It's not paintings."

"What is it then?"

"You could call them sculptures. Well, not exactly. They're animals. But believe me, there's nothing cute about it.

"What is it then?"

"I don't know."

"What do you mean?"

"Wait and see. It will be easier to show you."

"Woo mysterious!" said Don. "When do you want to do it?"

"You've probably a busier schedule than I have."

"Maybe you could call me nearer the time."

"Great!"

Don pulled out a felt tip from his denim jacket pocket and scribbled on a napkin, using the palm of his other hand to rest on. "Here's my number. You can give me the address and stuff when you call."

"Great," Joe said again, a bit surprised at how forward Don was. "I'll call." Don turned and saluted. Joe watched as he walked away. Don's jeans were a baggy cut, but his thighs still seemed squashed into them. Joe's eyes stayed on Don until he turned the corner, enjoying the view. Joe stared into space for a second then his sight drifted towards the step machines. David was drying his face and neck with a towel and talking to Ryan all with his eyes on Joe.

9

Autumn arrived and like many pink blooded, hard acting,
As the exhibition drew near Joe and Don spoke on the
phone more often. They got on well and both of them
seemed exited. Although David and Joe had a relatively
open relationship, other people didn't usually keep their
interest for long. David was concerned that Don would.
So was Joe.

On the evening Joe left to meet Don, David puttered
around the house, feeling awkward, as though he didn't
quite fit the space. One moment felt too hot, the next too
cold. Television was boring and reading too demanded
too much attention. Eventually, he decided to bake a
chocolate cake, Joe's favorite. The process of reading,
fetching, measuring and mixing, had a meditative affect
allowing him to relax. He was in a calm, if not a little
detached state of mind, when the doorbell rang. David
opened it, cup in hand.

"Judy!" There stood Ryan's mother. With her dyed
brunette hair, fake tan and an attention seeking lipstick,
it was clear that her aim was femininity and glamour,
but somehow it all fell short. David noticed a hard edge

to her.

"Thanks for getting him to call," she said sarcastically.

"I can't make him call."

"He knows I called, presumably."

"Of course he does. Do you think I kidnapped him? And yes, it's nice to see you too."

"Oh yeah," said Judy, clearly distracted. "Is he in?"

"No, but you can still come in."

"Thanks," she said as she walked in. "It's as fancy as ever."

"Well observed! I do believe that's the technical term for the style."

"Still quick with the tongue, aren't you?"

"Judy, I know you must be upset, but I won't have you take it out on me."

"I wasn't. I mean, I'm not."

"You mean you're always this rude?"

"No," she said and made the motions of a hug. "I'm sorry. I just got fed up with waiting for him to call." As she was led into the living room Judy put her hand to her mouth as though to stifle laughter. "My word!"

Resignedly, David decided not to dignify her reaction, but instead moved on. "Most kids leave home at some point."

"I know that but he wasn't meant to. That is, I want him to go to college."

"He didn't say anything about that."

"He wouldn't, would he?"

"Listen, first things first. Do you want anything to drink?"

"Tea would be great."

David continued through to the kitchen with Judy in tow. "Do you have a preference?"

Judy frowned.

"What kind of tea would you like? English Breakfast okay?"

"No! Teabag tea."

"Sorry, we don't have any."

"Well, whatever tastes the most normal."

"I guess that's Lap sang souchong then." Judy looked at him with a blank expression. "Just kidding!"

Judy shrugged. "Your London jokes are wasted on me."

"Right," said David. Facing away, he rolled his eyes, and filled the kettle.

Judy couldn't help but inspect the room. Something caught her attention, just above the doorway. She stared trying to understand. As David came back into the room, she said, "It's not right."

"What?" said David.

"Putting chocolate on that cross."

"It's just a joke."

"If God's not for you, fine. There's no need to mock."

"It's not about mocking God but about questioning the things we worship."

"*I* don't worship chocolate."

David was happier preparing a tray for the tea, anything to avoid his sister. He took two packets of biscuits out of a cupboard and milk out of the fridge, all with his back to her. "It's not just about chocolate. It's about all large companies, consumerism, capitalism generally, the worship of money and success, that kind of thing."

"I don't worship those things either."

"But some people do."

The kettle switched off and David finished putting together the tea things. "Shall we?" he said, leading them back into the living room.

Judy spoke as she followed. "Maybe your ideas are more about yourself than God."

"Maybe," said David sitting down and in doing so also suggesting where Judy should sit.

"But that's the beauty of God," said Judy with an exaggerated evangelist zeal. "It is whatever we want. Whatever we dare to imagine."

"Maybe."

David fell quieter than he'd previously been.

"Where've you gone?"

"Inside." He'd drifted off and was thinking about Ryan.

"Nearer your God?"

"I hadn't looked at it that way before." He smiled amused by the double meaning.

Judy smiled too, thinking she had gotten through to David. Although begrudging, still David tried to relate to her world. "It's not my fault."

"What isn't?" she asked.

"That Ryan came here."

"If you weren't here, he wouldn't have come."

"I mean, it's not my fault he left home."

"What makes you think I thought it was?"

"You seem intent on making me look a fool, or something."

Judy's expression switched, as though a different program had downloaded. "I'm sorry. I didn't mean to make you uncomfortable."

"That's even more disturbing. If it wasn't your intention it makes me wonder what's going on in your head." He paused. "Judy, do you even like me?"

"I like *you*. I'm just not sure about your lifestyle."

Somewhat angry, he stood up partly to not be near her any longer. "What do you know of my lifestyle?"

"David, I know what you get up to."

"How?"

"It's written all over your soul."

This remark made David think she was completely insane. "Why do you care? What business is it of yours?" Then as though to reiterate, "My life has nothing to do with you."

"David, you haven't changed. Always the blusher."

A key turned in the front door. Ryan walked in and when spotting his mum, turned as though to leave again.

"Ryan! You come back here," David said, quite amused by his playacting.

He turned back, casually threw down his bag, and kissed David on the cheek. Then he set off towards the kitchen.

"Ryan!" said Judy.

Hey, Mum! He stood at the door to the kitchen. "Can I help you with something?"

Judy was use to his cheekiness. "Look at your hair."

"Why, what's it doing?"

"I couldn't tell you."

David got off the sofa. "If you're going to have hair that misbehaves, it may as well be beautiful." He put his arm around Ryan's shoulder and led him back towards the sofa. Ryan sat so that David was in between him and his mum. He looked at the floor.

There was silence. David tried to help. "So what's this about college?"

Judy spoke in a much more timid way than she had to David. "It's what your father and I wanted."

"Are you sure?"

"Yes!" she said peering around David in an attempt to catch Ryan's eye. "And I'll forget about the smoke, or whatever you call it."

"What about the next time?"

"There'll be a next time?"

"There's always a next time."

"Does there have to be in this case?"

"*Mum!*"

Judy knew what this meant. She winced and reluctantly said, "All right." Ryan smiled. This made David smile. That and seeing that they were really communicating.

"I know I'm gong to sound a hundred years old, but you're really lucky that you can talk to your mum like this."

"I'd hate to see unlucky."

"I'll show you unlucky," said Judy, trying to sound like a mum.

"So what will you are studying?" asked David.

"Hey! We're jumping ahead a bit."

"Sorry," said David. "What *might* you be studying?"

"English and drama. There's quite a good drama course."

"It's one of the best in the country," said Judy.

"It's one of the *only* ones," said Ryan.

"Don't split hairs."

"So, you're going to be an actor?" asked David.

"Already am."

"That he is."

"Actually, going to college isn't a bad idea. With all the new HIV meds, I could live to old age. And to tell the truth I have thought about doing some more education myself."

"You could go to church," offered Judy.

"I've thought of it," said David, while shaking his head.

"Never miss a chance, hey, Mum?"

"She's right though. Religion is something to do, but I'm guessing it helps if you believe in the whole thing. There again, there's only so much socialising, drug taking and being completely fabulous that one can do."

Judy started to rummage in her bag. "Spare us the details. Anyway, it's nice to see you're having a good influence on him."

"Thank you." David looked past Judy and out of the window. He squinted and said, "I like to think we help him broaden his horizons."

"As long as that's all you're broadening."

"Mum!" Ryan began to blush.

David followed suit.

After a moment of awkward silence, David began to gather the tea things.

Judy broke the awkward silence. "What a pickle."

First Ryan, then David, then finally Judy laughed.

10

Dusk. Spitalfields meat market. As his cab pulled up, Joe glanced at his watch. On the other side of the road there was somebody waiting. Although silhouetted, he could make out that it was Don. He paid, got out of his cab, and called him over.

"I like a man who's punctual," said Don.

Joe reached out for Don's hand. "Me too. Any trouble finding it?"

"No, I got a black cab." Unless he had imagined it, Don seemed to linger on the handshake. "How are you?"

"Good!" said Joe. "Well, I had a *good* day."

Don put both hands in his jeans pockets. It made him look younger. "What does *good* entail?"

"You know, no death in the family. Didn't see any starving children. I didn't catch an incurable disease."

"Wow! You did have a *good* day.

Don smiled and then held his watch under a street-lamp. "So, I'm guessing the gallery's closed now."

"Right," said Joe, distracted by how iconic Don's jaw looked in of the light from above.

"Will there be anyone there?"

"Only security. Why, what do you have planned? Oh and it's not a gallery, ordinarily."

"What is it?"

"It's a disused shop.

They walked just a few paces up a Dickensian-looking alleyway and approached a door, its weather worn paintwork dull and flaking with age. It was the kind of burgundy/ox blood red that people had used as an undercoat about fifty years before.

Joe rang the bell. Answering the door was a man who could almost have been as old as the building. He wore a black uniform, but had a dark green cardigan underneath it. The buttons fastened wrongly so that the whole thing looked as though it was sliding off to the left.

"Hello, Shawn."

"Hallo, mate." He sounded even older than he looked.

Joe stepped inside first. "Everything okay?"

Although the light was dim, it was clearly run down with bare floorboards, plaster falling off the walls, and somehow it was colder than outside.

"Yeah. It's nice to have company." Shawn broke into a long cough. "I tell you, it gets spooky here at night. Are you thinking of staying long?"

"Not sure," said Joe looking at Don. "An hour. Maybe a bit longer?"

"Well, I'll be here if you need me."

"Okay," said Joe. "See you in a while." A cry came from down the hall. Joe winced. Don looked confused. "I'm afraid that's where we're heading."

"Nice!" said Don.

They set off down the corridor, the floorboards creaking under foot. Single bulbs lit the corridor, so one was never too far away from darkness, and corners that you couldn't see properly. At the end, Joe pushed open two big wooden doors. As he did, the whole spectrum of animal noises opened up; whining, snarling, and howling. The sound alone sent a shiver up Joe's spine.

"Jesus!" said Don. "I feel like I've just walked into hell."

"Great response," said Joe. "It's not too late to change your mind." Don faltered. "Really, it's not. You probably see enough hideous stuff at work."

"That's kind of my feeling about it."

"Let's skip it."

"I think I get the idea," said Don and walked back the way they'd come through the wooden doors and along the corridor. Once they were clear of the exhibition space he turned to Joe and said, "Sorry."

"No. *I'm* sorry." He paused. "Well that's how I'm meant to feel."

"What do you mean?""

"I hope I have some kind of conscience about creating this."

"I'm sure you do."

"Thanks, but I can't help wondering if I'm just really fucked up."

"That sounds like a good start. I would have thought it essential for an artist."

"Well counseled."

"We get training in it."

Joe burst out laughing. His voice echoed through the corridor. With the doors closed to the exhibition, the sounds of it were muffled but still audible.

"Let's get out of here," said Joe.

"I'm right behind you."

They went back to the end of the corridor, both feeling more on edge.

"We're done Shawn," said Joe. "Changed our minds."

"No offense, mate, but I'm not surprised."

"None taken."

Shawn blew his nose with a tatty off-white handkerchief. "So, when's the official opening? I want to look smart."

"In two days. I started putting it together about a week ago. I wanted it to be ready before the press saw it."

"Is it?" asked Don.

"Let's say, it's worse than I imagined it."

"And I'm guessing that's good."

Joe raised his shoulders, frowned, and then smiled at the same time. "I guess so."

"Good night to you both then," said Shawn, and pulled open the door to the street.

"Thanks, Shawn. I'll see you Tuesday, unless there's a problem."

"Tuesday it is then," said Shawn, and closed the door behind them. On the street, they had to wait a few minutes to get a cab. It was a beautiful evening, the air warm. Don stood in the same yellow streetlight, only now it was lighter. Clouds had cleared to reveal a bright full moon.

"God, look at that," said Don pointing.

"That's the kind of moon people fall in love under."

"Or turn to werewolves."

Joe turned and faced Don, who said something else about there being a connection between werewolves and love. He could only watch, see clearly Don's lashes, and mouth. It might have been the way his lips moved, puckering needlessly, or the look in his eye, or the angle at which his body leaned forward. Joe drenched himself in Don's smell, imagining how he might taste, and breathed him in deeply. Before he knew it, he had pressed his lips against Don's. They were warm, dry, and gave in to Joe's. After a few seconds, Joe pulled back.

"God, I was dying to do that."

"Wow. I think you're a beautiful man . . ." said Don, and then paused.

"It sounds like there's a 'but'."

Don made an expression as if it was painful to say what was going to come next.

"But?" said Joe.

"I'm straight."

Shit, thought Joe. "Jesus," he said. *Damn!* "Right." *What? Why? Wh* . . . Here his brain seemed to flat line. All he had left now was hollow, nonsensical speech. "I didn't think there were any of you left."

Don put up his hand in admission. "Afraid so."

"Hey, there's nothing to be sorry about. We didn't do anything. I was just checking, I guess."

"That's fair enough. I'd have done the same thing in your shoes." He saw a cab some distance off, and stuck out his hand. "I have to admit, a real ego boost. You must be able to get anybody you want."

Joe pulled an unconvincing smile. "Obviously not," he said.

11

Five-thirty. All week Flora had been working on a design, an art-therapy/theatre space for the elderly. It was within the shell of an old factory that had been used for many things since first being built, including ammunitions packing and a tea warehouse. It was a big project, but was finally finished. Not wanting to begin anything new, she answered some unimportant emails. For a moment, she wondered if she was killing time, but dismissed this idea believing instead that she was waiting for rush hour traffic to clear. Deep down she knew the real reason, it wasn't so much traffic she was avoiding, but going home to an apartment where she'd be alone. She decided to rearranged the desktop on her Mac, so, labelled items properly, organized them, emptied the trash and even chose a new screensaver.

One after the other, Flora opened and closed folders. She came across one called 'Miscellaneous.' It had been a long time since she'd noticed it, let alone opened it. If computer files could gather dust this would have a thick layer. Within it, she found a file titled You. She opened the file, her eyes glancing quickly over it. It was prose, a letter, but clearly not for anyone else to read. It was as though Flora had written to herself. Fascinated, she read on, became more involved, and then recalled the feelings that went into it, remembering the pain. When finished, she immediately started at the beginning again. She snickered a few of times then began to laugh. At the same time, it fuelled and burned her. She had to let it out, so began to write.

Love. It filled me as much as emotion can, and it emptied me. I never want it again. Maybe it wasn't love, and I still have that to look forward to. If it was, then love stinks. Abandoning me as quickly as it engulfed me. Making me rotten as slowly as it made me grow. Romantic love is small, fleeting, and arbitrary.

The love a mother has for a child. That is true love. It needs her. It can't live without her. It is a part of her and belongs to her. I believe there is no greater love. The child doesn't even have to reciprocate. Still, the mother knows. This love doesn't have to be fed by flattery, explanation, or sex.

Joe and David have a silly love. It will last as long as their desire. It is superficial. Deep within him, David still loves me. Things like that can't be stopped by a change of the mind.

Our love is eternal. Rather, as long as we both live. Joe is insignificant, an inconvenience. More than this, he's an annoyance. David's my baby.

Flora closed the file and shut down her computer. She sighed deeply and stared ahead of her. Slowly her lips pulled in tighter and her eyes squinted. There was a clanking noise. A door opened behind her.

"Sorry miss," said the cleaner. "I thought everybody was gone."

"Don't worry, I'm off now."

"What should I do with these drawings?" said the cleaner, referring to a huge roll of photocopies.

"Actually, we're done with them. We didn't get the job. You can bin them."

"Didn't you have your heart set on designing that place?"

"Umm hmm."

"Oh! I'm sorry, honey."

"It doesn't matter. There'll always be babies, so hopefully there'll always be a need for nurseries."

The cleaner picked up the roll and set off down the hall to the bins. Flora, taking her cue, collected a few things off her desk and headed home.

On the street, there was still a post-work urgency, everybody eager to get home. The traffic was thick; inches apart in places. Once home, she showered, hoping it would refresh her, but still she felt weary, worse still bored. The telephone rang.

"Baby! How's your bum?"

"Round, hard, a little hair in the crack."

Flora stood up. "I mean. How does it feel?"

"Beautiful. You should check it out sometime."

"I don't think I could be accused of neglecting it."

"I suppose you're right."

"Are you hooked yet?"

"Of course!"

A police car approached the building. Flora waited as

the noise of its siren peaked. As it died off she continued, "I knew you'd like it."

"I understand why gays do it now."

"Don't even think about it. I lost one boy to gays already. I'm not about to lose another."

"Only fooling. I like breasts squashing against my back whilst I'm getting fucked."

"That's my boy. You just keep thinking that." The man's voice fell silent. "Is Baby okay?"

"Yeah," he said, a bit of whine his voice.

"What's wrong?"

"Nothing. I'm just a bit down."

"It's hardy surprising after doing crystal. I know what you need."

"Go on."

"A few shops in Knightsbridge will stay open late for their good customers. How's about I give them a call and we go burn some of that stuff."

"I think it's called money."

"Yeah, yeah, yeah!"

"You earn too much."

"There's no such thing. Apparently one can't eat too much chocolate, lose too much weight, or earn too much money."

"Says who?"

"*Hello* magazine."

"Known for their highly accurate facts and subtle reportage."

"That's the one," said Flora. "Listen, I'll just make some calls, jump in the shower, and pick you up in 30."

"Thirty it is."

"Bye!" Just as Flora took the receiver away from her

ear, she heard the man speak. "What? Sorry, I didn't hear you."

"I said. You won't make me pay you back for this in some hideous, twisted, fucked–up, sexual way?"

"Of course!"

"Good. See you in 30."

Flora went to the toilet, brushed her teeth, reapplied her lipstick, changed her tampon, and left. Rush-hour traffic had thinned, so she made good time. Driving down a central street, Flora pulled over and honked. Within seconds the car door opened and a man jumped in. They sat for a moment looking at each other. Then smiles broke out on their faces. Flora pulled a joint from behind her ear, slapped the man on his thigh and shouted in an overexcited way, "Ready parrrdner?"

"Yahoo!" said the man, and they tore off up the street.

As promised, the shops she'd called were open. The couple spent over an hour in the first shop alone, totally engrossed by what they were doing, not noticing when occasional passers-by stopped to window-shop and ended up watching them. Leila was one of these. A pair of shoes had caught her eye, pretty, with primrose straps, and what looked like mother of pearl stones all the way round the soles. Assuming they'd be too expensive, she decided not to bother even trying them on. The man inside got his arms caught in the sleeves of the jacket he was trying on and he was trying to wiggle into it. Instead of sliding smoothly, the jacket seemed to cling to him. As Leila turned back towards the street, the waving of the man's arms caught her attention. His jacket finally slipped into place, the man turned to face the mirror. He stepped forward and turned to see how the jacket fitted at the back. For the first time, she got a good look at him and the woman behind. Leila recognised Flora from photos Ryan had shown her. Also, David had pointed her out in a theatre once, before insisting they sneak out and go to see another film. What surprised Leila was seeing her with Joe's friend, Don.

Leila immediately felt awkward, unsure whether she should say hello. If she tapped on the glass, she would feel trashy, and she didn't particularly want to meet Flora. Her thoughts were at odds with themselves. Within her head, a dialogue started, and got too loud. The shop window gave a good reflection, and so she saw her face expressing the jumble of thoughts and feelings within. She backed away into the street, embarrassed. A cab was passing. With a pathetic voice and barely a gesture, she said "Taxi!" but the cab sped by, the driver shaking his head and pointing above him to the unlit sign.

12

The exhibition opened at six. David and Joe turned up at seven. When they arrived, they had to make their way through reporters and animal rights protestors. Joe was getting used to this on opening nights. His exhibitions were getting more attention each time. One of the more 'respectable' newspapers wrote "It shouldn't be possible for Holtzman's exhibition to be more shocking than his previous, but one would be right in expecting it to be so." The "gutter press" outright condemned him, writing less coherent tirades, running headlines, like *"Art or Abattoir"* and *"Painfully Bad."*

Joe was busy being a charming host and was subtly trying to spot people with whom he might actually enjoy speaking. In between Mister and Misses whoever from whichevfund/magazine/establishment he scanned the room for familiar faces. He had invited Don, but after his aborted, pre-preview didn't expect him to show tonight. When he did turn up, looking both sexy and stylish in a fog grey suit, dung brown shirt and pale blue velvet tie, Joe was surprised to see him and quietly pleased. Still, even with him there, along his faithful favorites David,

Ryan, and Leila, they could only speak to him for so long. Otherwise, Joe would appear cliquish. Don commented that he thought the guests looked more tortured than the exhibits. In response, Joe burst out laughing, more as an emotional release than because he found it truly funny. But as he did, he felt a tap on his shoulder. He turned to see Flora right behind him, dressed in a beige dress made of suede, and over it she wore a real leopard skin fur coat.

"Oh my God! Flora." Joe was confused as to whether he was shocked to see her or the outfit she was wearing.

David cut in. "Oh Lord! Look what the cat dragged in!" During their last conversation over a year ago, they agreed they could both live in London, just as long as they were never both under the same roof, even if it were a football stadium. He couldn't believe she would have the nerve to show up.

"That sounds like I'm not welcome."

Joe was lost for words, but quickly gestured to the nearest waiter with a tray of champagne.

"Nice stuff," she said with an overdramatic gesture of her hand.

"Nice?" said David, clearly annoyed.

She looked him straight in the eye. "Yes, *nice*. How are you, David?"

"Fine."

"And?"

"That's it, I'm fine."

"That's *nice*," she added sarcastically.

"Joe suddenly found his voice. "Sorry, Flora, this is Leila, Ryan and Don."

"Charmed," she said overlooking both Leila and Ryan,

but offering her hand to Don.

He held his up casually in response. "Hi."

Feral-like Flora purred, "Haven't we met before?"

"I don't think so."

"You look kind of familiar."

"It's probably the man on the porridge commercial. Everyone says that."

"Oh, my God! That's right. 'Eat them good and hot.'"

Don let out a little laugh. "Everyone says that as well."

"Sorry."

"That too."

"I'd better shut up."

Flora made a zipping action across her mouth. All the while, Leila watched their playacting, confused. They were convincing strangers. Leila noted that the elegant shoulder bag Flora wore was by Prada, and the suede dress was so impeccably tailored, it must have been by somebody fabulous. If Leila hadn't known better, she would have thought her quite proper, and of course, Don was the classic "nice guy." Who would have thought they could be in cahoots, presumably scheming at something or other.

"A friend of mine said he was coming," said Flora. "So here I am."

"How *nice*," snarled David.

"Thank you, Pet."

"Stop it, you two! This is *my* night, okay?"

"Sorry," said David.

Next, Leila stepped forward, passed Ryan, and introduced herself to Flora who assumed a mildly grand gesture as if Leila's interest in meeting her were expected. Leila for her part regarded Flora with a respectful yet cool detachment. She was curious to take a closer look at the freakish older woman she'd heard so much about, and so she offered to show Flora around the exhibition.

Equally intrigued, Flora thought this was an ideal chance to get to know who Leila was. More importantly, what she was doing with David and Joe.

"Would somebody hold my drink?"

"Sure!" said Don, instinctively.

In an over familiar way, Flora linked Leila's arm as they departed.

David noticed this and said quietly to Joe. "She's too much!"

They watched the women as they worked their way through the crowd chatting and laughing.

"Do you want a line of coke?" said Flora.

"Yeah, great," said Leila. "The ladies' is this way."

They slid into a room that smelt of school showers, damp and general decay. As the door closed and the voices of the crowd faded out they were replaced by the sound of trickling and dripping. A single red bulb lit the space, which wouldn't have been out of place in a peep show. It had a ratty-looking piece of string attached for turning it on and off. The two women squeezed into small cubicle, which housed a big old toilet basin. It was a tight fit. Flora didn't mind, as she found Leila magnetic and in some way sexy. They had to clean off the top of the cistern to put the coke out on. There was no toilet paper and so Flora pulled a Versace scarf out of her bag and wiped down the surface until it was shiny clean. When she finished, she held up the scarf as though it was an old dishrag, scrunched her nose, and tied it loosely around the strap of her bag. Then she emptied out a whole wrap, and chopped two ridiculously fat lines.

"Jesus!" said Leila. "They're big."

"Don't believe a word they say. Size does matter. You don't mind, do you?"

"No!" Leila said, grateful despite being annoyed. "Don't you mind finishing it?"

"No, that's what it's for. Anyway, I've got more." Flora handed her an elegant silver tube. "You first."

Leila inspected the tube and admiringly. "Fancy!"

"It's Platinum, darling. Tiffany's."

Leila wondered if Flora realised she was standing in a puddle that had leaked from the toilet bowl. *Glamorous*, she thought, but said, "How camp! You've been hanging out with too many gays."

"That's a paradox, too many gays." Gesturing to the coke, Flora said "Ladies first."

Leila bent to do her line and said, "Do you do a lot of this?" She'd never done drugs with an older woman before and thought it a novelty.

"Not particularly. I just thought this whole fiasco would be more tolerable with a little help," said Flora. Then seeing that Leila had only done half a line, she teased, "Lightweight."

Flora did hers in one, so Leila went back down to finish her line. When she came up, she already had enough coke confidence to confront Flora, but thought if she played along she could probably learn much more. "What do you mean fiasco?"

"Those two."

This annoyed Leila. She already felt protective, but Flora was beginning to get under her skin. "You know them well?"

Flora looked self-satisfied. "You could say that. David

and I were lovers, for years."

Without a trace of self-consciousness Leila pulled up her skirt, sat on the toilet and started to pee. "You're messing with me. He used to be straight?"

"Well, it has a bit of a curve," she said, smiling smugly.

Leila's nose was about to run, and so she tipped her head back channelling it down the back of her throat. She looked down her face towards Flora, and sounding as though she had a cold said, "I can't believe you used to see him."

"Swear on my mother's grave," said Flora squeezing her nostrils together to make sure all the coke passed through the mucus membranes of her nose.

"What was he like in bed?"

"I knew you'd be thinking that." Flora felt like she had Lela's attention now, and so she put more performance into her words. She rubbed her thumb and forefinger together then looked at the back of her hand admiring her elegant long red nails. "He was good actually. You'd never know he didn't like it. I still can't really believe it."

"Leila took a tissue from out of her pocket, wiped herself and stood up letting her skirt fall back into place. "I guess people change."

"Perhaps. But he was *really* good, if you get my drift." Flora's big red lipstick smile looked moist and vaginal.

"I hear you girlfriend," Leila said encouraging. "If Ryan's anything to go by."

"*Ryan*! That's not nephew Ryan is it?"

"The very same."

Now Flora suddenly looked lecherous. "I used to

tease David about him. I used to say that he fancied Ryan. He was only little then . . . Bet he's not now!"

"Right! But did he fancy Ryan?"

"I don't know. I don't think so. Who knows? Well, like I said. I don't even believe he's really gay." She paused, alone with her thoughts. "But I must say Joe is a dish."

"You fancy Joe?"

"When you reach your 30s, your taste becomes much more, how shall I put it . . ."

"Desperate?"

"You bitch!" She laughed. "I was gong to say varied. Let's get out of here, I'm getting claustrophobic."

"Yeah, if we stay in here much longer, we'll need another line."

"Now there's an idea."

"I was messing."

They left the cubicle.

"You're bad!" said Leila, believing she had a 'new best friend' who just happened to be on the inside.

You've no idea, thought Flora, but said, "And that's good, right?"

They stood in front of the mirror.

"I love that lipstick," said Flora, talking to Leila's reflection. "Chanel?"

Suddenly, for some reason Leila had had enough. Her face changed and looked morbidly serious, but still she spoke into the mirror. "Flora?"

"Yes?"

"Cut the crap."

"What?" said Flora confused.

"What's Don up to?"

"Don who?"

"Listen to me. When I warn somebody, it means they're this far from being in deep shit."

Flora just stood listening.

"And you, bitch, are being warned."

"What are you talking about?"

Leila was still partly guessing. "I know about you and Don."

Flora's expression changed from acting confused to one of having been busted. "Oh!"

"And?"

"It's just a game."

Leila spoke slowly with gravity and an uncanny force. "Let me make myself very, very clear. It's going to stop. Right now. Got it?"

"Whatever."

"Flora. I'm serious. I'll hurt you . . . badly."

"Fuck you! Who do you think you are?"

Leila looked back at her own reflection, and tousled her hair girlishly. Then she went into her bag, pulled out a hairbrush, and left her bag wide open.

"Flora, do like my bag? It's got a beautiful lining."

Confused Flora glanced down at it, and spotted Leila's gun. She gasped, and stepped back in shock.

"That's right," said Leila, watching Flora in the mirror. "*Now* do you want to tell me what you're up to?"

"You're crazy!"

"No. I'm *fucking* crazy. And now that's clear, do you feel any more like telling me what's going on?"

Flora was used to being the toughest and the scariest, but she'd finally met her match with Leila. She panicked and gave in, "Don's just a tool."

"To do what?"

"To fuck with their heads, that's all."

Throughout, Leila remained eerily calm had kept the whole thing from getting out of control. "Okay. We're done here. Out! Or they'll be wondering what happened to us."

It was entirely out of character, but Flora did exactly as she was told. Then again, she'd never come across somebody like Leila before. They left the toilet and went back to the others.

"Girl talk?" asked David cynically.

"Yeah," said Leila, innocently and giggled, "Girl talk."

Ryan noticed that something was different about Leila, as she seemed distant, unreachable. It worried him. David's mind was on Flora and he watched her. Why was she so quiet? She seemed more timid, even traumatized. What had happened since he last saw them? David didn't know Leila well enough to guess. Regardless, if anything could make Flora cower in the way she was now, he approved of it. Still, it was oddly out of character. Joe was oblivious to both women, as his head was a mass of questions, possible problems, answers, and guilt. The exhibition. He excused himself.

Don had been studying Joe the whole time and so missed any differences in behavior in either Leila or Flora. He saw Joe beginning to look really frazzled and asked. "Do you need any help?"

"No. All I have to do is open some doors to another room."

"Why the mystery?" asked Don.

With a devilish look on his face David said, "Who knows!"

Don was surprised. "He's even kept it secret from

you?"

"Just for the fun of it."

As he spoke, there were lots of camera flashes and murmuring.

David knew to expect the unexpected, and said quite dryly, "What's he gone and done now?"

"Let's go see," said Leila excited. She led the way, and they joined the back of the crowd. There was still much fuss, cameramen moving, photographers kneeling, standing, clicking, and lamps flashing. When the guests did actually get to see the exhibit, after the initial gasps, a hush fell upon them.

"Fuck!" said Leila quietly to Ryan. "I feel so . . ." She searched for the right word.

"Humbled?"

"Humbled's good, actually, but I was going to say *irrelevant.*"

13

In a large, but simple white room there was a bed. Its antique cover was black and had red roses embroidered on it.

The phone beside the bed started to ring. Flora counted as she rushed from the bathroom. Two. Three. Four. Five. After one more voicemail would get it. Wrapped in a just a towel, she caught it, falling on her bed.

She held a peeled orange in her hand. "What?"

"Flora?"

"Who'd you expect?" she said with a smirk. Then she took a bite out of the orange. Juice squirted out and dribbled down her chin.

"I don't know. I might have the wrong number."

"But you've got speed dial."

"Oh yeah. You sound busy."

"No not really." Her mouth was full of juice so she found it difficult to speak. "I've just had a shower and now I'm having some lunch." Steadying the phone between her ear and shoulder, she reached for a tissue.

"And since when have you been ex-directory? It says *withheld* on my display."

"Huh? Since today."

"Why?"

"I don't know."

"You funny bugger," said Flora putting a flame to the tissue in her hand. It set alight easily and rapidly. She let it drop into an ashtray. Immediately, she lit another, and watched it burn, mesmerized. Silently it glowed, changing from incandescent orange to a dead matte black.

"So, listen. I was thinking about those two."

"You mean Joe and David."

"Who else?"

"Why do you let them get to you?"

"The first time I didn't really have a choice. This time it's just sport."

"I don't like hearing you talk like that."

"What's changed? It didn't used to. Do you like them?"

"No!"

Flora thought for a moment. "Anyway, I'm over them. They bore me. You can drop them. That's if you're not too attached already. Joe's a seductive bugger. And you know what I think of David."

"I don't, actually. Well, I'm confused. You said you loved him. That's not what it looks like."

Flora lay on her back with her feet in the air. "Love often turns to hate."

"No love I know. Obsession, maybe."

She admired the length of her waxed legs. Then her attention turned to her freshly painted toenails. "You're getting all soft on me," said Flora idly and sighed. With a playground lilt she sang, "Don loves Joe!"

"Get bent, Flora."

As she spoke, Flora moved her hand over her body.

"Sounds like you *already* are. Don loves Joe!" she sang again.

"That is so irritating."

Without thinking she flicked her nipple gently. "Only 'cause it's true!"

"If you don't take that stupid tone out of your voice I'm going to hang up."

"I was only teasing you." She squeezed her nipple and was suddenly aware of what she was doing with her hand. "Have I hit a nerve?"

"Absolutely anything said with that voice would hit a nerve."

"How about, 'Eat my pussy!'" she said squeezing her nipple more consciously, and still she used the same inflection and melody in her voice. She was about to run with this idea and play with Don knowing it would drive him crazy with lust. "Well." She stopped. There was a sudden loud thud at her window. Flora gasped.

"What!" said Don. "Are you okay?" There was no answer. "Flora! What's wrong?"

After a pause, she said, "I don't know."

She made her way into the living room. "Something hit the window?"

"What do you mean *something*? You're quite high up."

"I know that's what's so weird." She was tentative, keeping her distance and trying to look over the sill of her window for a clue. "I think it was a bird."

"This would only happen to you, Flora."

"Now, that's the concerned response I needed." As Flora stood squashed up against the window, trying to see below her, she became conscious that she had no clothes on. A naked woman, alone, pressed up against a window.

What a funny sight, she thought. She backed away from the window, went into the bedroom, got her towel, and covered herself up.

"Wow! I wonder what the likelihood is of a bird smashing into your window."

"Not content with having me half scared to death now you want me to die of boredom. When does this get interesting?"

"Some people would think it interesting."

"Yeah, my granddad, and his fascinating drinking buddy, Jeb."

"Flora, you're so cynical."

"Anyway, back to you and Joe. Yeah, Don and Joe. I bet you're with him all the time."

"I'm hanging up. Four! Three! Two! I'm hanging."

"I'm pregnant!" said Flora.

Don froze. He couldn't move or reply. His focus was far inside his head. After a moment he managed to say, "Jesus Christ!" He paused again. "Is it mine?"

"For the moment, it's nobody's."

Don was silent. He tried to digest what he'd heard and wondered about possibilities. Then, timidly, he said, "Might you keep it?"

"*Might*."

"If?"

"If I feel like it."

"What does it depend on?"

"I don't know yet. I'll get back to you." Don found refuge in the silence she allowed him. "Listen, honey," she continued. "I've got to get something ready for FedEx. Can I call you later?"

"Er, sure! No. I mean . . . I'll be busy . . ." He was lying and so had to think quickly. " . . . I'll be in the cinema."

"Whatever! This bastard's going nowhere in a hurry."

Although Don was used to Flora, still she managed to shock him. *How vulgar*, he thought. "Okay," he said. "Talk to you later then."

They both hung up. Don shuddered, and anxiety waved through him. Confused, he sat on the bed. Then he reached for the phone, but thought better of it, stood up again and left the room. He drifted along the hallway, down the stairs, turned through the living room, and then entered the kitchen.

"Hey! What's wrong?" said Joe.

"Bad news?" wondered David.

Don shook his head, bewildered. "I think so."

14

Sky's office appeared blank, but she managed to get David to furnish it with his memories, feelings, and experiences, or at least his understanding of these things.

A few months ago, David brought something else into their space when he told her that he'd begun to love her.

In response, she'd smiled sweetly and said, "I love you too."

Sky's naturalness often surprised David. "Are weallowed to say things like this in therapy?"

"We can say whatever we like."

This was one of the reasons David admired Sky so much. She never resorted to clichés as an easy option, but always appeared to say what she believed was the most compassionate, sensible, and mindful. Once, David had asked her, if they came across each other in the street, should they say hello. She looked puzzled. "It would be weird if we didn't. Don't you think?"

"Definitely!" said David.

Sky was warm and genuine. The things David hoped for with friends, exactly what he got from Joe. He knew it was rare and he cherished Sky. He'd been seeing her for several years now after being advised to seek counselling after his attack. She'd helped him immediately after and then continued to see him. David felt she taught him something nearly every time he saw her. Some kind of profound connection was bound to grow between them and neither of them was worried about its definition. Its shape and depth was simply accepted.

David looked up. He had been daydreaming. Sky stood at the door. In her hand, she held a folded piece of paper.

"These are my holiday dates. I wrote them down for you, so you wouldn't forget."

"Thanks. Isn't it simply that you're away for three weeks?"

"Well, tell me what you think of this. I thought I'd see you the day before I leave and the day after I got back, although those aren't the days I'd usually see you."

"That's very thoughtful of you. Am I your only patient?"

"No." Sky looked a little embarrassed, and chuckled as she put her head down. Then she lifted it again, while at the same time moving her hair off her face. Still smiling, she said, "I just thought you might like that."

"You mean *need* it."

"Do you need it?"

"I guess so." David watched Sky and noted that the blouse she was wearing looked more dressy than usual. Aware that she was under scrutiny, Sky caught David's eye and smiled again. "You seem happy today."

"I am."

"Is there a particular reason for it?"

"It's Wednesday?"

"That's so corny."

"Corny's okay. Saying *'I love you'* is corny too, but when you feel it, as you'll have experienced, nothing else will do but those three words. It's corny as hell, but if you feel it, what should you do, hold it inside, or . . ."

David butted in. "Say it, no matter how corny it is?"

"I think so," said Sky.

"You're a lovely woman."

"Thank you."

The window in the therapy room was open. There was noise in the street, children screeching and shouting. Some unpleasant memories came back to David, of playgrounds, of not fitting in.

"What's on your mind?" said Sky.

"How did you know there was anything?"

"Your face changed."

"I must try to control it better," said David.

"Why would you want to do that?"

He shifted in his seat. "I don't see why you should have to suffer because my mind is on something."

"I presume you are referring to me as another person, because as your therapist it's my job to deal with what's on your mind."

"I meant as another person. Others shouldn't have to see what I'm thinking, or feeling."

"But what if they want to? People spend time with you because they choose to. I'd imagine they'd like to share your thoughts and feelings."

"I hadn't thought about it like that." There was a pause. David looked at Sky and she back at him. "Still, people don't need to hear every neurotic comment to and from myself."

"I'm afraid I can't agree with you. It sounds quite fun."

"It's only because you're a therapist that you find it interesting."

"No. I'm a therapist because I'm interested in people, not the other way round."

"Ah! You've got a silk tongue, so you have," said David with an Irish accent he'd learned from his grandfather. Sky covered her face with both hands and suppressed her laughter. This was another thing he loved about her. Sometimes she let so much of her true personality show.

"Why do you cover your face when you laugh?"

"Do you really want to know?"

"Yes."

"Firstly, I was very self-conscious about my teeth as a little girl and I guess the habit must have stuck. Secondly, I was eating a salad when you arrived and was afraid some of it might have stuck to my teeth. Thirdly, I'd rather the image you have of me in your head isn't of me laughing. It's too easy to misconstrue."

"I'm not that paranoid."

"Still, laughter doesn't always mean happiness."

"I don't understand."

"I'm thinking of those clowns at funfairs."

"You're showing your age. Weren't they a Fifties thing? And, anyway, I don't think of you like that. They're horrible."

"You see my point, though?" She sounded so serious. "Laughter can be very cruel. Nobody likes to be laughed at."

"Why is that?"

"I'm not sure, but I'd guess it's because it's so potent. When somebody laughs, it takes a lot of effort. Imagine the feeling when that's turned against you. It's quite scary and it's very real, in that it's an immediate emotional expression, not a calculated thought."

"Right!"

"It makes me think of when dogs bark," said Sky. "*They* really are scary."

"It might be for similar reasons. Possibly something very natural."

Sky put her head to one side. Her face relaxed into a pleasant expression, one that David imagined was comfortable for Sky. He believed because it was natural for her.

"You never told me what was on your mind, before, when you heard the children playing outside."

David paused for a moment. "I was taken back to my schoolyard."

"This can be a source of so much unhappiness."

"And happiness," said David, pleased that he was being positive.

"Of course. Are you saying that it was for you?"

"No."

"That's what I imagined."

"From my face?" he asked. Sky nodded and smiled in a way she often did. To David it meant she understood. Also that she was concerned, even cared. David started to cry. Through his tears he managed to say, "Can't I get through a single session without this shit?" His acknowledgement made him cry more ferociously. He was determined to not let his emotions rule him, so he forced out more words. "What's this about?"

"What were you thinking of?" Like she'd done many times before, she handed David a box of tissues.

"Someone poking me."

Sky was silent. Clearly, David was very upset and being picked on at school probably wasn't the reason. Through a mass of emotion, he thought he knew what was on her mind.

"You think this is connected to the rape, don't you?"

Sky became more serious. "Possibly." She put three fingers over her lips and looked pensive. David wondered if it meant anything besides that she was thinking. Fragments of thoughts dwelt on this idea, whilst at the same time he continued to cry over more immediate responses.

"Why?" said David, and immediately felt like he'd said something trite.

"There's no reason. Nothing connected with you, anyway."

"There must have been something I could have done." Again, he questioned how it sounded. Some character from a TV movie came to mind. No person or movie in particular, just a victim. "I feel like a victim."

"You were a victim."

"When will the memories go away?"

"I doubt they will but you'll become more able to deal with them."

With that note of hope David stopped crying. "Will I?"

Sky nodded in a sure way and pulled a faint tranquil smile.

Again, voices could be heard on the street below. A bee flew through the window, buzzing noisily. It looped the room and left. Outside. Inside. Therapy. Real world.

Voices. Sky. David looked down, taking comfort in being distracted by the speckled pile of the carpet. For seconds, he and Sky didn't say anything. There was silence, but for distant city sounds. Then David burst out laughing. Sky's expression didn't change.

"I was just thinking how much I cry here. I wonder how much water I've left in this room, over the years."

Without missing a beat, Sky said, "Enough to keep a flower alive."

At first, David didn't get the double meaning of this, so looked towards the open window, thinking it was simply beautiful imagery. Then it clicked, and he turned back to face Sky who was already smiling in acknowledgement.

15

Leila's parents hadn't seen her for a while and asked her to visit. They told her that they were considering a review of her finances. If her allowance were in jeopardy, she'd be home quick enough. This much they knew, and so used it as leverage. In reality, they loved to spoil her, but would happily to stoop to threats, whatever it took to see their little girl.

On Friday afternoon Ryan took her to Euston station, which houses trains heading north; to Manchester, Liverpool, Preston, many places they'd both rather forget. Leila's eventual destination was Winslow, an affluent strip on the outskirts of Manchester.

Leila and Ryan sat in a burger bar. She had on a long black wig and wore a bright yellow flowing dress, referring to her look as *travel apparel*, with an emphasis on the "*el*" ending of both words. It made them rhyme better and sound more French. Opposite her, Ryan was in a bright blue t-shirt, green shorts, and a red baseball cap. Although Leila was aiming for an Orient Express feel, their mix of primary coloured clothing made them look like children's TV presenters. With only ten minutes before her train departed, Ryan wanted to get closer to Leila, so he stood up, and then sat sideways on her lap, turning his cap sideways, and away from her. His hips were very slim, but still it was a tight squeeze in the fast-food-sized plastic table/bench construct. With his arm around her, he said, "I wish you'd speak French during sex."

"I do," said Leila, as though they were already mid-conversation and it wasn't a random comment. Then she laid her face tenderly against his chest. "Inside."

He kissed the top of her head and stroked her cheek. "What good's it doing there, Pony?"

"It does me good."

Although Ryan often liked to act silly around Leila, today he was sensitive to the fact that they'd be apart. "You could share it."

She loved how soft he was being and looked up at him, their faces almost touching. "I'd feel silly."

"I think that's meant to be part of the deal . . ." As Ryan spoke, his breath made Leila blink. "It's like dressing up, or playing roles, it's liberating." He broke up his speech with soft baby kisses all over Leila's face. "Do you know what I mean?" Kiss. "My Pony." Kiss. "Hey! Come on." Kiss. "Or you'll miss your train."

"Okay," said Leila. "But I love those lovely little lip treats."

They walked to the main concourse and checked for platform information. It was a grim sight. Her train seemed to be stopping at so many stations along the way. Leila made a resigned expression, to which Ryan pulled a smile, and somehow this conveyed "*I know how you feel*." Then taking her by the hand, he led her onto the platform. Then in an overly earnest voice he said, "You will write me, won't you?"

· They'd played out what they called 'Merchant Ivory Moments' many times before, and so Leila knew her response. "I truly hope to have a moment for recollections of the heart." Leila stopped beside the entrance to her platform, placed down her bag, put her nose in the air, and acted as though she was carrying a parasol. "Sometime, perhaps, between engagements, should I find myself at a loss, I might put pen to paper and send news of my affection; its health and vitality."

Ryan took off his cap and tucked it in his back pocket. "Right!" he said, dropping out of character and taking Leila's hands in his. "So, call me when you get there, when you walk through the front door, then it's just sitting, drinking tea, and anything else you think to do," he paused. "Without me!"

"So," said Leila. "That's every 20 minutes. Sounds good to me." At this she threw herself around Ryan's neck. "I love . . ." she took a breath. "Your sense of humor."

"*It* loves you too." This was the nearest either of them had ever been to using the word *love* within their relationship, although they both felt it. They looked each other in the eye and all else seemed to mute; the bustle around them, trains pulling in and out, announcements, everybody and everything else. For this moment nothing external broke through. They drew into each other and kissed. After a moment, they pulled apart, but helplessly went back for more.

Suddenly, Leila pulled away abruptly. "My train!"

Picking up her bag, she ran down the platform and

stepped up into the carriage. Then she collected herself, leant out of the window and cried, "I like you."

Ryan tapped his head with his finger, did about three moves of a country-and-western line dance, then mouthed the words, "Mad cow," but when noticing Leila's face change, added, "I like you too."

The train guard whistled, the doors shut and Leila disappeared inside the carriage. Ryan watched for a moment smiling as it pulled off, and then he got on the tube.

Once he got back to Hampstead, he found David in the kitchen. He was sitting at the table by himself looking towards the back door.

"Hey. What you doing?" he Ryan asked.

"Nothing, I think."

He went and sat close beside David. "That doesn't look like nothing."

David broke into a smile. "I'm worrying over nothing I suppose. It's just that there'll be a TV crew at Joe's exhibition tomorrow."

"Wow!" Ryan made an exaggerated expression that meant he was impressed.

"It's the BBC. He's quite nervous."

"Does it always affect you like this?"

"Yeah. I have been known to go out and get trashed."

"Funnily enough, that's what I was going to suggest."

David's eyes flicked to one side as he considered what this might entail.

"Don't think about it too much. If we all did that, we'd never take drugs."

Through resigned laughter, David said, "I guess you're right." He paused. "I think."

"Less of that thinking nonsense. So, note this. The plan is; club nap, bath, dress . . . effortlessly, yet fabulously casual, and rendezvous in on the landing upstairs at two hundred hours." David pictured Ryan in the bath naked but was caught daydreaming. "Is anybody home in there?"

"Afraid so."

"Well, keep focused! Anyway, back to The Plan. We'll warm up here." Ryan rubbed his hands together like a crafty con man. Then he nudged his nostril with his thumb, "If you know what I mean!" As with most characters Ryan attempted to mimic, his cute real self shone through. "Then, we'll go for a little drink, hit a club, and somewhere along the way get really, really, really, really fucking cunted!"

David laughed, more from excitement than because of Ryan's performance. Then after staring into space for just a beat too long, he changed direction and said, "I wish I'd had my hair cut."

"Barbie!"

Then as if to excuse his last remark David said, "It's my duty to look as best I can."

"Listen, tonight you're with me, remember that. None of that gay malarkey."

"What's that?"

"You know eyes everywhere." Ryan made a scary monster face and in a Hammer Horror style voice said, "Beware the roving eye!"

"I don't do that. Do I?"

"You all do," said Ryan. "It's in your genes."

David couldn't help snickering at the *jeans* pun, but thought better of voicing it.

"I know what you're thinking," said Ryan. "Your age group likes innuendoes don't you?"

"That's because when we were kids, you couldn't be frank."

"*Frank*," said Ryan, then, in an exaggerated way, "Ha, ha!" This bugged David. "So, is it a deal? No cruising?"

"I'll try my best, but if I don't know I'm doing it, how can I stop it?"

"Just focus on me."

"It sounds like good old-fashioned jealousy."

"Maybe. Or I just like a lot of attention."

"Don't we all?"

"Yeah," said Ryan, then put the knuckles of his ring and forefinger under his chin as though posing for a photograph. "But it's what I'm used to."

"Eww! Arrogant. That better not be real."

Ryan didn't answer, but went to the doorway, stopped and turned. He lifted his nose in the air dramatically, and flicked some hair off his neck. With only a hint of a smile, he left the room, and bounded off upstairs.

Clearly, it was going to be a long night. David was too excited to sleep so took a Rohypnol. When he woke up, Joe was behind him, holding him.

"Hey," said David sleepily and turned to face Joe. "Puppy . . . I was going to go out with Ryan. I feel like I've been rattling around the house all day. For some reason, tomorrow's really stressing me out. What do you think, about going out, I mean?"

"It's fine by me. And I know what you mean about tomorrow. Actually, it'll be good for me to have some time alone. Plan for tomorrow."

"That's what I thought."

Joe rubbed his lips lightly against David's forehead. "Are you still going to come?"

"Of course," said David. "I wouldn't let you down."

Joe held him tighter. "I love you when you're insecure."

David looked down, avoiding Joe's eyes. "Am I being too clingy?"

"No." Joe lifted David's chin so that they had eye contact again. "But it wouldn't matter if you were. You can be as clingy and as clumsy as you want."

"Where did *clumsy* come from?"

"I thought I'd just throw that one in." He smiled and brushed the hair off David's forehead.

The room fell quiet until the sound of music rose from Ryan's room. David pulled the sheets pulled up around his neck. They where white, and accentuated his tan.

"It may be some freaky trick of the light," said Joe, "But you're looking absolutely delicious."

"Really? I feel ugly today."

Joe nuzzled into his neck "How could you feel ugly?"

David contorted his face and body. "Like this."

"Give up. You can't do ugly."

"What are you after?"

"Your bum hole." Joe put his hand on, and slid his fingers into David's butt crack.

"Okay then!" David answered before Joe had finished speaking.

"I hate that it always so hard to convince you." David's face lit up. "It would be purely therapeutic, you understand, to alleviate stress."

"Of course!"

Joe knelt up on the bed. He got in between David's

legs, and with reassuring certainty, he nudged his thighs apart until they spread open with his butt crack visible. He looked down at David who had his hands behind his head, attempting to feign a casual cockiness. They both knew this was an act, because they also knew what could happen next and how there would be nothing casual about it. What would be much more likely was that within minutes David would be writhing and squirming, asking Joe to stop and yet insisting he fuck deeper. At this point Joe would be grinding, teasing, and then with power he'd lunge. But for now David could pretend, and so lay on his back, with his torso making a very pretty V-shape.

Now there's a sight I don't get bored with," said Joe, his voice heavy with a gravel texture that David recognised and knew what usually followed.

"Funny, but now matter how many times your dick goes in and out of my butt, and no matter how repetitive the motion, I never get bored with *it*. Funny that!"

There was a knock on the bedroom door. And a weak, gentle, old man sounding voice said, "Is everything okay in there?"

Joe and David laughed, covered up, and told Ryan to come in.

He continued, but in his normal voice. "I was worried about you."

"Why? We weren't making much noise," said David.

"Yet," added Joe, his eye squinting with playful menace.

"Let's put it this way," said Ryan, disregarding their privacy and pouncing on the bed. "I wanted to make sure you were up."

David tickled Ryan who wriggled and screeched. Soon, this turned into a boisterous all-inclusive wrestle, which ended up with them all in a heap laughing hysterically. They took it in turn to assemble their limbs and get off the bed.

"It's getting late," said Ryan. "That's why I came to get you. It wasn't just to ruin your fun. So . . ." he stopped and looked at David with Disney innocence. " . . . Me thinks, chop-chop?"

David made a shocked face. "When'd you get so knowledgeable about drugs?"

Ryan pretended a jaded yawn. To which Joe shook his head, as if to say, "What am I going to do with you both?" He decided to leave them to it and headed out of the room, but before closing the door behind him, he turned to David and said, "Oi! Just remember. We have unfinished business. Okay?"

David saluted. "Got you, sergeant."

Then Joe left them to it and went downstairs to work on some notes for his interview the following day.

Ryan and David got ready quickly and both became a little overexcited. After a few lines of coke and as many drinks they were buzzing before they even left the house. They stopped into the club Heaven to kill time and buy more drugs. David bumped into a few people he knew, but nobody with whom he wanted to spend any time. When Heaven closed, he and Ryan went on to Trade. It had been their endpoint all along, although neither had mentioned it. The next few hours were unpunctuated, a stream of haphazard shapes, personalities, and attitudes, one blending with the next. Noise and colour merged with cigarette smoke and neurosis. The evening mainly consisted of drinking, snorting, popping, squeezing past bodies slippery with sweat, monotonous beats, dancing, more chopping and popping, the odd suggestion of a melody, within one seemingly continual track, confused, racing thoughts, and more repetitive beats. Then resting, sitting, zoning out, intimate conversations with strangers, erratic obsessions, irregular shifts in mood, the sudden emptiness of the toilet cubicle. The chaos of its stillness, not changing colour, or flashing, or banging, or heaving, or catching somebody's eye, or noticing somebody's triceps as they lean and order a drink. Without all this distraction, it's easy to turn inside, turn over thoughts, useless ideas that lead nowhere but the next stream of consciousness. Occasionally, a practicality arises, like focusing on pissing, trying to open the cubicle door or navigate the stairs. Then there's safety, sitting, talking nonsense, and, by chance, arbitrarily making sense, and sometimes more than normal.

David and Ryan sat sweating and huddled in a dimly lit corner of the chill-out room with their backs against a wall. They'd had a little too much ecstasy and couldn't get any coke, so they felt loved up but didn't have the energy to talk to anybody else.

The chill-out room wasn't as hectic as the rest of the club, but the people around still moved too much, and did it with too much attitude, but at least the music was muffled.

"You're lucky you slept earlier," said Ryan, his mouth moving more than was necessary to say the words.

"Luck had nothing to do with it."

The door opened and a wave of louder music swelled

and then died. "Did you have a little help? About so big?" Ryan held his forefinger and thumb about three millimetres apart. "I'm seeing purple? You know what? I can't hear the word Rohypnol anymore without picturing you and what's-his-face."

"Rob," said David. "How do you picture it, if you don't know what he looked like?"

A man with cropped hair and tattoos stood in front of them, only inches away from them. If he was at the proper distance they might have enjoyed looking at him, but he blocked their view and invaded their personal space too. The most annoying thing was that he didn't seem to notice them. This pissed them off. They felt too full of love not to be appreciated. Ryan also thought it odd that the man stood all on his own.

"Rob. Let me think. Well in my head he changes; even within the same scene." Ryan paused, looked around him, and took a gulp of his vodka/Red Bull, not sure if he wanted to admit to David what he was going to say. "I like it."

He offered David his drink. David sipped and then said with clarity that surprised him, "Let me get this straight. In your head . . ." David stopped. It must only have been a wave of lucidity, because within the sentence his brain coughed, "I'm with this monster thing," then died. "Right?"

"No. It's not like that. He's people I know, but he changes. Like that effect they use on music videos."

"Morphing," said David. Ryan didn't respond. "Joe told me it's called morphing."

"Oh! Well, sometimes he's Joe, other times he's somebody completely random."

"It sounds very hectic."

"It doesn't feel like that."

"How does it feel?"

"Really horny."

"You freak."

"Sometimes, the other person . . ." Ryan stopped. Cropped Hair and Tattoos was joined a by another one, shorter, slimmer and more heavily tattooed. He looked like a condensed version of the first. This made Ryan smile. *At least Cropped Hair and Tattoos has a friend*, he thought.

"Don't tell me," said David looking nonplussed. "It's Leila?"

"No," he said in a low voice. "Sometimes, it's me."

"I take that back. You're not a freak. That's very sensible."

"It doesn't feel *that* sensible."

David wiped some sweat off his face with his equally sweaty arm. "You don't know until you've tried it."

"I guess so," said Ryan, with what looked to David like a charming mix of uncertainty and curiosity. In actual fact Ryan was thinking that he couldn't believe he hadn't told David that he'd *tried it* many times before. Still, David watched him, thinking perhaps that he was playing out scenarios in his head, possibly even options. The side of their bodies, arms and shoulders touched, their sweat mingled. They were absorbed by each other. David rested his head on Ryan's shoulder and wondered if he might be considering - at this very moment – having sex with a man. Ryan wondered if now as the right time to tell David. For some reason, it was so much more difficult with David than anybody else. Leila was cool about it. Even Mum was adjusting in her own fruitcake-mixed-with-denial kind of way. But there was something difficult about coming out to a gay uncle. Despite the airlessness and humidity, David thought he could smell Ryan.

Surely there's nothing wrong with desire, David thought. *That's if, I don't act on it.* He lay back onto Ryan's lap and looked up at him. *Desire is an emotional response.* Ryan bit on his lips, which made them redder, more inviting. *All I have to do is process my response before reacting.*

Ryan looked down at David and saw vulnerability, love and concern. *Surely I should say something*, he thought. *If only just an intimation.*

I'd take Ryan, Joe, Leila, and even Judy into account. I'd be careful.

Ryan put one hand under David's head; simply to hold him, appreciate him. David reached up to give him a hug and gently pulled him down. Ryan went with this, bent forward, lost in his own train of thoughts he put his lips on David's.

This is okay, thought David, as *long as I don't kiss him.*

Opening his mouth Ryan thought, *I love you David.*

David's mouth opened also. Ryan moved his lips and so did David. *So soft*, thought David. *That's okay.* They both continued to move their lips. *This isn't a kiss.* Dry, and warm. *But it feels so nice. I love it. Ryan. Ryan? Ryan!*

David squirmed. Ryan noticed, and so lifted a couple of inches from him, but still he looked down into David's eyes. There, he saw pupils large with ecstasy, loaded with love. Ryan bent forward again. David's mind continued to ramble, his thoughts cascaded, and his desire tumbled, his resistance collapsed and here - now - in his nephew's arms, it finally quit.

Maybe you'll understand this, thought Ryan.

The name *Ryan* echoed in David's head, but now he wasn't able to access even the scraps of conscience he'd previously had, and the little armour he'd had dissolved into nothing. Now, he was of no use to the will he'd strived for, and only of use to his lips.

After a few seconds Ryan lifted his lips from David's. Neither had a definitive idea in their heads but instead they swarmed with confusion. Impulses surged, and because of reason they fell aside. Both men were silent, and considering they were still less than twelve inches apart, neither looked in the direction of the other. Ryan lifted his head further, and through a mess of other club-bers he noticed that Cropped Hair and Tattoos was watching. He had a curious expression on his face. Ryan's immediate response was to assume that the man knew his relation to David. It made him feel a rush of panic. He had unhinged and unexpected thoughts of legality, propriety, and social norms. This wasn't com-pletely irrational, because all these things were relevant in varying degrees. Whether the man knew anything about him and David or not, it didn't matter really. Still, Ryan felt paranoid. This was complicated by the fact that he was lying to David. Ryan excused himself to go to the toilet saying that he was, "busting for a piss." Graciously, David sat up off him and let him leave. *Busting*. In all his years of taking drugs, David had never known anybody to be *busting* for a piss in a club, the shits maybe, but not piss.

Left alone, all that was on David's mind was the kiss. Considering it couldn't have been more than thirty seconds long, his mind was stuffed, cram-packed with thoughts, feelings, and loads of things that either hovered in between or fit neither category properly. During those seconds his memory tore through the past, throwing up notions of Ryan, each one tripping over the next. There was a potent and completely beautiful image of when he first saw Ryan. At the time, David had wrestled with what became a common dilemma about him being only seven years old. This merged into an acknowledgement of the hundreds of times he'd jerked off about Ryan. David flipped through nine years of jerking off, and the different images he'd had in his head at the time. Then he wondered if he should be questioning the fact that they're related but justified this by thinking that it would be more an issue if their intention was to procreate. One concern stuck and meant too much. Joe. Why hadn't he ever told him? He hadn't even mentioned it. If there was nothing to be ashamed of, how come he hadn't? Finally, at no fixed point and for no reason that he was aware of, David abandoned himself completely to the moment. Here, he let go and kind of poured himself into his mouth and by default, Ryan's. This lasted only a moment.

Now, sitting alone and waiting David felt surprisingly self-conscious. The music seemed louder, the crowd more annoying, and the reason for being in Trade escaped him.

Ryan returned quiet and sulking. "I've had enough of this place."

"Me too," said David.

"Shall we split?"

"Yeah."

David stood and balanced. Then he and Ryan silently made their way upstairs. Both behaved as though something traumatic had just happened. Once outside, they chose one of the shouting, haggling cab drivers to take them home. Whoever they chose was guaranteed to rip them off, so they went with one because David liked the color of his T-shirt. Then another slid in at the last second and nearly halved his fare, and so they went with this man, not because they cared that much about the price but more because he seemed so determined.

In the cab they stared out the window. Then when they pulled up outside their house, they got out off the cab, paid the man, and walked up the garden path towards the front door. They managed to do all this using as little dialogue as was necessary to complete the task.

The morning sun was beginning to rise and because of the drugs all colour in the garden was heavily saturated. Also, it had a weird stillness, as though it was actually just a photograph of itself, but in 3D.

As they approached the front door Ryan reached out ahead of him for David's arm. "Hey!" David turned. "It's okay, you know."

David looked at him wondering if he'd said what he had and also if it was true. "I feel so weird."

"Don't Sweet Man."

"How did that even happen?"

They spoke with lowered voices, not that they could be heard inside, but they were acting on instinct not logic. In an attempt to make David feel all right about the kiss Ryan managed to access a part of himself that he didn't usually need, and David didn't know existed.

"The way I see it is, if you take drugs you have to accept that freaky things might happen sometimes."

Without conviction, David nodded.

"It's partly why we do them isn't it?"

Again, David nodded, but this time more in agreement. Then he looked down the path to the street. "Is it me or do cabs seem to linger when they drop us off?"

"It's probably you."

"It happens every time."

"What reason would they have to hang around? They've got better things to be doing than stalking us."

"You'd think so wouldn't you? Anyway, let's go inside. I'm a bit cold."

"Me too," said Ryan and link David's arm in a reassuring and buddy-like way.

When they stepped inside David mouthed, "Shall we go to the kitchen? I still feel funny. Don't want to go to bed like this."

Ryan followed David's lead as far as communication was concerned and he mouthed, "Listen. Go up to my room. I'll get us a drink and follow you."

David didn't move or respond much at all.

"Go!"

At this, he did what Ryan said and crept quietly up the stairs. It made sense to go to Ryan's room, as it was warmer and more comfortable and Leila was away. David made his way into the room and sat at the bottom of Ryan's bed. He expected him to come up with hot milk or herbal tea, a comfort drink, but instead he appeared with a bottle of Tequila, two shot glasses, salt, and a lemon cut into quarters. This too was a comfort drink, but in a totally different way.

From David's expression Ryan could tell it wasn't what he was expecting.

"What?" He didn't need an answer to this question, but busied himself with putting down the glasses and preparing two Tequila Slammers. "I think we have to let go of that kiss thing. It was something that happened when we were cunted and we shouldn't freak out about it."

David couldn't be as gung-ho, but at the same time he was still pretty high and so was no more capable of decision-making than he had been at the time. "I guess so," he said with uncertainty.

Ryan knelt in front of David and prepared the Slammers as he spoke. "The thing is *Uncle*," he said teasing. He took hold of David's hand and turned it on its side. "I know you love me, and that you know I love you." He poured salt on the back of David's thumb. "And so that means we both know that neither of us would harm the other." Ryan stuck a wedge of lemon in David's free hand. "So, whatever happened happened. We're still us, and we still love each other. Let's drink to that."

"Okay," said David as he copied Ryan's actions. He licked the salt, bit the lemon and took a swig. Then he made the obligatory oh-my-god-how-sour face, and with a mouthful of excess saliva he said, "How did you get to be so mature and cool?"

"I'm sure I learned a lot of it from you and Joe." David raised his eyebrows. "Well it can't have been my mum, can it?"

David let out a short soft one-syllable burst of laughter. "That's funny."

"We know we crossed boundaries tonight, but I think we shouldn't be hard on ourselves. We're cool about what happened. Right?"

David nodded unconvincingly, not sure at all.

"My thoughts are, we should take some Rohypnol, cuddle up and go to sleep. And let it pass. What do you say?"

"Ryan you're such a lovely man."

"And I want you to feel loved going to sleep tonight. You did nothing wrong. Please don't beat yourself up about it."

With his head hanging low, David didn't look like he believed this and they sat in silence for a moment as the old house showed its age by making noises around them. When David looked up next, Ryan could see that his eyes were wet. "It's confusing, Ryan."

"I know it is. Here take these."

Ryan plied David's mouth open using the Rohypnol and pushed three in one by one. 'Let's be old school. Swallow them down with Tequila."

Passive and receptive David accepted what he was given, including the suggestion of how to wash them down. Ryan rolled a joint, and they drank a lot while talking little. David began to slur his words. Ryan didn't. At some point - about twenty minutes after taking the Rohypnol - when reaching for another Tequila David stopped and slumped forward. This was what Ryan had been waiting for.

First Ryan finished the joint he was working on. Then

he held it in his mouth, the smoke making him squint, as he pulled off David's T-shit and lay him down on the bed. He lay down on his front beside David and smoked on his joint. He watched David's chest going up and down and put his arm across it. He could feel the heat from his body. It felt lovely. He rubbed his lips against David's chest then rested his head down on it. For minutes Ryan lay still, gazing ahead of him. Then he eased off David's boxer shorts, and turned him over and took off his own underpants. Next he pushed David's legs apart, lay between them with his face close to David's butt. Ryan pushed his own hips into the bed, clenching his butt, and grinding his hard dick beneath him. As he raised his hips, his butt-crack opened slightly, and when he thrust forward his cheeks formed two smooth, hard bumps. Ryan breathed in deep, hoping to absorb some of David. For a moment, Ryan's face hovered over David's butt, before nuzzling into it. Again, he breathed in deep. David smelt musky, gorgeous, and more wonderful than Ryan had ever imagined. He knelt upright, and looked down at the sight below, trying to freeze-frame it, so he'd never forget it. For seconds he thought about consequences. Then he threw them aside in favour of indulgence. Besides, he'd thought this one through long ago. He hadn't planned on David being asleep, but this did tap more directly into a fantasy he'd had since David had mentioned the scenario with Rob and Rohypnol. Almost falling, he pushed his face into David's butt. He stuck out his tongue, licked around the hole, prodded it by making his tongue stiff and pointed, then slid it right inside. It was incredible. Warm like a mouth, but more erotic. Like Leila's cunt, but less moist, with a completely different taste and smell.

For half an hour, Ryan kept his face never more than three inches away from David's butt. Slowly he began to come down from his drugs. With each passing minute, he questioned himself further. He pulled back, emotionally and physically not wanting to be inside David anymore. Some kind of fear took hold, overcoming his desire. He turned and sat on the edge of the bed. Even his surroundings seemed silly now. What would anybody want to paint a room in such this way? With the big circles of color, it looked as though it were that of a child's. What were they, David and Joe, trying to say about themselves? Ryan thought he heard a floorboard creak, and so quickly slipped his underpants on. Waiting and holding his breath, he strained to hear if Joe was on the landing. Not that he was particularly prepared if he did come in the room. There wasn't any further sound except the wheezing and spluttering of the heating coming on. It sounded like some futuristic hybrid of old man and machine engine.

Ryan turned his attention back to David. Suddenly he seemed foolish, naked, with his legs apart, so vulnerable, careless, and stupid. In slow motion, Ryan put his head in his hands, and he continued to perch on the end of the bed, as though he didn't want to be on the bed, but didn't want to get off either. He also continued to come down. There was nothing here for Ryan now. Well, nothing to do with sex, and so he pulled the sheet over David's feet, his calves, thighs and shoulders, everything that only a short time before he'd wanted to coat, with himself. He kissed the side of David head, smelled his lovely scent, and then he went to his jeans to get

Rohypnol for himself this time. He swallowed three, and lay beside David once more. He nuzzled into his neck, said goodnight in David's ear and waited for the relief of sleep.

16

To give the interview an authentic feel of a night at an exhibition, the BBC had invited thirty or so guests. Along with these, there was also about half as many film crew. Amid the mess of people, Joe was calm. He wore a black fitted suit, had his hair slicked back, was clean-shaven, and altogether immaculately groomed.

"So," said the reporter. "Would it be too simplistic to say you believe art is more important than life?"

"Yes . . ." he said looking at the woman's tweed skirt, synthetic looking cream blouse and pearl twin set. In response, she raised an eyebrow. But he hadn't finished his sentence. " . . . That would be too simplistic." Now she raised both eyebrows showing more alarm than she'd have liked to on air.

The camera pulled in to a close-up of the woman interviewer, with people passing behind her. As well as the 'naturalistic' smile she held throughout the whole interview she now gave a quizzical, reporter kind of look, as though Joe had just said a curious punch line, that she didn't quite get, and she'd leave it for the viewers to work out. Although she'd already made it clear what she thought their response should be.

Knowing he was out of shot, Joe reached for his drink. Lots of people were looking at the exhibition and others just watched Joe. He scanned them and spotted David, who was keeping a respectful distance. Joe beckoned him over.

As he approached, David stuck his thumb up. "Well done, puppy. That was great."

"How long have you been here?"

"About twenty minutes."

"I didn't see you."

"The light was in your eyes."

"Oh, yeah, I forgot, you're used to being in front of a camera."

"Not any more."

Joe stepped closer to David and spoke quietly into his ear. "Do you think they got it?"

"They'd have to be stupid not to."

"Just between you and me, I think they are." Joe walked away and returned with another drink. "How was last night?"

"Interesting?"

"Did you have Rohypnol?" David nodded. "That's why I don't like taking them. If I'm going to go to such lengths to have fun, I at least want to remember."

"Good point." David had put an inflection on the word *interesting*. By this, he didn't mean to express that he didn't remember, but that he was confused. Regardless, he went with Joe's take on it for now, until he had the time or inclination to explain. He didn't want to bother Joe at this moment. Well, that's what he told himself. Like Ryan had said, 'Shit happens when you get

fucked up', or words to that effect, although this sounded less like a reason now, and more like an excuse.
Whatever! David thought. *I'll deal with it later*. "You
know me, I hate coming down."

"I know you, Pumpkin."

Again, Joe spoke into David's ear. "Don't quote me on
this," he said. "But I'll be glad to scrap this foul exhibition."

"Right!" said David not really concentrating. "Did you
see Don?"

A grip squeezed between them carrying a chair.
"Sorry mate!"

They stepped apart. "No, problem," said Joe. Then to
David, "No, I haven't. Have you seen Flora?"

David was instantly distracted from last night and
Ryan and everything going on around him. "You are kidding!"

"I'm not." Joe stood on his toes and tried to look over
the people milling around. "I saw her helping herself to
the crew's refreshments. Did Leila tell you?" David
looked lost. "About seeing Don and her together?"

"Weird, hey?"

"I don't get it," said Joe. "I thought I trusted Don."

"Do you think that's wise?"

Another person wanted to get by. "Sorry," said a non-
definable member of the crew.

"Let's stand over here," said Joe pulling David to a
doorway that led to the toilets. "I find it hard to believe
he'd go along with any nonsense. What do you think?"

"I don't know."

"Are you okay with him?" asked Joe, concerned.

David suddenly looked about five years old. "He sort

of intimidates me."

For a moment, Joe looked surprised but on a deeper level he identified with the expression David had made, so he said, "I can see why." He thought for a moment. "Of course, nothing Flora does surprises me."

"She went beyond that a long time ago. Do you think she's up to something?"

"Probably."

"Do you care?"

"Maybe."

The door behind them opened and three young women came through. On seeing David, they giggled flirtatiously. In response to them, he smiled, and then he rolled his eyes at Joe.

"Jesus!" said Joe. "It's like a zoo in here, and I'm not talking about the dogs." He shook his head in disbelief. "How many people does it take? I'm sure most of these don't do anything. Speaking of zoos, where is Mad Cow?" Again, he tried to see over or around the bustling people. "Can't see her." Then he said, "She headed this way ages ago, but she must be done by now."

"Oh that reminds me, I have to piss."

"You know where it is," said Joe.

"Yeah." At this, he kissed Joe on the nose and turned to go.

"Pumpkin." David stopped. "Don't forget when we get home tonight you owe me."

To show Joe he knew what he meant, David scratched his butt and said, "I know." Then he looked down, as though embarrassed. Joe thought this an odd response, as he expected something sexier, or at least cheeky, even *I love you* would have done fine, but *I know*, almost verged on the all-time worst response, *"that's nice, dear."*

Joe watched David walk away, thinking that there was something off about him, and although he couldn't put his finger on why, he felt sad.

The toilet was in the basement down two flights of stairs. As he was about to leave the room Ryan stepped in front of him.

"Where you off to?"

"Er, toilet. . . I'll catch you in a minute." He started to head off.

Ryan reached for him. "Hey, Baby! Slow down." Ryan reached for David and they hugged awkwardly.

"You okay?"

"I don't know. *You*?"

"Not sure. You weren't there when I woke up, so I began to worry. Thought maybe I'd scared you away."

"That'll be post-drugs paranoia. No. When I woke up without my boxers on, I got out of there as soon as I could. What if Joe had come in?"

David spoke earnestly, but also as though it was almost too painful to utter his thoughts. "Please tell me I didn't get all sleazy on you before the Rohypnol kicked in. Old habits die hard."

Ryan put his hand on David's neck. "Let's just say I've no regrets, and if you can't remember you can't have any either."

David looked confused. This wasn't enough informa-tion. "You know if my ex Rob had been there he'd have dived right in." He frowned. "Our legs would been in the air as soon as we hit our pillows."

"Wow!" said Ryan, not giving anything away as to

whether that would have been a good or bad thing.

David stared into space. "The good old days." His was only partly a joke, but on a more serious note. "It was simpler then."

"Anyway, before you get lost in nostalgia, I still love you. And I meant what I said about the kiss."

David managed a half-baked smile. "I wondered when you were going to use the K word.

Ryan sensed his uneasiness, took hold of him, and squeezed him. "You silly-manilly. We're good, right? Listen, in the future, let's refer to it as special K."

David nodded, but didn't like this collusion, and he felt just as uncertain about the whole thing as he had before they spoke. He opened the door to the stairwell and darted through.

Once out of the main exhibition space, David noticed how much quieter it was and away from the lights much cooler also. In the hallway, there were screens, half open paint cans, and cartons of turpentine with brushes sticking out of them. The turps was lying on its side creating a large pale green puddle. The fumes were strong and as he passed them, he held his breath and tried not to get any of it on his shoes. He half expected to have to deal with Flora, but she didn't seem to be there. *Perhaps*, he thought, *she was still in the toilet*. Just in case he crept quickly down the concrete steps quietly and went into the toilet without a sound.

Ryan milled around until he caught Joe's eye. He wanted to give him encouragement and winked and gave him a comforting smile. Then he went to the refreshment table and got a drink.

Flora arrived, acting manic. She seemed nervous

about something, jittery. Maybe she'd done too much coke in the toilet.

Joe was just about to go on camera for his final take when Don tapped his shoulder. "Hey, Buddy," he said, less confidently than Joe was used to.

"Hey, dude!"

"Since when did you get all Californian?"

"Just now. Does it suit me?"

"Kind of," said Don, and took hold of Joe's hand. "Listen, there's something I want to talk to you about."

"They've just got to do the closing shot."

"It's quite important," he said with his head down.

"Can it wait?" said Joe, trying to establish eye contact. "It won't be long."

"Yeah," said Don. "It can wait."

With her face powdered, the interviewer was ready. Her plan was to criticize the exhibition, hoping to get the support of the viewers, and then close with some pithy remark. Then she'd give her concerned but warm smile and say goodnight. She looked around at the mirror to rehearse her expression and had to bend to see herself. When she stood upright again, she fluffed her fringe gently with her fingers. As she turned back towards the camera her heel caught. She tripped and fell against a light. It tipped, hovered, and crashed onto the floor. There was a lot of commotion and noise, as people rushed about.

Over this racket, there was a single, terrifying cry, "Fire! Fire! Fire!" In the stairwell, out of sight, it had begun only minutes before. Within a short time, flames coated the hallway, floor, walls, and ceiling. The old dry wood of the double doors set alight quickly. Streams of smoke started gushing through the crack in between the doors. Don took charge immediately and started to evacuate the building.

Once outside, all anybody could do was stand and stare. Don helped the other firemen when he could, but he knew they had a routine to follow and team roles to play, so mostly he stood beside Joe, out of the way. He thought to ask if David had gone home already. Joe looked suddenly bewildered, almost blank. Then he set off, running, towards the entrance to the building. Don caught him, pinning him down.

"Let go," Joe shouted words. "David's inside."

"Where?" Don yelled, as Joe continued to kick and scream.

"The basement."

Don called to one of the other firemen, who in turn spoke into his radio.

Earlier, when still at home David had prepared a joint. This was the perfect time to smoke it. There was no way that he wanted to bump into Flora on the stairwell and he knew Joe would be a while before he finished shooting, so he took it out of his sock and for a moment admired how well it had stayed intact. He took his time, relishing the relaxing effect it had and enjoyed the savoury smell. Joe came to mind and without trying to, he smiled. When done with his joint he splashed some water on his face, looked in an old cracked mirror, and absentmindedly fiddled with his hair. He made a pretend model face and then the smell of smoke caught his attention. His immediate response was to check the cubicle to make sure he hadn't set anything alight. No, nothing. Next, with hesitation he opened the door to look up the stairwell. It took only seconds for him to realize what was going on. He knew then that there was no way he would be able to make his way up two flights of burning stairs. He thought of Joe and began to cry. His mind became a rush of memories, all mixed with fear and love and frantic questions of what to do. He knew there was no hope whichever way he went, but in desperation, he backed up into the toilet and knowing it would do no good, still he ran all the water taps. *Water puts out fire*, he thought. Therefore, he blocked the toilet by sticking paper in. Then he flushed and tried to flush again even before the cistern had time to fill. *Where did all the water come from when it overflowed at home*, he thought. How could he just stand there and wait for the fire to burn him to death. What else could he do though? Panic messed up his mind and it made him move without direction or goal. Then a thought sprung up, clear and loud. He could try one more thing. At the sinks, he drenched himself with water, took off his jacket, and soaked it too. Then he held it dripping wet around his head. Now, using all the courage he could muster, he ran. Desperate and terrified, he set off into the corridor coated with flames. On adrenalin alone, he made it up both flights of stairs, stumbling and banging into walls. He could feel nothing now, as he'd left his body back at the foot of the stairs. If he could just make it into the main room, he might have a chance. Maybe there'd be firemen there. He headed in the direction of the double doors, but slipped on the spilled paint and smashed to the floor. He tried to scramble to his feet, but wailed with fear and pain as he breathed in flames and the fire engulfed him. Falling to his knees once more he screamed, "Joe!"

17

David's funeral service took place outside. At one point,
just for a short time, the clouds cleared and sunlight cut
through the leaves of a huge oak tree. It covered everybody in attendance in a camouflage-like pattern.
Ordinarily, this lighting, along with such a beautifully
dressed gathering, the dramatic gothic setting, and the
feeling of togetherness might have created a pleasant
mood, but not today. The context was wrong and their
being a part of the funeral meant they didn't notice
much about things like surroundings. Grief governed
every thought and influenced every feeling. Joe was so
absorbed that he wasn't even aware that he needed comforting, but he did, desperately. Leila stepped up to con-
sole him. This surprised some, especially Flora, but a
more accurate way to describe her reaction was *put out.*
She felt it was strategy, but this was how Flora saw the
world and the people operating within it. From experience she knew Leila to be a fierce rival, with desire and
probably profound feelings too, so it was obvious that
she had motive for moving in on Joe. It was true that
Leila cared for Joe and welcomed getting closer to him,

but her reasons were perhaps not as devious as Flora believed.

Ironically, it would usually have fallen on Joe's 'nearest and dearest' David to make him feel everything was okay, but this is one of the eternal tragedies; that when the person we love most dies, they'd be the very person we'd ordinarily have turned to for solace.

The trouble was, as happens with many couples, neither David nor Joe had bothered to develop close outside relationships, mainly because Joe hadn't the time, and David had become more of a homebody in the last few years of his life, especially after he had been raped. Naturally, Joe had had more sex partners than David, but not that many and not that often and certainly there was never anybody who was allowed to get close. It wasn't a rule, agreed upon, but simply a preference, one that went unquestioned.

Everybody knew what a special relationship Ryan and David had, so Ryan was expected to be devastated and nobody expected him to be fit to comfort anybody else. Unlike Joe who had lost people in the past, especially gay friends in the 80s and 90s, Ryan was still inexperienced. In practice, this meant he had a *get out of jail free card*, so everybody kept a respectful distance and didn't even think to ask him to say anything at the service.

Don had found David cold and never bothered trying to get to know him. He even felt a bit self-conscious about this during the service. It wasn't difficult for him not to feel that much about David specifically, but funerals always made him upset. Not that he rose to the occasion and cried, but his face did twitch at times. This was mainly because of the impact of David's death on Joe and Flora.

Joe wrote a eulogy, but wasn't fit to read it. Judy offered to read it for him.

"This is Joe's eulogy," said Judy, and began reading.

"What was David to me? It would make more sense to ask, what wasn't he? I'd like to praise him, but you all knew him. This leaves me wanting to tell you how he made me feel, loved, adored, and so at ease. When everything made so little sense, he was my sense. When I couldn't comprehend others, their actions or the things they said, he was my link. He fixed what was broken in me, making order of what I saw as chaos, simply by letting me tell him that I loved him. Through him, for the first time in my life, everything made sense. Although I was bitter, cynical, and jaded, he made me comprehend love."

As Judy finished reading, Joe closed his eyes. In his head, he had an image of David sitting at the end of their bed, facing away, so Joe could see his back, and his beautiful waist. He smiled. Judy looked over for some kind of acknowledgement, but Joe was lost in his private thoughts. The service continued.

A little later, it was Flora's turn to read what she had written. She hadn't been sure that she'd be able to do it. Filled with doubt, she repeated encouragement, as though a mantra. She left her seat, and by the time she reached the microphone, she was able to begin. Although she sniffled all the way through, she carried on reading, determined. She read,

"Things won't be the same without you. You selfish thing. What about us? I'm sure I'll forgive you in time, but remember, I'll think of you every day, my precious, my puppy."

She looked over at Joe, who now had his eyes open. Then she said, finally,

"*Our puppy.*"

At this point she began to sob noisily. Don went up and collected her. She was all little girl now, pathetic, unable to walk without being led, her eyes full of tears. Joe's heart went out to Flora. She'd been emptied. Over the years since she and David had split, she'd at least been able to take comfort knowing he was around, if only in the same city with somebody else. At this moment, Joe had the urge to hold Flora, make sure she was okay. They had, after all, loved the same person. Albeit in a twisted way, *love* connected them.

Somebody had to go through David's address book and make sure people knew what had happened. Joe wasn't in any shape to make such calls. Judy couldn't be trusted to say the right things in the right way and it was presumed Ryan would feel too raw. So again, Leila stepped in. She had to make sure she wasn't calling the dry cleaners, a car service, or some decorator, and she found she had to keep catching Joe at the right moment. Then she'd run a handful of names by him quickly as if he wouldn't notice it was happening.

Sky was on the list. Out of everybody, she responded with such gravity and even asked if she could say a few words at the service. Although distracted by everything going on; David's death, everybody's individual pain, and the task of making the phone calls, still Leila was curious as to what Sky wanted to say, so when she got up to speak she listened carefully,

"I'm here to say goodbye to a dear man. I will miss him, his gentle nature, and his softness. Fortunately, a trace of him remains in me, and I'm guessing in us all here. Goodbye, David."

Maybe because Sky represented somebody not close to David, what she said seemed somehow more objective so her few simple words touched on something that made everybody, apart from Flora, cry. Flora found Sky's sentiment incidental and she thought to watch everybody else's responses. In Leila's peripheral vision, she noticed Flora's head move and so followed her eyes. Nothing seemed out of the ordinary, and Leila, not knowing the mind of Flora, didn't understand why she'd even want to look around, but then she did notice something odd. Ryan wasn't crying. This wasn't strange in itself, but what was stranger was the vacant look in his eyes. It disturbed her, not just that he was doing it now at his uncle's funeral, but also because she'd never seen him wear an expression like this. What did it mean?

Before everybody left the church, Joe told Flora to call him if she needed to talk. Taking him up on his offer, she phoned that night. Joe was glad to talk with someone who had also loved David as he had. The next day she called again, in the morning, when trying to face her day, and in the evening when trying to face the night. On both occasions Joe was more than happy to talk about David. He was conscious not to trample on Flora's feelings. At the same time, Flora was careful not to undermine Joe's. Flora and Joe began to feel comfortable with each other. They had something in common, which made their relationship up to this point seem petty. At first, they spoke on the phone. Then they started to meet, occasionally, then more often. Flora had softened and Joe had opened. Both were more able to accept each other. Their friendship began to grow.

Flora had an ultrasound to make sure her baby was healthy and was told she was carrying a boy. She was excited when she got the news, but generally she seemed to get milder, and calmer as the months went by. Joe began to think she'd make an incredible mother. Flora decided to call the baby David. Everyone thought this right somehow. As the pregnancy drew to a close, Joe helped out, more and more. Whether he realised this might be the nearest he'd come to having a baby or there were deeper paternal instincts at work, he was there when she needed him. He kept her company when bored, indulged her diet, massaged her feet, even drove her to the hospital, when the time came. Flora asked if he'd be the godfather, and Joe was very flattered. He said *yes*. The baby was stillborn.

They stood on either side of the tiny coffin as it was lowered into the earth, and slowly, in one's and two's, the crowd trickled away. Joe walked with Flora to her car, his arm linked in hers.

Don caught them up. "I've just been talking to the priest about fire regulations." he said.

It took a moment after he'd finished saying this before he noticed that Flora and Joe had been already having another, unspoken conversation. Feeling a bit left out, he said, "Let me in."

"Well," said Joe. "I was saying a couple of things, I miss David. And, Flora you're a lucky bitch finding a guy like Don."

Flora turned to Don. "It's surprising what one can say." She paused, and smiled. "Without words!" She kissed him to make sure he knew she wasn't serious. Next she said to Joe, as though in mid-conversation, "And I was saying, you're very special. I'm glad that David found you and loved you."

Joe reached out for Flora with both hands. They held each other.

"Look what you've gone and done," said Flora, pulling away. Joe could see she was crying.

"Don't Flora, you'll make me . . ." Joe couldn't finish his sentence, because he held his mouth firmly shut. He was trying to stop himself crying. He looked down, then into the sky, then up to Flora. At this, seeing each other so upset, and looking ridiculous, they both burst out laughing.

"Enough of this thought stuff," said Don.

Sniffling, Joe said, "I guess we could use that speech thing, like the humans do."

"In that case," said Flora. "I'll state that I've had enough funerals for one year."

"Too many," said Joe.

"I guess any is too many," said Don.

"So it's a deal," said Flora. "No more."

Joe smiled, despite the topic of conversation. "It's a deal."

18

The stage was only a few feet off the ground. The audience, sitting in rows of dining hall chairs, consisted of mums and dads, a reporter from a local paper, and a talent scout who was there to watch one person in particular.

A blue spotlight came up on a young man. This was his soliloquy, part of his end-of-term assessment. He felt relaxed and comfortable, verging on showing off. His stage presence was self-assured, his acting subtle and controlled. The lights dimmed to black. He spoke into the dark. Putting only the slightest melody into his voice, he started to sing the last sentence, and dropped back to his speaking voice for the final few words.

There was silence in front of him.

It broke with some hesitant clapping, which turned into a noisy and vigorous applause. Someone in the audience shouted, "Well done, kid."

The lights came up, and Ryan stood, smiling. He put his hands together in front of him, about waist high, tipped his head forward, turned and walked off stage left. A high-pitched "Woo!" followed him. This time Ryan recognised the voice. It was Leila's. The crowd kept clapping.

Backstage, Ryan couldn't contain his excitement. His friends squealed and patted him. Uli, the only person at college Ryan considered a friend, rushed forward, and jumped up. He wrapped his short legs around Ryan, and gave him loud, theatrical kisses on either cheek. Ryan liked Uli's softness, it reminded him a little of David, although physically the only resemblance was that they were both blonde and had the same baby eyelashes. Uli wasn't tall, and he certainly didn't have David's commercially viable facial features. Ryan liked him because he wasn't afraid of showing affection and Uli liked Ryan mainly because he was more open-minded than most their age. Regardless of the fact they had little in common besides their enthusiasm for drama, they hung out at college and increasingly in the evenings also.

He was not heavy, so Ryan spun him around. As they turned, Uli leant back with his arms outstretched, screeching, *darling*, and generally being outrageous. Uli's brother appeared backstage. He looked like a bulky, overfed version of Uli, without the any cute elements. Instantly uncomfortable, Uli jumped down off Ryan, and dropped the camp theatrical behaviour. On seeing this, Ryan felt sorry for Uli, realizing that he probably couldn't be himself at home.

One of Ryan's tutors introduced him to a woman, the man's wife. She was effusive and somehow managed to turn the center of the conversation to herself. Immediately, Ryan felt bored, but understood that he had to perform once more. This took effort, but he appreciated Mr. Kenwood's advice so he rallied as much charm as was necessary. Moments after he'd resigned himself to this task, he saw Leila over Mrs. Kenwood's shoulder. She winked. Ryan responded. Mr. Kenwood noticed and turned.

"I'm sorry. My girlfriend's here," said Ryan.

"Oh don't worry, I'll see you tomorrow."

Then as though to validate his leaving Mr. Kenwood, he added, "She had to take time off work to come."

Mrs. Kenwood smiled. "Get over there. You shouldn't keep her waiting," she said, giving what she thought the more female take on the situation.

Ryan laughed convincingly, said goodbye, and rushed over to Leila.

She stood with her arms out to welcome him. "You nailed it," she said.

"I hoped so. Like the outfit." He was referring to an elegant long black dress that would have been more appropriate at the glamorous opening night of an opera.

"Did you hear that applause?" said Leila. "The audience was right with you." She took a step back as if to marvel at him and possibly get a more objective viewpoint. Then she shook her head. "Oh my God! Especially that stuff about your mum. Genius!"

"Did that really work?" Adrenaline still rushed through him.

"God yeah! I just feel sorry for everybody else who performed. Your piece clearly stood out. Theirs were childish in comparison."

"Thanks Pony." He pulled in close to Leila and spoke in her ear. "Listen, I've got a couple of beers in my bag. Let's go find a quiet place somewhere."

She knew the college well as she'd spent many a lunch break with Ryan. "How about the refectory?"

"Good idea."

They made their way there, only having to stop a couple of times to be congratulated. One of these times was by the agent who'd been in the audience. Ryan was surprised, but acted cool. He was given a card with a number to call.

Only one door was open to the refectory. It had been left for the cleaners. Inside it was empty except for upturned chairs on tabletops. Usually full of glances, and angst, it felt strange now. Although the lights were off, it wasn't dark. The full moon provided plenty of light.

They went to the far side of the refectory. It was the furthest point from the door and was partially hidden by a screen. The windows covered the whole wall and so they stood close looking out onto the ruby pitch. "Check out the moon." said Ryan. "Spooky!"

"I was thinking romantic."

"It's quite exciting isn't it?"

"What the agent?" asked Leila.

"Well yeah, but I meant in here."

"Are you getting fresh?"

"Maybe."

"Give me a kiss."

She didn't hesitate. Then turned her cheek to Ryan. He took hold of her chin and turned it towards his lips. Leila intimidated most men so she appreciated the novelty of somebody else taking control like this. Her strength left her and she simply gave into being kissed.

Leila pulled away, "I . . ." she said, and then stopped.

As Ryan was facing the moon, his face looked powdered by it. "What's on your mind, Pony?"

Leila took a deep breath, and sighed, "I love you."

"Ah Baby!" Ryan watched Leila looking downwards for a moment as she collected her thoughts, then when she raised her head again, and their eyes met he said, "I love you too." He paused for a couple of seconds. "Regardless."

Leila smiled and looked down again. This time, Ryan lifted her chin. He waited until he could resist no more and then kissed her.

This kiss and the intention she believed was behind it made Leila feel as though her stomach, being made of butter now began to melt, and in doing so it massaged and tickled the walls that lined it. "I've been dying to say that."

"Me too."

Leila's voice was breathy, "Baby!"

"I say it in my head every time we kiss."

"Every time?"

"Well . . ." he said, and then thought hard to make sure he was telling the truth. "Definitely when we get fleshy."

"That sounds cannibalistic," said Leila, whose face was in shadow. This had the effect of being mysterious and very sexy and a little devilish, which was also very sexy. "I've been thinking it for ages," she continued. "The love thing, I mean."

"Why didn't you say it?"

"I don't know . . . Scared?"

Ryan leaned with his back against the window and moved her around in from of him. Now her face was soft focused by the moonlight. "Scared of what?"

It was obvious to Leila what the answer should be.

Firstly, she thought it too corny to say, but also, in her heart of hearts she felt this wasn't the real reason. She considered the question and couldn't think of another reason so said, "Rejection, I guess."

"I thought it was obvious how I felt."

"Not to me. I, on the other hand, follow you around like a dog. You move to London, I do. You come back to Manchester, I do. Do you think I wanted to do this stupid BA?"

Ryan opened his feet wide apart so his head lowered beneath Leila's. He looked up at her with a confused look on his face, "Didn't you?"

Leila knew what she was going to say wasn't cool, but continued anyway, "I only did it so I'd have something to do while you were at college. And . . ."

She fell quiet.

"What?"

"After the whole David thing, I thought you needed my support."

"Pony I do, but I thought you liked the course as well."

"It's okay, but seriously, could you really imagine me as a magistrate? If I'm not careful, that's what I'm heading for."

"I think it's sexy. Your Honor."

"Well, that's the important thing," said Leila a little bugged because she's trying to be serious.

"Isn't it?"

Leila thought for a second and as she did Ryan ran his fingers through her hair and stroked her face with the back of his hand. "Actually," she said giving into his touch. "It's quite important."

Ryan pulled Leila towards him again. They kissed. This time more passionately. Ryan rubbed his hands up her body, inside her dress. It made her shiver. He slid his hand under her bra, took hold of her breast, and started to massage it, flicking her nipple with his forefinger. Leila responded with a deep, seemingly endless sigh. When she next gathered her thoughts, she undid his fly, and pushed her hand inside his jeans. His dick was hot compared to the air around them. Ryan pushed his tongue into her mouth. This drove Leila on. She pulled out his dick, and bent her knees to get to it. Muffled sounds could be heard from the main hall. There were glass doors and curtains separating them.

Leila took Ryan's dick in her mouth, making him groan.

His head fell back against the window. "Jesus!" he said. Leila crouched and took his dick into her mouth. With one hand, she stroked his dick up and down in a twisting motion, while the other gently massaged his balls. He looked down at Leila, "I love you Pony. I'm glad I can say that now."

Leila pulled her mouth off his dick, but just long enough to look up at him and say, "I feel exactly the same." She smiled a pretty, yet sexy smile and once again closed her mouth around Ryan's dick.

"Be careful. I could cum anytime."

Leila pulled back. "Not that I wouldn't love a mouthful of your cum, but let's take this home. I want to get naked."

Ryan helped Leila up. "I guess now that we've admitted to loving each other we don't have to bother having sex anymore."

Although it was obvious that Ryan was teasing her, she didn't get the joke.

"Why no sex?" she said and wiped the corner of her mouth with her ring finger like she'd seen 'loose' women do in movies.

"Because now Pony, we can make love."

Shyly Leila looked down and smiled. "I can't wait."

19

Flora squashed awkwardly through the doorway of a West End bistro. Her red trouser suit, with a black blouse and heels made her look conspicuously glamorous, or at last showy. This outfit and the fact that she carried a huge black portfolio under her arm meant that everybody turned and watched her entrance.

The bar was full in as much as there were couples sitting at every etched glass table. All of them were dressed in varying degrees of chic office wear, most had glasses of wine in front of them, and a few had tapas. Nobody was laughing or even smiling. Ambient music played low enough to talk over, and although it wasn't yet dark outside, dim shaded lamps gave the impression that the place was cozy.

"Sorry, I'm late," said Flora, to Joe, while miming at the waiter, asking his permission to put her portfolio on the mantelpiece over the fireplace.

"*A bit*?" said Joe.

Flora looked at her watch and made a shocked face. "God!"

"Is that who kept you?"

"Aha! Her and every other bloody driver in London, it seems."

With his thumb, Joe gestured to the portfolio behind him "Why didn't you leave that in the car?"

"I know this sounds stupid, but I was scared of it getting stolen."

A glamorous but drunk looking couple fell in through the doorway. They straightened themselves up, looked round the room, then at each other conspiratorially, burst out laughing, and left.

Neither Flora nor Joe said anything about the couple, but they shared a knowing look about what they thought. However, at their departure, Flora smiled faintly, delighted to be the person that Joe related to, and he raised his eyebrows pleased that they understood each other. Then they continued the other conversation they were having previously. "But you're not bothered about the car?"

"I'm bored with the color."

Acting as if he was a concerned councillor he put his hand on Flora's and said, "I wondered when you would be."

"Is it that bad?" Flora flicked his hand away in mock annoyance.

"Aha!" said Joe, in exactly the same way Flora had.

"Really?"

"Yeah!"

"Now I know you're teasing me. If you really thought so, you wouldn't tell me."

"Got me. Maybe I knew you'd think that, and I'm actually telling the truth."

Exasperated, Flora let out a cry. It was a little too loud, and so people looked around at her. The waiter also glanced over to see what the fuss was about and not being one to miss an opportunity, she beckoned him over with what could have been a cute finger wiggle, but because she had quite large hands and long red nails, it came across more like a posh woman beckoning her butler.

The waiter felt this and immediately took a disliking to her. "How can I help you?" he said.

"Kier Royal, please. Actually, make that a double," she added.

The waiter looked confused. "We don't do champagne in doubles."

"It was a joke."

It wouldn't have taken much for him to be annoyed by her and this was easily enough. He let his face drop into a caricature of somebody clearly not amused. "That was extremely funny," he said. "Let me get your drink while I laugh my head off."

Flora looked at Joe, pointing to the waiter with her eyes, and said, "Dry!"

"Crispy," said Joe.

"*Crispy*. I'll have to remember that."

"I got it from David. He had a whole list, crunchy, brittle, arid, and many more."

Flora smiled sadly, frowned, and sighed.

Joe fell into a reverie, staring deep into the fire and his own memories.

For months after David's death, Joe blamed himself. He felt partly responsible. Therapy and a course of antidepressants helped him change his perspective to a certain extent. Still, as far as he was concerned if he hadn't had his exhibition in such a rundown building David would still be alive. A year had passed and so he'd began to think less about the man he loved being burnt alive, and more about getting through each day and night, just filling time without him.

Joe and David had woken, ate, rested and slept together everyday for over four years. After his death, he had to get used to David not being at arms length, whenever he needed a kiss, a hug, or an expression that showed he understood and cared about what happened in Joe's life.

"Hey! Come back!" said Flora.

"Sorry," said Joe turning back to face her.

"Let me guess. David?"

"I was actually thinking about the first time I stayed at your house." The waiter reappeared and put Flora's drink in front of her.

"Would you like to run a . . ."

Joe cut him off. "No! Put it on *my* tab."

"Okay," said the waiter. Then, to Flora, "You know, I'm still having trouble keeping a straight face."

"Looks goddamn *straight* to me," said Flora. At this the waiter turned, flicked his butt at them and left their table without saying another word.

"He looked *gay* to me," said Joe.

"Oh yeah, I forgot you can all tell, can't you?" Joe nodded. "Anyway! What about the first time you stayed at my house?"

"Oh yeah!" said Joe. "The artwork in my bedroom. I asked David about it, but never got round to asking you. It was a crazy time."

"Thanks to me."

"I don't mean to put down your role, but you were only an extra." The waiter was looking at Joe, and it distracted him momentarily.

"Thanks, I think. Were you being bitchy, or sweet?"

"Yes," said Joe, and raised his bottle to Flora's while his eyes flicked imperceptibly at the waiter.

"Cheers to rears."

"Yeah! Cheers to rears."

"And so?" said Flora. "The artwork? Hey! Eyes on me. I know what you're up to."

Joe snorted a laugh. "Sorry! Do you still do any?"

"You make it sound like drugs."

"Isn't it?"

"I guess so." Flora thought about what Joe said for a moment. "If it's so addictive, why aren't you doing any?"

"Don't feel like it."

"Guess that's why, in answer to your question, I haven't done any since David left me." Flora zoned out. Then in a flash returned. "Around that time anyway."

"It was a significant time."

"Aha!" Flora turned away. "Waiter! Same." She turned back to Joe. "Drink?"

"Beer, please," said Joe holding up the bottle he'd been drinking from. This time the waiter attempted a cruiser swivel before leaving. "You sure have a way with waiters. But you know what I think he quite likes you."

"But you said he was gay."

"That's never stopped you before."

"If you're referring to David I was lucky enough to have caught him on the cusp."

"Lucky?"

"Yes fucking lucky!"

Again they shared a look, only this time it stretched and felt bitter sweet. Of course they were intensely sad, yet enough time had passed that they also felt lucky that they'd met David at all.

"No doubt you blamed yourself."

"*Of course.* I've always found it difficult to grasp the idea that the world doesn't revolve round me."

Joe burst out laughing.

"The artwork! I have to confess, you've almost got me interested now."

"Right!" said Joe. "So, how did you hang it?" He looked at Flora earnestly. "I've always wondered."

"Don't even bother."

"No, really. I was wondering if you had any more."

"Why do you ask?"

"I'll tell you in a minute. First, can I just run some questions by you?"

"Sure," said Flora looking slightly puzzled.

"About painting."

"I feel I better warn you, my knowledge is limited."

"Maybe that's a good thing. Don't think too hard just tell me what you feel, intuitively."

"Fire away."

"Okay," said Joe. "What do you think of Symbolism?"

"If the viewer doesn't know what the symbols refer to, it won't communicate much."

"Impressionism?"

"Oh, come on, it's just stupid, isn't it? I guess they were ahead of their time, anticipating chocolate box design by a hundred years or so."

Joe laughed. "Landscapes?"

"Unchallenging. Too safe."

"Abstraction?"

"Childish, but pretending to be adult."

"Cubism?"

"This I find confusing. Someone has an idea then a

generation of duds reproduce different versions of the same thing."

"Ouch!" Joe thought for a moment. "Op-art?"

"Scratches the surface. It shows shape and colour have an effect, which is useful."

"Very good. What about figurative art?"

"Ah! It definitely has potential."

"So, there is some art you think worth bothering with."

"Yeah!"

"Carry on."

"Expressionism. It's simple, evocative, understandable, and again effective." Joe nodded. "Then there's portraiture. You can't go wrong with portraits. They're indicative of the age, yet give insight into the person portrayed and the artist. Rather, the person in that time." Joe pretended to seriousness. "Pop art was fun. It made sense of art and industry. Mondrian had a good eye for placement of colour."

"Wait a minute. Your tornado montage used symbolism, didn't it?"

"Very easily understood symbols. You could call them icons. They are pretty universal. A mean-looking dog, an erection, a tornado, destruction, the fragility and vulnerability of a baby bird."

"David isn't a universal symbol."

"Actually he is, within the Western world. Youth and beauty are understood, even if somebody isn't sexually attractive to you. Generally you still know if they're beautiful, or not."

"Get you lady. You know your stuff."

"Only my stuff. Don't know Jack-shit about anybody else's."

"It's a good start." Flora forced a laugh, unsure. "I'm

serious. What better place to start than knowing what is right and good and true for you?"

"You came over all Emerson then."

"My God! You're not referring to his essays on self-reliance are you?" Flora nodded, shook her head, and then nodded again. "You are, aren't you?" This time Flora made her head roll around, neither nodding, nor shaking. "Please say yes."

Flora opened her mouth into a thin slit, just a couple of millimetres apart, and squeaked in a voice that sounded like it might belong to an elf, "Yes!"

"Brilliant!"

"Who, me, or this Emerson lady?"

"Maybe both."

"You're too kind. But why all these questions?"

"I was thinking, maybe . . . Just maybe, we could work on something together."

"What like an aberration?"

"I hope not. I was thinking of collaboration."

"You're still teasing me, right?"

"No. We could have an exhibition."

"What! An exhibition with you! But Joe, you're so famous. People will think it strange."

"That's good."

"Oh my God! You *are* being serious."

"It would be hard work. There'd be stupid journalists to deal with. I'd boss you around. I'd be a fascist about every shape and colour you choose. I'd use you, starve you, and be opinionated and arrogant."

"Sounds wonderful, but . . ."

"What!" said Joe in mock annoyance.

"I won't have you being fascist about color. It's my baby."

Joe winced. "Mine, too."

"And all you want is my soul? Where do I sign?"

"Seriously, though, if it doesn't work out, there's no harm done. It's just an idea."

"Not for long." Flora raised her glass to Joe's bottle.

"Needless to say, we can both back out whenever we feel like it."

"You mean, like a relationship," said Flora. Before Joe had time to digest this comment, she continued, "So, how about coming back to my place?" Flora paused. "And looking at the rest of my stuff. If you don't back out when you've seen the rest, then it's a deal."

"You drive a hard bargain." Then to the waiter who was lingering nearby, "Excuse me, can I have the check?" Then back to Flora, "Sorry, are we ready?"

"Ready as I can be."

Joe paid the bill and exchanged numbers with the waiter. Momentarily, he even imagined the sex they might have, but his was as far as Joe could take it. He wasn't ready yet. Heavy rush-hour traffic waited with cars inches apart the whole way home.

"You know the deal," said Flora as she took of her jacket. "Treat the place like it's your own."

"I know . . ." said Joe. Then in a pretend Flora-voice, "But no decorating!"

"Have I made that joke so many times?"

"That's what's meant to be funny about it, isn't it?"

Flora felt slightly embarrassed and so lied. "Of course!"

Her joke was more relevant than she knew. Whenever Joe was at her place he couldn't help but mentally color it in, move furniture, and add or throw out things that offended his sensibility. Generally, he found that he could read someone accurately based on his or her apartment, but with Flora, he couldn't. Perhaps it was because she was incredibly witty, and so utterly dry. Alternatively, she might a sociopath. Possibly her taste so evolved that he simply couldn't fathom it. Some might have referred to it Zen, others bleak. The furnishings were more comfortable, and the colors marginally more interesting, but still the living room had the feel of a jail cell. This struck Joe as odd especially considering there were wall to ceiling windows spanning the whole of one side. Admittedly there were no personal items; things that might intimate the character of person who resided. Maybe she didn't read, because there weren't any books around. There weren't even any magazines and not even a TV. Of course, these were ways to pass time and maybe she was too busy. But what did she do when she was alone. Things that usually gave great clues like photos, or notes to self were absent. There was no indication of anybody's character, like funny mugs, or kitsch memorabilia from trips away. Also there didn't seem to be anything that gave the impression that Flora had contact with others, no gift like things, or mail, nothing that showed a person lived there. Oddly enough, there was a chessboard and it appeared to be mid-game. Joe registered this and made a metal note to ask her whom she played. But currently, he had other things on his mind, and later he forgot. What he didn't know was that Flora actually played herself. This was because she felt she was her only fitting adversary. Well that's what she liked to believe. There was another reason, which she wouldn't admit even she was aware of it. There wasn't much more she hated in life than losing, and if she played herself she never lost.

Something Joe found stranger was that there were no full-length mirrors in the entire place, especially for somebody who dressed with such relish.

All of this created a weird and profound suspicion, which sat in the darker depths of Joe's thoughts. It happened whenever he was in her home, surrounded by so much her. Regardless, he continued to project his interior design on to everything that came across his path as he made himself a cup of tea and poured a gin and diet tonic for Flora.

Meanwhile, she slid off her shoes and rolled a joint. He joined her on the sofa and they kicked back, taking deep relaxing breaths looking out the windows at the setting sun and cityscape beneath. Gradually, a sense of calm returned.

"Phew!" said Flora. "That's better."

"Much."

"Oh I get it!" Joe said, as this he'd just discovered the atom. "This view is your TV. And it's so much better, because you can still think, as well as be entertained visually."

"Right!" Then after a long pause of doing exactly what Joe had just said, she got up. "I'm going to have to look around a bit for that artwork. I don't think I've thrown it out.

"I never throw artwork away," said Joe. "It shows where my head was at the time."

Flora dropped her head back on to the sofa, and blew smoke into the air with such force she might have been trying to kill a passing bug. "Maybe I didn't want to remember where my head was."

"Sounds kind of a shame. Whatever you've been

through makes you what you are today. And I for one wouldn't change anything about you." As Joe said this, he realised that it wasn't exactly true, because in reality his feelings towards her were inconsistent, patchy. There was still so much he didn't know about her, and whenever he probed - no matter how casually or direct-ly - he'd always get the same evasive humour. Still despite everything he did know about Flora, he was cer-tain there was something about her he admired, although he couldn't pinpoint what.

Jaded and bored of hearing her own voice she said, "If memories are worth remembering, they'll probably stay."

"I like to encourage some." He paused, and gazed out the window. In the distance two planes crossed paths. They looked incredibly close but in actuality were prob-ably miles apart. This crisscross of aircraft exhaust became the spot Joe let his eyes rest on as he reminisced. "Things about David, say."

"My point exactly, I don't have a problem remember-ing *David*."

"Flora, I'm kinda becoming accustomed to y'all."

"Hey Joe, don't act so sweet. It doesn't suit you."

"Sweet does suit me."

"Since when?"

"Since I realized it works," said Joe. "About 13, I think." Flora responded with an expression that didn't mean anything specific to Joe's comment, but intended to show she was still listening. "I just don't have much call for it these days."

"You soft bugger!" Then, realizing that her wording was harsh, she gestured that a hug was in order and then reached for Joe. They stayed in that position for a few minutes. "Baby, you know I'm always here for you. Really, Joe, day or night, any hour of any morning, please let me show you I care." Joe rolled his eyes. "I mean it, Joe. You can only avoid the feeling thang so long."

With a wave of his had to gesture *enough*, he said, "I know, but this is how long I'm doing it."

In earnest Flora tilted her body slightly towards Joe. "I'm sorry. I didn't mean to push you."

"I know." He cupped her chin with his hand. "So, how about finding that artwork?"

"Okay, boss."

Flora sprung to her feet, and disappeared into her bedroom. Cupboards could be heard opening and closing, boxes being shifted and dragged, until Flora returned dragging a large box. Joe jumped to his feet to help her, and together they carried it to the table.

"What's the smell?" said Joe, angling his head, to better catch the scent.

"I'd say probably a putrid mix by now. They used to all have individual smells, essential oils, boot polish, perfumes, household bleach, and all sorts of stuff."

"It's part of the art?"

She hesitated not sure what would response impress Joe the most. "Whimsical, hey?"

"Cute."

"Somehow, I don't mind being patronised by you."

"Good! It's part of the work package." Joe emptied the box carefully, and looked through the work with deliberation. With each one he held it up to the level of his face, stretched out his arms in front, in an attempt to get a more objective view of it then he turned the pieces to side and then the other - sometimes on its head - to get yet further perspectives. As he considered each one in this way, he uttered things like, 'I get it,' 'witty,' 'clever,' or 'ugh.' Sometimes he barely formed words, but simply responded with an emotion. At one point, he pursed his lips; another time, he laughed heartily. This was followed by a frown, which continued through several pieces. Lastly, he rubbed his hands together then clasped them.

When he arrived at the bottom of the pile, he said, "Just a couple more quick questions."

"Fire away."

"What is sex to you?"

"Joe. Don't get fresh," she said, pretending to be coy and bashful.

"I'm not."

"Never mind." This obviously wasn't playtime, so she became more serious. She thought for a second. "At best it's an expression of feelings of love. At worst, it's isolating, like how I imagine dying feels."

"Flora, you're such a poet." Joe took a second then asked, "God?"

"At best it's love. At worst it's fear."

Joe smiled. "I can't wait to start working with you. How busy are you this week?"

"Not at all."

"Great. Let's start next week, just brainstorming, I'll bring some pads and some felt tips and you bring your pretty brain and your not-so-pretty attitude."

"Okay! Got it," said Flora. "You'll bring some lads and your svelte hips. And I'll bring the shitty rain and the platitudes.

"My loft at teatime. I'll call you."

20

Next to Joe on the emerald green velvet sofa in his living room sat a large man who bulged out of his ill-fitting suit as though trying to escape it. In comparison, Joe looked miniature. The only thing they had in common was that they faced the mint green wall opposite, and more specifically, had their eyes fixed on the monitor there. They watched a DVD of an advertisement that Joe had directed. It was a close-up shot of cocoons, hundreds of them. In dim light, they twitched a little making the whole screen a mass of movement. Slowly, the scene became brighter. With the light came heat and as it got hotter, the chrysalis became more agitated. The movement caused some to sink, others to rise to the surface, all the time making a crackling sound. As this process continued, the sharp snapping noise they made increased in volume.

Like a symphony conductor Joe lifted his palms. "Wait for it . . . And zoom . . . Watch . . . Lovely." Violins began to make sharp, stabbing sounds. The camera pulled out to show thousands of the grubs.

"Makes my skin crawl," said the Scent rep.

"Makes mine tingle," said Joe, brimming with smiles.

"The spray's beautiful. How did you make it glow like that?"

Putting a finger to his lips Joe shook his head and said, "Sorry! Trade secret." He paused a few seconds for dramatic affect then added, "I'm kidding you! It's just well-angled side lighting."

"Stunning! Really, Joe."

"You wait; the best bit's coming any second." The perfume mist seemed to dance in the air, finally landing on the chrysalis, coating them.

"The mist?" asked the rep.

"Animated."

"Subtle. I couldn't tell."

In fast motion suddenly the grubs began to hatch. Many different species of butterfly started to appear. The violins began to make sense. Melody emerged out of the previous cacophony. The screen became saturated with gently fluttering wings iridescent in color; each leaving ghost-like trails, a spectrum of colours as they moved.

"Magnificent!" said the rep.

"Wait for it," said Joe.

The voiceover was clearly an elderly woman's: "Scent. Draws out the beauty in you."

"Clever," said the rep, holding up his finger as if to imply what he said was fact and not opinion.

Joe crouched forward, excited by his own work. "Clean, don't you think?" he said into the air, then tuned to face the rep. "No nonsense. Right?"

"Yes. Not too much, but just enough."

"I'd never give you not enough."

"That wasn't our fear."

"My reputation precedes me." As he said this, he ran his fingers through his hair, leaving his hands resting on his head, clearly pleased with himself.

The rep sat back and crossed his arms and rested them on top his belly. Then shaking his head slowly he said, "We nearly didn't go with you on this project,"

His ego knocked, Joe looked puzzled and at the same time hurt.

To answer Joe's response, he said, "You're a bit of a wild card. We thought you might produce something too controversial." The rep said the word controversial as though he didn't like it being in his head, or mouth. Joe realised that he was supposed to feel ashamed, but couldn't. "Something tells me you're not as hard as everyone thinks you are." Joe looked down at his feet. "I knew it." Now Joe started to go slightly pink. "They won't believe this back at the office. I made Joseph Holtzman blush."

"You make me sound like a monster."

"Aren't you?" The rep asked, but the same intonation and speed as *oh-come-on*.

Of course Joe was aware what the papers wrote about him, but still he felt put out by the rep's implication. "No," he said, trying to sound convincing, but in actuality it sounded unsure. "Not that I'm aware of."

"What about your last exhibition?"

"Not again." Joe knew exactly where this conversation was heading, and couldn't help but sound cunty like an L.A. teenage girl. "Will I have to carry that around my neck forever?"

"Probably. People don't forget things like that easily."

"I should be flattered, I suppose."

The rep knew he had the upper hand now and he wielded it with self-satisfaction. "I think it's definitely a talent to be able to cause such response, but . . ."

"Blah, blah, blah."

"Sorry, does that annoy you?"

Joe was beginning to lose his temper. "Actually it bores me."

"Sensitive subject?"

By this point he finally felt like he'd had enough. Still he spoke in a measured and calm way. "Get out of here," he said with a spooky amount of control. "You've got your ad, hope everyone likes it and all, but, you don't pay me enough to listen to your shit as well." Joe led the man to the front door. "If there are any questions, e-mail me."

The man was left outside Joe's front door confused, trying to work out how things got so out of hand. He wouldn't be able to say anything at work. It was his job to be good at interacting with the talent.

21

Flora's bed had the characterless look and feel as one you might find in a hotel chain. It was midday. Her mental state was bored and antsy. Beside her lay Don. After a night at the fire station with no sleep, he was worn out.

Flora knew Don was exhausted, so she took the opportunity to goad him. She sat with arms folded perch up with her pillows. "So?"

Curled up in the hope of attaining comfort, Don laid facing away from her. "What?" he grunted.

"I'm bored."

His face was squashed into the pillow and so his words were mumbled and distorted. "Okay Baby," was his unrelated and noncommittal response.

A loud rumbling sound came from the sky as the storm brewed. It can be exciting, and drag you back to childhood and fears that lurk there.

But Flora was more bothered by Don than the world outside and continued, "I can't tell what you're saying." She clipped her own words as though it was for maximum clarity, but in fact it was because she knew it would irritate him. "Speak clearly!" she demanded.

Purposely Don's response was incoherent.

"Very funny!"

This time he raised his head and overly enunciated, "Okay. Leave me god damn alone!"

"I'll let you alone when I'm ready."

"What's your problem?"

"You."

He was being kept more awake than he wanted to be and he began to get a bitchy. "Why don't you go shave your legs, or rearrange your hair, or do whatever it is you do when I'm not here?"

"I'm not some little missy who'll put on an apron and go do the cleaning while my man sleeps the day away."

"Jesus! There is something in between."

"Joe?" she said all pleased with herself. She turned and plumped up her pillow as though settling in for a fight.

"Joe? What's he got to do with this?"

"He's your something in between isn't he?"

"Jesus. You're obsessed!"

"Arh! Does it wound your masculinity?"

Don couldn't be bothered to rise to this. "Yeah. It kills me," he said dryly.

"What? When he fucks you?"

"Yeah. That's exactly what I meant. And you wank about it right?"

Now Flora leant on one elbow facing him. Whether he wanted to or not, she was going to have her argument. She poked him hard in his back. "Oi!"

As tired as he was, and as hard as he tried to not to be drawn into her world, he was beginning to lose his cool. "I told you. Leave me alone!"

Outside came a massive crack of thunder, loud

enough to make Flora jump slightly, but still she recovered enough to say, "Sore point hey?"

It was clear she wasn't going to let up and so Don decided to roll over onto his back, so at least he wasn't facing away from her. Maybe this would appease her, and she wouldn't be such a bitch.

"*Sore* point. No, it's not a *point* at all." Don rubbed his temples. "Listen Baby . . . I've got a shitty headache." He looked at her sincerely in an attempt to appeal to a better side of her nature. "Can't we just be nice?"

"Don't try to get round me by calling me 'Baby.' And I don't feel like being *nice.*"

He lifted the pillow from under his head and placed it over his face. Then he removed it as though this simple action might have the power to somehow shift the time continuum so that he wasn't in fact in the middle of an assault by Flora. More practically - based on desperation - he tried to change the conversation.

"How was last night?"

If she wouldn't shut up, he might at least be able to get her to mellow her mood. No such luck because although Flora's train of thought did shift, it went somewhere even nastier.

"He was great."

"Spare me!" Don said as exasperated as a person could possibly be before becoming completely weary.

"Don't you want to hear?"

"No." He sighed. When was she going to let up? "I know it's just a Flora idea of a joke . . . Right?"

Her response was a smirk.

"Bitch! Whether you did or didn't. Bitch!"

"Boo hoo!"

"You didn't?"

"What if I did? You don't own me."

"Of course I don't, but I do have an emotional invest-ment. Don't I?"

"I don't know . . ." Considering that she had been on the attack Flora suddenly adopted a defensive pose. She sat up, pulled her knees in tight to her chest and wrapped her arms around them. Either this betrayed her feelings or it was a clear indication of something lurking in her depths. Failing to listen to her own body language she continued with her tirade. Again, as though talking to a child, "I mean, I don't know what goes on in your Priddy widdle head." As she said this she also stroked his head.

If Don hadn't been so tired, he'd have been more annoyed at her, but her gentle touch was so welcome by this point.

With a mix of emotion, breath and actual words he said, "That feels nice."

This moment of peace was shattered by a terrifying roar of thunder and was immediately followed by an intense burst of lightning. "Fuck!" said Flora. "The storm must be close now."

Don was so pleased that Flora's mood had passed. "Sounds like it's right above us."

"Anyway. His dick was juicier than yours."

This lull was brief, because now Don was tormented and felt overwhelmed with jealousy. "What are you try-ing to do?"

"Just playing."

"Why can't I get through to you? I'm too tired to play."

"Because I'm bored and to me that's more important."

"So go and do something, see a film, read a book, anything, but just stop getting at me."

"Maybe I'll give Juicy-dick-Rick a call."

"If you're intending to drive me away, it's working."

Although not completely aware of it, she was trying to push him out of her life. She was bored, not just with the day, but of their routine, and their interaction, even the sound of his voice. Things about him had begun to irritate her. Once it had started, it snowballed. She didn't like him smelling of smoke; it made her think of David. And when she did this two things happened, one her heart broke some more, and two, she couldn't help but compare them both. Despite the fact that Don did deliver the goods sexually, in all else he paled to nothing. And another thing Don was always so tired. This was boring. She didn't like his work hours. They were so hard to remember, and he was impossible to plan around. When David died, Don had been comforting, like a flannelette sheet, an old cardigan, or a cup of warm milk, but now that she was beginning to climb out of the pit created by losing David, she had less use for a 'comforter.' He became an embarrassment, a reminder of how needy she'd been. It made her cringe to think she'd depended on him. Flora never wanted to depend on anyone again. These weren't thoughts with a clear beginning and end. They were feelings, causing responses. Attacking Don seemed to be a solution. If questioned, she probably would have denied being cruel, but he definitely felt it, and it muddled his thoughts and feelings. There were times when he couldn't even face seeing her. Sometimes, creeping back to his own home after an exhausting night was all he could bear. This wasn't the case today. He was exhausted, but didn't want to be alone, and felt insecure, and needy. Still, the last thing he wanted from the person keeping him company was to be provoked, harassed and made to feel more alone than if he was on his own.

Flora continued to amuse herself with Don, comforting him; then, just as he was softening and letting down his guard, she'd ridicule him. When she was lovely, he couldn't refuse her, but when she wasn't he wanted to be nowhere near her.

Finally, after he'd taken as much as he could stand, he said, "I'm going."

This annoyed Flora. He couldn't just walk out. She'd planned her day around him. It didn't make her feel sorry, but indignant, and harder than ever. "I'll call you," she said, and paused for effect. "Sometime."

"Or not," said Don grabbing his belongings and dumping them in his rucksack. "By the way, I've been meaning to tell you, your breath stinks. You rancid fucking bitch! Cab my stuff over. I'll do the same."

"It's all mine. I bought it for you anyway."

At first, he had attempted to cope with her attack. Now he spoke without thinking, about her feelings, or his dignity. "You're absolutely pathetic."

"People don't seem to mind."

"What do you mean? You've only ever had one boyfriend."

"Don't bring David into this."

"He must have been a fucking angel to put up with you. Oh, no! That's right, he left you."

The mention of David's name fanned the flames of an already blazing row. It triggered something previously unlocked in Flora and left the world of the rational behind. She became unhinged and rabid with eyes wild and unfocused. Now she had no thoughts at her disposal, only unfettered feelings.

With a terrifying scream she lunged at Don with arms flailing. "You fucker!"

He managed to grab hold of her by her wrists. "You're pathetic," he said again with a mocking tone.

At this, she kneed him hard in the balls. No matter how big he was, or how strong, a knee to the balls – if it hits the right spots – is completely debilitating. Instantly, he let go of her and fell to the floor, crying out.

"Not so pathetic," said Flora, and grinned.

Don got hold of her ankle and pulled it from under her. She fell onto her back, Don crawled on top of her, pinning her down.

"You've gone too far this time," he said.

Don got up off Flora, but she stayed sitting on the floor.

"I'm going. And you're going to have to do some pretty apologizing if you want to see me again."

"I'm sorry! I'm sorry!" She paused. "That I ever met you."

"Oh my God. I can't believe I nearly had a kid with you."

As he put his hand on the doorknob to open it, Flora got to her knees and shouted, "It wasn't even yours. It was Joe's."

On hearing this, Don opened the door and left. He walked out knowing he would never see Flora again. As the door closed, she looked around, grabbed a glass ashtray that David had bought her as a joke when she'd failed to give up smoking for the tenth time – the only thing in the room that had any sentimental value - and she threw it against the door. It smashed into pieces.

For a moment, Flora had a hard expression on her face, pure anger and hatred, but slowly this softened. She began to sob.

After a short time, she got up and went to the window. She stood there wiping her eyes. The storm had passed. From deep inside her, she began to laugh. *How absurd*, she thought. The storm had timed perfectly with her argument. Gone With The Wind, sprung to mind. Then she said to herself, *Hollywood or what?* Flora knew herself better than most people did, and so questioned if she'd staged the whole thing. *How fabulous*, she thought. T*hat lighting was almost too much!* With modesty, she admitted - quite out of character - that even she couldn't control the heavens. In consolation she thought, *that did still leave Hell up for grabs.*

22

Trade was relatively quiet. It was the weekend after a long holiday weekend and so many had exhausted themselves, but more importantly their finances. Only the die-hard core was showing their worn out faces.

The music sounded like it had been on a loop since the club opened. It was always on when you arrived, and on when you left, so who really knew if it ever stopped.

Even though there wasn't the usual three of four rows of people waiting to get served, whatever she tried, Flora couldn't get the attention of the man at the bar. She tried flashing her wrist while absentmindedly twiddling her earring - which often worked with straight barmen - but to no avail. The air was wet, hot, and loaded with other people's breath. It was Trade's unique but usual climate. Joe had taken her, but had gone off to dance about an hour ago. Several people had stopped and spoken with her and so having been distracted, Flora felt like Joe had just left. It felt like she'd been at the bar over half an hour. It had, in fact, been ten minutes.

A well-built man with no shirt on squeezed in beside

her. As he leaned into the bar his torso faced Flora. She watched him raise his one of his vascular arms and flag down the barman, who came straight over. Within a minute he had his drinks in front of him and waited for his change.

Because she hadn't been concentrating she'd missed the barman. "Hey! I've been here ages."

The man stood in silence for a moment just looking at her then he said, "You should check out the dance floor. It's more fun."

His timing and simple response threw Flora. "I was joking."

Again there was a pause. "So was I."

"Oh . . . "It took a moment to get her head round this man's sense of humor, or lack of it. "I'd prefer to be dancing."

Another pause. Flora couldn't tell if he was really dim, really drug fucked, or really, really clever and funny. "Your E no good?" There he went again, with his weird, dry, almost retarded answers.

Flora spoke slowly and enunciated, just in case he was mentally impaired in some way. "The pill's not the problem. I'm just trying to get served."

This time he answered within a more normal time frame. "Why didn't you say?" He must have made some signal to the barman, because he returned instantly. "Would you sort this lady out with a drink?"

"Anything for you Paul," replied the barman, while not acknowledging Flora in the slightest. "What would she like?"

"What do you want sweetheart?"

To not feel invisible, she thought to herself. "Err. Um.

Large Red bull and vodka?"

It seemed that her saying it didn't really count. Paul relayed the order. As he was busy Flora pulled her head back a little and gave him a quick once over. He was over six feet tall, had a short back and sides barber cut, with a little more left on top, which leant to one side. *That was it*, she thought. He looked like Richard Gere in *An Officer And A Gentleman.*

The barman left them, and Flora nudged Paul, partly to be cute, but also to make sure she had his attention. "Thanks. That was nice of you. So you're name's Paul?"

The pause returned. " . . . Yeah . . . You?"

Shit, she thought. *Now he's breaking mid-sentence as well.* "Flora."

The barman returned, and as he held out his hand for Flora's money, he faced Paul with an "I'm-all-yours-if-you-want-me" expression.

"Let me get this," Paul insisted.

"Thanks. Wow! Gallant and generous."

A weird expression flashed across Paul's face. It was the first time he'd used one. Up till now, she wouldn't have known it was in his repertoire. "You know what they say about dirty money."

Intrigued, Flora briefly, wondered what the reference to *dirty money* meant. She was distracted from this train of thought when noticing that the barman was still waiting with what looked like affection while Paul tried to retrieve money from his pockets, but in doing so pulled out the entire contents.

She had already presumed enough to come to certain conclusions about Paul, based on the way he dressed and carried himself. Only she saw none of the usual suspects; keys, gum, tissue and telephone numbers. But instead a miniature pen, an acorn – way to early for the coming season, which begged the question had he carried it since last year? Also there was a red tartan handkerchief. This she noted was just like one she'd given her Uncle Len for his birthday last year. Lastly, there were some foreign bills. Nothing she recognized, but from the lettering she guessed it was from somewhere in the Middle East.

No joy in finding usable cash. Patiently the barman watched as Paul put his hand in his other pocket and this time pulled out money and something more predictable, but also more than seemed humanly possible to receive in an evening; a bunch of business cards and scraps of paper with phone numbers. Paul looked at both of them in turn, and then hunched his shoulders with an apologetic look on his face. For a laugh, he acted as though they couldn't see him and push the whole lot into a pile on the bar. Flora found herself raising her eyebrows again.

In reference to the numbers, he said in a matter of fact tone. "Saves time this way." Then he pretended to be overly sincere and said. "Somebody might get use out of them. It's best to recycle tricks." Gesturing to the barman as he walked away, Paul said. "I think he fancies me."

"Do you think?" said Flora with complete irony. Then she started to wonder if Paul was a bit slow. She didn't know whether her humor was lost on him.

" I've seen you here before."

"Really? You're a bit of a funny bugger Paul."

Like a broken clockwork toy, he wound up again, *but* Flora wondered, *how long would it last*? "Funny, 'titter', or funny, 'kooky'?"

"*Titter and kooky*, will cover it."

"Right. That'll be the drugs. They'll probably be making me seem more *titter* and *kooky* than I really am."

A farm of bulky men tumbled by, all wearing rugby outfits. One of them fell clumsily into Flora knocking her drink to the floor. *Typical*, she thought, but played out her response with grace, and even managed to convince them that they didn't need to replace her drink.

Paul took a swig of his drink, and offered it to Flora. She understood it as a symbol of something bonding like a peace pipe, and so she took a similar size swig, with a similar gesture.

He watched her. " I like you. You get me."

Quiet the opposite, she'd never met anybody she understood less in her life. Yet she knew what he meant by it. There was a strange draw between them. Something connected on some – albeit unfathomable – level.

"Shall we?" he said stepping away from the bar and into a mash of sweaty bodies. She nodded and followed him. Just before reaching their destination a club kid threw his arms around Paul. The man was naked and wore a prosthetic cunt over his real crotch. To complete the look properly he wore a red striped bikini top to hold his fake breasts. After a fleeting hello they flittered away.

They stood facing a wall so nobody would bother them.

"Paul. I don't know if you're aware of this, but you're huge."

"Yeah. I'm trying to address it."

"It's not as though it's a problem."

Off he went now to a new hyper speed. "If you had to stick needles into your flesh, inject steroids through them, spend so much time doing repetitive, painful, and really uninteresting movements, than you don't have time to do anything productive or worthy. If you had to read the nutritional information on everything you buy, and then eat huge amounts of the thing you choose, which puts a real strain on your entire system, and in turn, makes you shit for England. . ." Now came the pause. "Then . . . you might think it's a problem."

"This may be a stupid question, especially here at Trade, but, why?"

" . . . Cause I'm insecure, got hang-ups about my masculinity. Shall I go on?"

"I get the picture. You mean you're gay?"

This made Paul laugh. It was the first time she'd seen it. And somehow it was really attractive. Now seemed like as good a time as any to find out more about him. There was something about him that fascinated her. "Paul. Do you mind me asking what you do for a living?"

"No . . . I don't work."

Flora waited for him to fill her in but then remembering his fits and starts pace, she thought to encourage him.

"So how do you pay for this lifestyle?" As she said this, she couldn't help thinking the word lifestyle was completely inappropriate for the stuff that happened in Trade. Surely *life* was the antithesis, and style had long since had anything to do Trade.

"I have HIV, and was quite sick for a while." Flora didn't know what to say. "Don't worry I'm okay now. I'm still positive, but . . ."

"Oh! So you get some kind of disability benefit?"

"Yeah.

"And?"

"I'm not dead."

"But still claiming?"

"Yeah."

"How do you spend your time?"

Paul must have been on some mongy E, because although Flora hadn't particularly noticed the change, he'd gradually stopped pausing. He also became brighter, quicker, and more importantly, consistent. "I'm a writer–cum–artist-cum-drug-taking gay."

Flora burst out laughing. "God! You're different."

"From who?"

Flora made a gesture with her hand, meaning everybody around them.

"You'd be surprised," said Paul. "I know lots of cum-sucking-bum-fucking-drug-taking-gays."

"I bet you do, looking like that," said Flora. "Like flies round shit."

"Nice metaphor."

"Sorry."

"I do okay," he said a little coy. "Are you with friends?"

"I thought so, but I'm beginning to wonder."

"Would you like to meet mine? They'd really get you."

"That would be a nice change."

"We're in the far corner. It might be best if you get hold of my belt loop."

"Okay."

Paul seemed to know everybody. He couldn't go a few feet without somebody kissing him, hugging him, at least nodding, or mouthing hello. As they entered the main dance area, a blotchy, red-faced man put an ecstasy in Paul's mouth. Paul made a tastes-horrible face, bit the pill in half and popped it into Flora's mouth. Looking around, he gestured for a drink, to a group of people. One of them handed him a small bottle, nearly full. After taking a gulp, he appeared to keep the water in his mouth. He gestured for Flora to come closer. Although confused, she did, and realised he wanted her to put her mouth against his. She did this too. When their lips were touching, Paul squirted some of the water into her mouth. She accepted and swallowed her ecstasy.

Paul thanked the water person, and the red-faced man and said, "Ugh!" to Flora. "What can you do? It would be rude to refuse." As they got to the where they were heading, he said, "Can I tell you one of my poems?"

"Sure," said Flora, shouting over the music. Paul pulled her to one side into an alcove. Then he cupped his hands around her ear, which cut out a surprising amount of background noise. The beat of the track had a metronome affect, which added a modern twang. He spoke said;

"Looking for meaning is something to do
And has something to do with
Expecting
Wanting a need
Blaming the air
Not accepting

Dissatisfaction with the day
Uncomfortable within it
Pampering a desire to be more
And in trying becoming less"

Pausing, he pulled his head back to see her face.

"Don't worry. I'm listening. Carry on!" He gave her a warm smile and continued putting a more performance element into his voice, both urgent and exact.

"It is familiar
And unfriendly
Cozy and restrictive
The hum of unblurred nothingness
Affecting a lot by its littleness
Its stationariness
Its aggressive pining
Its indolent desperation
Its enthusiastic depression
Its lively and perpetual lethargy
Its sluggish and glue-like insistence
Its assuming human habit
Of being something to do"

Paul pulled back again. Flora was silent.

"Is he telling you a poem?" said a woman from behind them.

"He *is*, actually," said Flora.

"Good?"

"Really good!"

"I'm Josie."

"Flora, this is one of the friends who I said would get

you. Josie, Flora. Flora, Josie."

Josie's appearance surprised Flora. Everybody else in Trade usually stripped off as many layers as possible. They did this for different reasons, but mainly because it was so hot. Not Josie. Dressed like Morticia Adams in an ankle length, long sleeve black dress, she looked cool, and un-hot. To take the edge off her elegance she wore a pair of black Doc Martins. These contrasted with her dress so much that they actually made her look more feminine, but not at all girly. With only a trace of lip-gloss and pale base, she had mastered the art of looking like she wasn't wearing make-up. A straight black bob framed her face, and turned in cleverly under her delicate, fine looking chin. To showcase her features to their very best, she had skin that looked as though it had never been worn before, and certainly not out in winter wind or summer sun, let alone the rank, damp and germ-saturated stuff that passed for air in Trade.

Oddly, she didn't appear to be high, or drunk, and most unusual for Trade was that she had control of the muscles in her face. But beyond all this strangeness, Josie used her face to smile, not the chemical induced hall-of-mirrors-scary kind, which prevailed at Trade, but one that looked genuine.

Flora was confused, but still was happy to hang out with them, even if it was under a flight of stairs. "What are you doing here? And before either of you joke, I mean here in this club."

"Am I not welcome?" said Josie.

"Of course you are, but you look so out of place."

"Thank you!"

"You're right to take it as a compliment." She looked Josie

up and down. "You must be dying of heat."

"I am, but I'm not about to strip off."

"Sure! The funny thing is you don't even look flushed."

"She's cool," said Paul.

"Are you sober?"

Josie shuddered. "Please! Do you have to use the '*s*' word?"

"Sorry! But how?"

"Speed-ball."

"Oh!" said Flora, shocked, not letting on that she didn't know what it was. She knew it entailed shooting up, and possibly involved smack mixed with another drug.

"Hence," said Josie. "The long sleeves." Flora smiled knowingly, feeling out of her depth.

"So." Paul paused. "What do *you* do?"

Unlike most other things, Flora didn't feel cynical about her work. "I design buildings. Well actually just parts of them usually."

"What do you mean?" said Josie.

"I adapt areas of buildings for people with special needs."

"Nice!" said Paul impressed.

"My sister's an architect," said Josie.

"Mine's a cow," said Paul. "Who did you say you were here with?"

"Just my friend Joe."

"Not Joe Holtzman?" said Paul.

"Yeah. Do you know him?"

"No! I was joking." Now Paul was very impressed. "Are you really a friend of his? He's incredible."

"Paul's got a crush on him," said Josie.

"Josie!" said Paul.

"Get over it! Flora. Can you introduce them?"

"Of course. He'd like you, I'm sure. That's if I ever find him."

"He went that way a minute ago," said Paul, pointing upstairs. "You were talking to Josie, and he was holding on to somebody's shoulders."

"Who?"

"Don't know. Some man with a beard."

"Sounds like George. He edits Joe's commercials."

"That Levi's one he did was fantastic," said Paul.

"Everybody likes that," said Flora.

"Clear this up for me," said Paul. "The leaves on that tree were animated weren't they?"

"Of course!"

"Guessed as much, but you never know."

"Listen," said Josie. "I'm bored of having to talk over this noise. It's like working in a factory. Let's go up to the café?"

"I have to sort out some shit with this dealer first," said Paul. "I'll follow you up."

"Josie?" said Flora.

"Right."

As was common in Trade, she took hold of Flora's hand so as not to lose her, and led her away upstairs.

23

The phone rang. Flora rolled over, and picked it up
simultaneously looking at her bedroom clock. It read,
eighteen thirty-six.

"Flora. It's Paul."

"Who?" said Flora. Still partly in sleep, she didn't
realize that she had been woken up, and so didn't feel
annoyed about it either.

"Paul, from *Trade*." Flora was none the wiser.

"You don't know who I am, do you?"

"Sorry, Paul. I took downers to get to sleep."

"It's nice to know I'm so memorable. No worry. Can I
speak to Josie?"

"Josie," said Flora, reallocating her thoughts, and putting this one in the right place, somewhere that made
sense. Then she rolled back into her original position
and waved the phone above Josie's face.

"What?" said Josie, barely out of sleep.

"It's *Paul*," said Flora, saying the word Paul as though
she didn't know who he was. A couple of times during
sleep, she'd got up to pee, so was aware of Josie lying
next to her, and why. Each time Flora got back into bed,

she'd wrapped herself around Josie, as though she'd been doing it all her life.

Without opening her eyes Josie put the receiver to her ear. "Hey, little thing."

For the next few minutes, Flora could only hear the tinny buzzing sound of Paul's voice through receiver, and Josie's replies. "Rotten . . .Yeah . . . I think it's actually just one long track . . . Really? . . . Probably . . .! I don't know. I'll find out. Hang on." Still with her eyes closed Josie rocked her head towards Flora. "Any idea what time we'll be functioning?"

"None. I *could* get up now," said Flora. "Why?"

"He wants to know if I want to go see a friend of ours in Brighton."

"Tell him you'll call him back."

"Paul. Can I call you back? We're still asleep, I think . . . Sure . . . Do you mind going by yourself? Okay . . . I'm sorry. Give me a call when you get back." Josie looked at Flora, and was awake enough to make a resigned face. "Okay," she continued to Paul. "I'll speak to you later. Yeah. Love you, too." She handed Flora the phone. "Sorry!"

"It's no biggie. Sounds like you got yourself a regular family."

"Closer."

"Yeah, mine too. My friends, I mean. Do you think that's because we don't have close family, or we have particularly close friends?"

"Yes," said Josie, leaning towards Flora and kissing her. "Definitely!"

Kiss finished, Flora said, "Breakfast?"

"What a fast it was? Juice would be good."

"Does a Bloody Mary sound better?"

"Like butter to the ears."

"Sounds messy."

"You should try it."

"I get the feeling you're going to show me lots of new stuff."

"If you want."

Flora looked Josie in the eye. They were barely apart, so it was more of an intense gaze. It also meant a great deal, that Flora had difficulty putting into words. Things about David, Don, and every other man she'd ever had a relationship with, or at least intimacy. All she knew was that it felt right in Josie's arms. Complete.

Even as they'd walked upstairs at Trade, there seemed to be something different about the way Josie held her hand. Then when sitting in the café, there seemed to be a communication between them that was on a whole other level than Flora was used to, so when Josie moved Flora's hair out of her eyes, this rudimentary touch signalled so much more. From then on, they didn't need to discus the details. It seemed only natural that Paul and Joe both went off and did whatever with whoever, and inevitable that the "girls" caught a cab home together.

Now in the morning, already it felt like the next phase in life. She pulled Josie towards her. Josie complied. Flora kissed her, and felt gorgeous inside, warm, fluid and at ease. Something important had begun between them.

24

In Joe's house, his studio was the only room that was all one colour. It didn't even have color, as it was a dark grey tone. The paint had a matte finish so that neither the walls, nor ceiling reflected light. It had the same effect as being in an art gallery space entirely devoted to Rothko paintings. As much as you like to think that you are taking them in, they draw you in too. After a while, it becomes difficult to know where you finish and their surface begins. This was exactly what Joe wanted from a studio. Rarely was anybody invited in. Even David used to check the position of the door first. There was a code. If it was wide open it meant *come on in*. If it were ajar, he'd knock gently and wait to be invited in. If it was closed this meant *do not disturb*. Tonight Joe brought Flora in to thrash out some ideas. He had dimmed the lights, so low that it was impossible to ascertain where the walls and ceiling met. This environment was ideal for brainstorming. There were simply no external stimuli and so everything had to come from within. As Flora walked in the room, she was too deep in her own head to notice, let alone comment on the décor that surrounded her. If she had been observant she'd have noticed that her three-piece trouser suit was as near a color/tone match with the walls as you could possibly get from two such different materials. The vacuum-like quality of the room engulfed her visually.Not surprisingly, her mind was on her work, as she was both excited and intimidated. "I brought some notes," she said pulling a folder out of a Louis Vuitton shoulder bag."Professional!" said Joe referring to the folder, adding, "And stylish," when he noticed the bag."It's my idea of power dressing to fool you into believing in me.""Good. I'm a great believer in presentation."There was a polished concrete table, which was about seven feet in length it and roughly four in width. It seemed the obvious place to put her folder down, but as she did, she raised her finger, breathed in, and looked as though she was about to start a lengthy explanation of her work.

Joe cut her off. "What you got, then?"

"Just some writing."

"Writing's good." He folded his arms, not so much to cut her off, but more to go inside his head, and ponder what he'd said.

"Actually, it's more words than writing."

Joe couldn't help thinking he was behaving a little like a schoolteacher. "Words are okay too."

Flora looked flustered. She'd wanted to excuse herself somehow, but Joe didn't seem to be letting her. "They're just ideas."

"Yep! Those, too. Let me see."

Flora pulled away, and took the opportunity to take off her jacket. Her figure looked stunning in her waistcoat and flared trousers. Hesitantly she edged her way back behind Joe. "Shall I read them to you?"

"Hey! Back off. What are you scared of?"

"Very little."

"I believe that."

Hovering, she moved from side to side, hoping to see what he was looking at so that she could explain it. She lied. "It's just that you might not be able to read my writing."

"Okay!" said Joe, not quite believing Flora's explanation. He opened his palm towards the work as if to say "be my guest." Then he cocked his head to one side, his listening position. "Fire away."

"Beyond fear." She paused, scratched her nose and watched for a response from Joe. He didn't give one. This made her nervous. "Beyond hate." Again she looked, but this time with a look of do-you-approve?

Joe simply nodded, which meant carry on.

"Beyond pain." She stopped, and rubbed her eyes. This wasn't going as well as she had hoped, and she knew that she was stalling.

After a pause, he said, "Nice! Is there more?"

At this affirmation, Flora confidence grew a little. "Beyond self-doubt?"

Joe looked bewildered. "Is there anything beyond self-doubt?"

Flora crouched down onto her hunches, so that her elbows were table height, where they comfortably rested. She looked much more at ease now than she actually felt. "Yes." She paused so that he'd have time to guess and to accentuate the impact of her answer. "Complete doubt."

Here was a statement that needed more consideration,

so he turned away from her and into himself. He did this by walking to the other side of the room and facing a blank wall. From this place of no distractions, he could focus more easily, and after a moment he spoke with his back to her with a fraction more space between each word than usual. "This . . . from . . . a . . . woman . . . who . . . fears . . . nothing?"

An explanation was in order so to the back of his head, she said, "Instead of doubting yourself, doubt everything else . . ." Although this wasn't a question, she somehow expected a response, and when given none, she added, "Why not?"

This got Joe thinking and to show he intended to answer he raised one finger. More than a minute passed before - with uncertainty in his voice - he finally said, "I don't know." With this answer, he surprised himself.

Acting humble, she said, "Do you wish you hadn't asked me to work with you?" She was also fishing for a compliment, and intellectual validation. Even an intimation that Joe finally realized she was his equal artistically. In actual fact she believed she was superior to him in every other way. David had been her weakness and her failing. Alternatively, she felt that Joe had always coveted David as his prize and trophy. *Smug bastard*, she thought. But that was all in the past. The future looked bright now.

Oblivious to her thoughts, Joe turned from the wall excited, with his hands clasped. "No! No! No!" said Joe. "Quite the opposite."

"You would tell me, wouldn't you?"

Even though she was currently pretending to be insecure, ordinarily Flora used arrogance as a front. Of course, any psychologist would guess this was to mask self-doubt. In this case, it was true. She lived in perpetual fear. At times she used clothes in an attempt to hoodwink others into thinking she was a tough, go-getting, ruthless bitch. Superficially they succeeded in being visually distracting. But on a deeper level, these costumes fooled the eye like the best trompe l'oeil giving the illusion of a three-dimensional object. Clever enough. But in that case, did she not have depth.

Surprised and charmed by Flora's childlike need for his approval, Joe nodded. "Anything else on that paper?" he leaned over to look. Flora pulled away but it was too late. Her notes weren't illegible, but very precise, and beautifully written. It looked like it had taken her hours, more like design than text. Arrows led to boxes and circles. In these were groups of words, or simply letters, numbers, and some unrecognizable symbols.

"Joe!" said Flora, annoyed.

As though he'd just seen some complex mathematical equation or ancient hieroglyphic, Joe made a surprised sound that almost resembled "*wow*!"

"It's just how I'm used to working."

"Fuck!"

Flora carried on as though all was normal. "I thought about your last exhibition, how it made me feel, what those feelings meant, how important they were." She paused and looked away from her notes to somewhere on the floor in front of her. "David's death is somehow intrinsically linked to this exhibition, because it links to both of us in a profound way. In a way it welds us together 'until death do us part' . . . so to speak."

"Stop! Let me digest this."

Flora paused for only a second. "This all loops, convolutes, and goes I don't know where."

"Are you talking about karma?"

"No. I think karma's about a belief in some sort of universal justice and let's face it, what bollocks."

"So?"

"So, let's talk, and see what happens visually. Hopefully, something will be expressed that we are incapable of saying in words."

"My God! You're good at this."

"I've tried to communicate before. That's what we're doing here, isn't it?"

"I think some artists forget that."

"They're not artists."

"I agree."

"It's part of the whole process. Live, sense, interpret, consider, articulate, and communicate."

"For some people the process is feel, respond, express, full stop. The expression is more about catharsis than communicating."

"And that's fine. But I think, don't exhibit it. Just have your catharsis and throw it away. Otherwise they may as well show us their shit."

"Sounds like my last exhibition."

"I think we can safely say that was everybody's shit, not just yours."

"Thank you."

"The way I see it, *beyond* can mean a couple of things. Either, whoever's saying it has left these things behind, or they've taken it to an extreme, to another level."

"I must admit, I quite like both."

"Me too. That's exactly where I was heading with this.

Maybe going beyond is an extreme response, a reaction, or device."

"Could be. It's subjective, isn't it?"

"Whoever's feeling the state of *beyond* is the one who decides. And they're hardly the best judge."

"Where are we going with this?"

"Just wriggling in the shit."

"I like the image, even if it has a negative slant to it"

"No. Not this time. Even shit becomes nutrients . . ."

"For growth!"

"Now you're with me."

"So you're saying, beyond all our shit, whether it's perceived or otherwise, there's growth?"

"There can be."

"It's naive to think that good always prevails."

"But we do want to show some kind of progress, or if you're not careful we just end up moaning."

"Which is okay, and it's more fun than selling your butt," said Joe.

"Is that why we're doing this?"

"No," said Joe. "It's because we feel like it."

"And that's a good enough reason for me."

"Actually, I do it because I have to. It hurts not to."

Flora looked confused. "Hurts?"

"Well, annoys me, irritates me, makes me feel there is something wrong, and I can fix it."

"I know that feeling," said Flora. "I deal with it by writing, drawing, or having sex that interests me."

"Really?"

"If *really* refers to the sex bit of that sentence, only sometimes."

Joe started imagining what she meant by this, what

she got up to generally, and how Don fitted into this picture.

"That reminds me, I haven't seen Don lately. He hasn't called or anything."

"I wonder why," said Flora vaguely, then with more enthusiasm, "I'm dying for a coffee."

"I'm the opposite, I live for it." The conversation had successfully been steered away from Don.

"Is coffee just a distraction from this work?"

"Distraction's okay."

"Only from first thing in the morning until last thing at night."

"You mean there are moments when you're not distracted?" said Flora in mock horror.

"Just before I fall asleep, that hazy, groggy, blurred state of consciousness. I just about cope with not being distracted then."

"That sounds tormented," said Flora. "Are you unhappy?"

"What! You mean despite thinking of David . . . every hour . . . of every day!" His eye filled with tears and he shook his head as though it might dislodge the feelings storming his head. "Of course I'm *unhappy*. Why in God's name wouldn't I be?" Tears ran down his cheeks, "He was the love of my life . . . He was my everything!" A moment of silence followed a reverence for what had just been said. Then as though he had gotten something out of his system he calmed, and in a cute, pretend, throwaway manner he said, "Anyway . . . who the hell is happy?"

Unsure if now was the right time to confess, sheepishly she said, "*I* am." She paused. "I think. No. Yes I am. I smile sometimes."

"On drugs?"

"No."

"I don't understand."

"It happens for no reason."

"Weird."

"I'm sorry!"

Flora and Joe talked for hours, made some notes, argued about colours they liked and disliked. Joe was quite bossy but Flora didn't mind. She considered Joe was doing her a favor, by letting her be involved. Their thoughts wove in and out of each other, connecting, clashing, or sometimes spinning off only to arrive at a dead end. This was the first day of their collaboration, and it was much like their tenth and fortieth. The weather, their outfits and mood changed, but at the core was something consistent, even potent. They would meet about three times a week. Joe postponed all video projects during this time, and Flora put all extraneous activities on hold. She didn't try to keep in touch with Don, feeling she'd had enough of him. It was convenient that he wasn't around. It was that much easier to lie. She started seeing Josie regularly, who conveniently filled the space Don left. Flora felt she was the happiest she'd been for a long time. Her love life was incredible, her career was taking an interesting turn, and her plan to get closer to Joe was working.

25

It was opening night at the Anthony d'Offay Gallery. As was expected at a show bearing the name Joe Holtzman there was a media buzz, and because there were so many people waiting outside the gallery it looked like a street fair, but for sophisticates. Most weren't going to get inside the gallery to see the work today, but at least they'd be able to say that they had tried to get into a Holtzman show.

In preparation, photographers checked that their flashbulbs worked and took light readings. They were so busy getting ready and looking out for a limo that they didn't notice Joe and Flora edging their way through the crowd on foot. He wore a snug fitting dark-blue Gucci suit, a brown shirt, black tie and shoes. On his arm, Flora complimented him beautifully in a dark-blue satin dress that showed off the shape of her body, and hovered just off the ground. They had dressed up, but so had many others, so they didn't look conspicuous. Still, more than most, and especially together, they had a 1950s Hollywood glamour about them. It wasn't until they were at the entrance, and Joe spoke to a woman on the door that somebody in the crowd recognized him and shouted, "Holtzman!"

With knee-jerk reaction, both he and Flora turned. Cameras burst and the noise level rose with popping and clicking and cries, as individual photographers tried to get their attention. This trick worked on Flora because she wasn't used to it, but Joe who was much more seasoned when it came to paparazzi, gently touched her elbow and guided her inside.

Some heartless photographer who wasn't ready for Joe to go inside shouted, "David's dead!" And he got exactly wanted when Joe looked round both shocked and annoyed. Of course only paparazzi would sink so low to get the necessary shot that would go beautifully with the tabloid gem of a headline that read Horrible Holtzman Strikes Again.

This put a damper on an already dreaded evening. At home, Joe had been sick with nerves, whereas Flora had been to the gym and maintained a sort of calm. Still, it wasn't enough. So she resorted to the more chemical solution Valium. She tried to help Joe by giving him some coke. They polished off a gram before leaving the house and started on another shortly after entering the gallery.

Journalists waited in line to speak to Joe and Flora. One of them, a woman, sat in front of them.

"Hello. I'm with *Hola* magazine."

"Hola!" said Flora.

The woman strained to smile. She'd obviously heard this response hundreds of times. "Right!" said *Hola* woman. "Joseph Holtzman." Joe nodded with a serious expression. "This is your first collaboration. Why now?"

"It's her fault," he said, leaning his head toward Flora.

"Some are saying that after your last exhibition, you've lost confidence."

"They're probably right."

Flora thought this was below the belt, and retaliated. "In journalists."

Joe continued to nod slowly. The interviewer appeared shocked.

"What happened at the last exhibition was extreme. It made me lose confidence in most things."

"But in your work?"

This subject and its association with David would've had him in tears if he weren't so coked up. "I imagine so. It comes from me. How could it not be affected?"

"Are you less sure about your ideas?" said the woman.

"I feel surer of this exhibition than any before."

Flora turned to Joe, feeling as though he were giving her a compliment. The journalist picked up on this.

"Because of Miss Evans?"

The way *Hola* said Miss Evans really grated on Flora. "Journalists are behind the scenes for a reason," she said.

Joe raised his eyebrows, surprised. He looked at Flora, who didn't look back, but smiled slightly, just enough to let him know she was aware he was looking. Then she bit her bottom lip, and squinted, as though trying to workout her opponent. Joe was on the verge of laughter.

"That is?" *Hola* said a little baffled.

Flora had had too much coke and so came out with something even more childish, inappropriate, and defensive. "Cause they're not interesting enough to be in the scene."

"And so can I assume that you are?"

Flora hesitated. The cocaine only gave her so much confidence.

"She is. I'm not."

"I think I've got all I need."

"Oh!" said Joe. "Please don't forget to mention the website."

"Right," said the woman. "Sure thing." She collected her Dictaphone, scarf, and mints into her bag.

"You'll need the address."

"Yes."

"It's www.blahblahblah.com."

Sounding more bored than offended, she said, "Of course it is."

Then she stood, acknowledging the man waiting to take her place. He said hello to Flora and Joe, who responded with deadly charm. The *Hola* journalist refrained from showing a response. But then addressing Flora, she said, "You've got something white on your nose."

As Flora went to wipe it, Joe shook his head, but not soon enough. Flora assumed that everyone must have been able to tell she'd been doing cocaine, and felt ridiculous. In reality, there was nothing on her nose. Joe looked at the journalist.

"Just kidding," she said, and smiled.

Flora and Joe both burst out laughing.

"Well done, bitch," said Flora.

"Thanks! I'm right in taking that as a compliment?" said the woman with genuine humor.

"You bet," said Flora.

"Don't worry about the article," said *Hola* as she turned to leave. "I'm on your side." Then she nudged the journalist now in front of them and said with affection, "I'd treat these two nicely, if you know what's good for you. They're a right pair." At this she winked at them and left.

26

Joe sat alone in his living room. He was looking at photos
of David in his portfolio. The photos were for work,
taken professionally and they lacked a certain amount of
realness. However, Joe could see through this façade of
posturing and poses, to the man he loved. Tears were
drying on his face. He stared into space. The doorbell
rang. With no interest in whom it might be, and no
desire to answer it and find out, Joe stood, moved
towards the front door and answered it without his feelings leaving David. For a moment, it crossed his mind
that he should collect his thoughts and more significantly his feelings before he opened the door, but he could-
n't be bothered.

"Hey, Joe!" Immediately, Ryan could see that Joe had
been crying and he took hold of him. "Baby! What's this
about?" He stepped into the hall, revealing somebody
who'd been standing behind him. "This is the Uli I told

you about."

Joe couldn't remember. His thoughts were still swirling with images of David. He tried to focus, to drag his attention to the present. "Right! I mean, yeah. I think so."

Uli stepped into the hallway. His messed up curly hair and freckles that made him look like he should also have scraped knees and elbows from doing something outdoorsy. With an unusual amount of formality, Joe reached out to shake his hand.

"I'm sorry," said Uli. "They're a bit clammy."

"Don't worry," said Joe, and held out his hand further, as if to imply, that shaking Uli's clammy hand was what he intended to do. Afterwards, Joe resisted wiping his hand on his jeans. Uli noticed this. He'd been conscious of his hands sweating ever since he was a kid, and very aware that people didn't like them. Therefore, he appreciated how Joe responded. It made him feel at ease and welcome. Joe led them into the living room, but with deference to him, Uli remained at the doorway.

The place looked different from when Ryan last saw it. All four walls were an intense bright green colour, artificial grass covered the floor, and hanging from the ceiling were long threads of silver tinsel. Also all the edges, along the ceiling, down the corners, and along the floor all had red plastic roses.

"Hey!" said Ryan, bending down to feel the fake grass. "What's with the park theme?"

"It's actually meant to be Hyde Park."

"That's where David used to make us go boating."

"Exactly. God you understand the mind of a sad lonely queen."

"You're not old and you'll never be lonely. Everybody loves *you*."

Joe went and stood in front of the window, and gazed wistfully through it. "Then how come I spend so much time by myself?"

As soon as he finished saying this, he thought maybe he'd been too open in front of somebody he didn't know.

Ryan thought the same, but overlooked it because he loved Joe and wanted to help. "You spend time alone because that's what you're used to." He went and stood beside Joe, but faced into the room, so as not to exclude Uli. "You forget that you were so comfortable with David that you used to be able to be alone even when you were with him." Joe nodded slightly, although it was difficult to tell if he was listening. "Other people can't offer you that." He put his hand on Joe's shoulder, partly to comfort him and partly to make sure he had his attention. "They need more from you than you're ready to give."

Uli already knew quite a lot about David. After his death, Ryan talked about him persistently, and being a sensitive and considerate young man, Uli let him, all the time learning more about a man that - sadly - he'd never meet. Up until this point in the conversation he'd still been standing at the doorway from the hall, his head lowered, but now he walked tentatively into the room, still keeping a measured distance. He raised his eyes and added sheepishly, "Yet."

For a moment, Ryan felt put out, thinking Uli's remark was a bit intrusive, but then he found that he agreed. "Yeah. *Yet.*" He felt this put a positive spin on the whole thing and so nodded in agreement thinking *well done*. "Give it time. Of course nobody is ever going to replace

David, but they might be able to give you companionship."

"It's early days," said Uli.

Out of politeness, Joe turned and smiled, but there was absolutely no joy behind it, and so this was precisely what it expressed.

"I just got it . . ." said Ryan, purposely changing the conversation. He had so many unresolved issues of his own surrounding David. Nobody knew anything about their night together. At times this felt like something personal and he was fine with it staying that way. At other times, the whole subject, loaded with complexity, felt ready to erupt. On Don's advice, he had some bereavement counselling when David died. However, he couldn't bear to even breach the subject anymore than David could with Sky. "The rose garden in Hyde Park . . . was your special place. How romantic."

Joe nodded sadly.

In an attempt to shift the mood, Ryan walked into the center of the room as though he was on stage. He opened both hands and gestured to all that surrounded him. "David would have loved this."

Still facing out of the window Joe nodded again, but now in a more resigned way. "Yeah but you know how he was, he liked the real thing. He loved his nature . . ."

"Right . . . So . . . Can't wait to see the exhibition." Joe didn't respond. "At the gallery." He definitely wasn't listening now.

Ryan looked at Uli . . . for some kind of consolation and noticed that he was attempting to point at something with his eyes. Ryan followed his sight line and saw the open portfolio. His response was to go take hold of

Joe, and give him another longer, more reassuring hug.

"Baby!" he said gently close into his ear, "You missing him?"

Joe's eyes darted about quickly, and when they stopped, they fell on an indiscriminate point in the garden.

Ryan tried to get his attention, to bring him back from his reverie. "Baby!" Joe could only manage an erratic and broken looking nod. His eyes filled with tears.

"You caught me at a bad time. I'm sorry."

"Don't be daft. Looks like we caught you at exactly the right time."

After a moment, Joe smiled through his upset. "You're a sweetheart Ryan."

"Learned it all from you and David. Listen, you sit here." He guided Joe on to the big wooden chair beside the window. It was the nearest seat, but also it meant that Joe now faced into the room, which made him more connected to the others. "Let me get you a drink," he said as a diversionary tactic. Then, "What will it be?" already heading towards the kitchen.

Absentmindedly Joe said, "A Coke, I guess . . . Diet."

"A brew please," said Uli and sidled over to the window. "Oh! Milk. Three sugars." He wanted to be not so separate from Joe. He perched on the sill.

"Coke light and tea extra coming up."

Left alone Joe and Uli felt uncomfortable. Uli because he was socially a bit awkward and Joe because he wasn't concentrating enough to address his thoughts on the situation. If he had been, he'd have realised that he was attracted to Uli, and noticed that this attraction was being reciprocated.

Fortunately, Ryan eased the situation by returning with their drinks. He put Uli's on the sill beside him, and the other on the arm of Joe's chair. Then from out of his back pocket, he pulled a bottle of larger, twisted off the cap and sat in the floor in front of them crossed legs, and took a big swig of his drink. "Don't let me stop you chatting," he said.

Joe tried to smile. "Sorry, I'm not on my best form."

"You're still better than most," said Ryan. As Joe wasn't paying attention, Ryan looked at Uli and gestured for him to talk to Joe.

Uli blushed and gulped at his tea. It was still too hot, so he spat it out. "Shit! Sorry."

"Nice!" said Ryan.

Joe looked over at Uli. "It doesn't matter about the floor." He noticed that he was making a cute expression, and it made him feel a bit better. "I think it's made from some kind of plastic, waterproof." He continued to watch Uli as he spoke. "Just between you and me, I don't think it will last long. I don't think I like it." Then he addressed Ryan, "I'm more of an urban type aren't I? Rural isn't really me."

"I hardly think this synthetic, toxic green version would be classed as rural." He rubbed his fingers through and cringed. "Lovely! It feels so authentic."

"Proves my point," said Joe. "I think it's positively wilderness."

Uli laughed, and then continued to sip his still-too-hot-but-gave-him-something-to-do tea.

"When was the last time you let your hair down?" said Ryan.

"I know exactly where this is heading."

"Come on! It'll be good for you."

Without a trace of humor, Joe raised an eyebrow.

"Oh, come on," said Ryan. "I want Uli to see it."

Joe made a series of expressions that communicated, no, then maybe, and eventually okay. He paused; his face motionless for a moment, then squinted and said, "Get my bitch on the phone."

"If you're referring to Flora, *My* bitch, is nicer than her previous name *The* bitch."

"Yeah. I couldn't pull it off without some moral support."

"By that you mean someone who'll score the drugs and make sure nobody bothers you."

"Etcetera. Etcetera!" said Joe.

"Couldn't you just tell them to leave you alone?" asked Uli.

"That's like telling them not to take drugs," said Ryan.

"You must understand," said Joe in a fatherly way. "At *Trade* there's a suspension of belief in the real world."

"What Joe's trying to say is nobody gives a fuck."

Joe released some air from his mouth, his version of a half-hearted laugh. The nearest thing to a real one since Ryan arrived.

"That's more like it," said Ryan. "The bitch's number?"

"You can just hit redial."

He set about doing this, and left the room.

Uli edged his way slightly towards Joe, sipping continually as he did.

"So, you must be taking the same subject as Ryan . . ."

Nervously Uli spewed out what he wanted to say.

"Well, we're at the same Uni, but doing different modules. Still, we do have four classes . . ."

Joe cut him off. "In sweetness." As soon as he finished speaking, he wondered if it was inappropriate. He felt embarrassed. Uli noticed, and started to bite his lip. This made Joe uncomfortable. Fortunately, Ryan didn't take too long and he kept up communication with them from the kitchen.

"She'll have a friend with her, some Josie character."

"I feel you're missing something."

"Yes, yes, yes! She'll have the stash."

"Do you mean drugs?" said Uli looking up at Joe and pronouncing the word drugs as though it was completely alien.

Being a little patronizing Ryan said, "Yes, dear!"

Joe noticed, but quickly moved on to his next thought. "Sounds like Flora has fallen for Josie."

"What! Flora a dyke? Fuck! That one's full of surprises."

"Oh! Flora said to tell you she's meeting Paul at the club. Who's Paul?" said Ryan defensively.

Joe took his seat in the big chair again. "Just some geezer."

"Since when have you used such slang?"

"Okay, some bloke."

"I assume you're trying to impress Uli 'cause it ain't washing with me. Try guy, or boy."

"It worked for me," said Uli, and without warning, or explanation. Uli stepped over, put his hand on Joe's neck, and started rubbing it. Joe wore a hooded sweatshirt, so Uli wasn't self-conscious about his hand sweating. Ryan watched Uli and had a feeling that something significant was happening. Meanwhile Joe became pure physicality, and gave into Uli's touch as though it were life giving. He moaned.

"Sounds like you could do with a massage," said Uli.

"Yes please," said Joe.

Embarrassed, Uli laughed. "I'm not a masseur."

"You sure as hell feel like one to me."

He saw this as an invitation and so stepped in behind Joe and massaged it as best he knew how.

Ryan couldn't help grinning with excitement. "I knew you two would like each other."

Joe relaxed, becoming soft, pliable, and responsive. "Um!" he moaned appreciatively. "So Uli, tell me. Do you think my Ryan's a good actor?"

Uli was pleased Joe was addressing him about something more serious, even if the topic was somebody else. "His tutors think so."

"You saw me at during my end of term performance before. Did you or didn't you like it?

"I try not to have like-dislike reaction to things. Anything somebody has put time into deserves more than an immediate reaction. Otherwise it might be based on what kind of day I've had or who phoned me last."

"Okay! I get your point. But how will I know if I'm good or not?"

"Somebody else isn't necessarily the best judge. My advice would be to wait and see how your own response differs over time."

"Why is yours a reaction, and mine a response?"

"Yours is deeper. You know it, understand it, and feel the need to do it."

"It can't be just a simple yes or no with you Joe, can

it?"

"I can't think of a single question, where a simple *yes* or *no* would be the appropriate answer." Joe looked at his watch. "So, anyway! We've got quite some time to kill. Anything at the cinema you fancy seeing?"

Ryan flicked through the pages, not really concentrating.

"Actually, I wouldn't mind a kip. I'm knackered."

"Why don't you lie down," said Joe. "Your room's the same as you left it." He paused. "But tidy."

"Ha ha!" said Ryan.

"Uli can keep me company." He looked at Uli. "Unless you want to sleep, too."

"I'm not tired," said Uli.

"Okay," said Joe. "I'll try to entertain Uli for a few hours and you can sleep."

"Is that okay?" said Ryan. Uli nodded. "You're in safe hands."

Ryan ran up the stairs, four at a time.

"Long legs," said Joe, listening to the footsteps. Uli nodded his head again, and sighed.

"Why the sigh?" said Joe.

His face going slightly red, Uli said, "Did I sigh?"

"Think so."

"God knows what I was thinking."

"Are you okay?"

"Do I seem not okay?"

"I don't know." Joe laughed a little exasperated. "Do you feel not okay?"

Uli was about to answer but Joe put his hand over his mouth. Joe's fingers felt lovely against Uli's lips. The smell went straight from his nose to his balls. He thought of sex, abstract and unfocused. He breathed in deeply. Joe let his hand linger, and only slowly pulled it away, sliding it over Uli's lips. Considering he must have been 20 years old; he still had soft downy hair over his lip. As Joe's hand left his lovely mouth, Uli's lips puckered slightly, as though kissing, reaching out, or wanting Joe's hand to stay.

Joe thought it very sexy, held-back, and gorgeous. "I felt your lips move," he said softly.

"I was rubbing them together. I could do with some lip balm."

"Here." Joe got his out, and with one hand, uncapped it and applied it to Uli's lips.

This time Uli didn't rub them together purposely, but instead waited. Joe put the cap back on. Then he did what Uli had hoped for, he rubbed his lips with one of his thick, warm and slightly rough finger. Doing this made Joe's dick throb inside his jeans. Uli saw it move and couldn't help but look down at Joe's fly. It moved again. Uli didn't have much choice now, so he opened his mouth and took his finger inside. Driven by a craving he didn't understand, he started to drop down in front of Joe, his intention to kneel, but Joe could see where this was heading, so took hold of Uli under his armpits and lifted him back up. He hadn't had sex since David, hadn't even kissed anybody. He just didn't have the inclination. But here, now, for both of them there was a battle between their thoughts and the impulse to act on their desire. Uli looked at Joe, for any sign that meant he might be able to have more of him. Joe felt a mix of reserve, desire, sadness, and something he hadn't felt in along time, excitement. Oblivious to the reality of

Joe's feelings, Uli convinced himself that he saw approval in Joe's eyes, and so he leaned forward. Joe didn't pull back. Closer, and Uli opened his mouth slightly, his mind full of a kiss. Now, closer, and he could feel Joe's warm breath. Now they were so close that all Uli had to do was pucker his lips and their mouths touched.

27

At two am, Ryan woke and made his way downstairs. Again, he strode several steps at a time, but more slowly, with a just-woken-from-sleep-weight to them. As he entered the living room he yawned, scratched his tummy, and vaguely noticed a smell, but because he was still unfocused from sleep, he didn't register what it was.

The film Blue Velvet was playing on the monitor. Although Joe and Uli were both watching it, because they sat at opposite ends of the sofa, they looked like they weren't doing it together.

Ryan rolled his eyes and said, "Joe won't bite you."

"How do you know?" said Joe.

"I guess I don't . . . I love this film. Is it just me, or is this the only decent thing Lynch ever directed?"

"Arguably," said Joe. "I think it's perfect," he continued. "The lighting, the colors, the casting, the acting, and a whole bunch of stuff I can't begin to put my finger on."

"Stuff you wouldn't want to put your finger on. It'd get covered in something."

"Sssh!" said Uli feeling excited. It might have been

that it was late and he was waiting to go to a 'cool' club in London. It might simply have been that he was staying at Joe's. He had no clear answer.

Ryan was restless and wanted a distraction, so went to the kitchen. A few minutes later he returned with a beer. "Nice to see someone finally broke the ice."

"In our own time," said Joe.

"Sure," said Ryan. "I was only messing."

"I know," said Joe. "But you're wrong about me not biting. I love nothing more than fresh blood."

"Vampires wouldn't last long these days," said Ryan. Uli looked puzzled. "Cause of HIV." Turning to Joe he said, "I guess you'd be okay though." Joe's face winced involuntarily. Again, Uli looked puzzled. "Cause he's already got it." Uli gasped a little. "What's wrong?" said Ryan. Uli started to say something, but nothing came out. "It's all right," said Ryan. "You can't catch it by watching the same film."

Uneasy looking Uli said, "Have you?"

Joe nodded.

"What's with the sudden interest in HIV?" said Ryan.

Uli answered with a vague, "Just . . . wondering."

"Is there something you're not telling me?" asked Ryan, feigning suspicion.

"No!"

Joe reached for Uli's head, tousled his hair, and said, "If you want to know more about it I'll fill you in later. But from the little I know of you, I'm certain you wouldn't have caught it."

Ryan looked baffled. "Enough HIV talk," he said. "What should I wear tonight?"

"It doesn't matter what you wear," said Joe.

"Everything suits youth."

"You've got a point," said Ryan, pretending to be arrogant. Then he sat on Joe's knee. "You seem much better than earlier."

"I'm holding up."

"Maybe it was my dear friend Uli here."

"Maybe," said Joe, not wanting to give anything away. In reality, it was more than a *maybe*.

As if it needed to be said, "I was only kidding." This statement served no purpose but to offend Uli, and when Ryan noticed this he tried to rescue himself, "Just kidding again. I'm very, very fond of Uli's company too."

Uli's expression softened and he smiled shyly.

In the hope of changing the conversation, Joe looked at his watch. "My God! We better get ready. Flora will be here."

"I'll jump in the shower," said Ryan. "If that's okay."

"Sure!" said Joe. "That's if you don't mind me hopping down here."

"You're funny," said Ryan, completely deadpan. "I'm out of here." With this he left and bounded up the stairs.

Uli and Joe were left in silence, and acutely aware of it.

"Um," said Uli.

"Yeah?" said Joe.

"Nothing."

"Doesn't look like nothing."

Now that Ryan had left the room Uli's whole demeanor changed, becoming more relaxed, and connected to Joe. "I just don't like the idea of you being sick."

"You sweet man. I'm not sick. I take medication. My health is tip top."

"I surprised you're so casual about it."

"Guess I never would have believed it either . . ." Joe

looked off to one side thinking about it. "When I lost David, from something as arbitrary as a fire, it put HIV in perspective, and it kind of lost its sting."

The doorbell rang and with it came the sound of high-pitched laughter through the front window.

"Saved by the bell," said Joe. "You get it. She'll be so confused."

Already he felt the urge to please Joe so got up to answer the door. When he did the laughter stopped.

Surprised, Flora said, "What have we here?" Uli didn't respond and after a moment she said, "Is Joe in?"

"Joe?" said Uli. "Sure." He opened the door and Flora walked in followed by Josie.

"So who might you be?" she said passing him and heading straight into the living room. Then, without waiting for him to answer, "For a second I thought I'd come to the wrong house."

"Flora!" said Joe.

"Darling!" said Flora uncharacteristically.

Uli followed them in.

She turned and looked at Uli, waiting to be introduced.

"Sorry. This is Uli." He paused for a second wondering how to explain. Then he opted for the easy route. "He's down for the weekend with Ryan."

"Oh. I thought you and he might be . . ."

Joe forced a relatively believable laugh. "And who's this lovely creature?"

"My name's Josie." As she spoke, her eyes, mouth, even the skin on her face seemed to smile. "So you're Joe. I've heard far too much about you."

"I'm sorry."

Flora was surprised at how different his mood was to

last time they spoke. "You're a lot perkier than earlier. What have you taken?"

"Nothing, but thanks. Yeah! I do feel better."

"All good. Ryan. Of course! Where is the sweetmeat?"

"He's having a shower," said Uli.

Josie looked around her. "Cute space."

"She already knows I did it," said Flora.

"It's still cute."

"Thank you," said Joe. "Or should Flora thank you. I think *I'll* take the credit, for having it in *my* house."

At that moment, Ryan came running down the stairs holding the banister with one hand and his towel with the other. "Flora!"

"Puppy!"

"Josie, right?"

"Correct," said Josie and went to shake his hand. It was the hand holding the towel.

He went to shake, and his towel began to drop. He switched hands quickly, but not quick enough.

"Big boy," said Josie. "That trick works every time."

Uli blushed and looked at Joe, who was busy distracting himself with his cuticles. Flora merely widened her eyes then took the opportunity to check out everybody else's responses. "That gave us all a bit of a rush," she said.

Joe noticed her noticing. "It's a gay thing, I mean a guy thing."

"It must be," said Flora. "I didn't even notice his smooth muscular thighs, his blond pubic hair, and his thick, brown, uncircumcised boy meat."

There was a brief pause whilst everyone laughed, and as it subsided she said, "Right! What are we waiting for?" She pulled a wrap out of her clutch bag, and as she looked Joe in the eye, she threw the drugs to Uli. *Busted*, thought Joe, as he realized she'd clocked something was going on between Uli and him. She smiled and said, "Come on sweetheart. Show us how it's done"

Instead of catching the wrap neatly, Uli knocked it from one hand to the other. When he finally had it in one hand, he said, "I don't know what you expect me to do with this, because I haven't a clue. I've seen it done in films. They use a credit card."

"Okay!" said Ryan. "Cute, but don't over do it. Nobody's that naïve."

"I'll do it," said Joe, and squeezed Uli's neck affectionately.

Ryan noticed this. "Have I missed something?"

Only now did Flora realize that Ryan didn't know. "Well! Well! Well!" She looked at Joe, who shrugged and pulled a strained looking smile.

"Dear me, what have I walked into here?" said Josie. "The intrigue of it all. I feel like I'm in a scene from *Dangerous Liaisons*."

"Will somebody tell me what's going on?" said Ryan.

"It's nothing," said Flora. "Just some joke I made earlier." She paused. "It's not worth repeating."

"Do tell us," said Joe mischievously.

"I couldn't," she said. Looking at Joe pointedly she added, "It's far too tedious, Joe." She placed extra emphasis on the word *Joe*, implying that it was he who was tedious.

Within just a couple of minutes, Joe had five lines cut. He didn't stand on ceremony and did his line first. "Who's next?"

Everybody, apart from Uli, was pretending not to

notice the lines ready and waiting. Before having a line herself Flora graciously handed Joe her Tiffany platinum snorting device. Joe took it, bent, and did his line without saying a word. Josie was next. Then she handed it back to Flora, who again thought to hand it to somebody else, Ryan.

"Go on kid," she said. "It'll make a man of you."

"It won't do that to me, will it?" said Josie.

"No, but it *will* put hair on your chest," said Joe.

"Josie with a hairy chest?" said Flora. "Stop, you're giving me a hard-on."

Without any fuss, Ryan did his line and hesitantly offered the straw to Uli.

"Do you want some?" said Joe. "It's only cocaine,"

"I don't know," said Uli.

"Joe will look after you," said Flora. "And if *he* doesn't, I will."

Reassured by this, Uli knelt bent forward. He paused, and then looked around at Joe, who simply watched. Uli thought Joe looked warm. He felt he'd be safe. Joe would make sure of that. Uli could think of nothing more incredible than going out with Joe, coming home with him, and falling asleep naked with him. Waking up next to him was almost too much to contemplate. At that moment, Uli wanted Joe more than anything in the world. Joe nodded, smiling. Uli leaned forward and snorted.

Flora started clapping. "For a moment, I wondered if you'd back out." Joe looked at her and shook his head. She noticed and changed her approach. "It's not so bad, hey?"

Uli smiled, feeling quite proud. "Just one more line,

please. I'll do anything. And I mean *anything*."

"Good, we've got him hooked," said Ryan. "It won't be long now before he's on heroin."

Josie added, "Then it's just slavery, pedophilia, and murder."

"Don't forget incest," said Flora.

Ryan looked at her, wondering if she knew about him and David.

Six lines of coke, four vodkas, two speed-bombs, and an ecstasy later, they remembered they were going to Trade. Once they did, it took them about three-quarters of an hour to get out the door. Luckily, a black cab was just across the road from the house.

"Are you waiting for somebody," said Josie.

"No."

"No, I was just sorting out some stuff," said the driver.

Ryan recognised him. "I've seen you here before."

"Yeah, I live just round here. Jump in!" This was the last thing the driver said during the journey. A couple of times Flora caught his eye in the rear-view mirror, but he looked away quickly.

28

Inside the club, they headed straight to the downstairs bar. They were already high enough to not mind the heat and people generally being too sweaty and too close. Shirtless men stared at them wide eyed. Josie ordered drinks. They all asked for alcohol, except Uli. Flora organized the collecting together of the knackered, school-canteen-like chairs. Then she directed the arrangement of them around an equally chic table. In 'real life' these would be thought grotty, but here they were prized. Besides, caring about anything in Trade apart from drugs was unimaginable. Now, they had everything they wanted, they were set for the evening.

Their clothes alone made them stand out. Of course Josie looked just as out of place as she always did, but now to compliment her slightly punk-gothic dress sense, Flora had her hair in pigtails, and she wore tailored short-pant trouser suit in navy blue pinstriped. It looked 70s and Heidi gone berserk and office wear, all at the same time. And, who would have thought she'd have such great legs, model long, but more athletic, and waxed to a perfect sheen. On her feet she wore trainers and football socks. She looked photo-shoot ready. Now Paul understood why she could take so much of Josie's time and interest in the last couple of months.

Although their crowd sat in a conspicuous place, Paul pretended he hadn't seen them. At the same time, he couldn't help but watch them. It seemed many other people had the same problem. They attracted a lot of attention. Their playing-up, flirting with each other, asides, and even their intimate conversations were all on show. Regardless, he hoped Josie would notice *him*, and come over. This was the only option. He was too nervous to approach her, not when she was with somebody that he fancied. The fact that he was famous, and more significantly Joseph Holtzman made it more difficult. Part of the problem was she was bang in the middle of them, walled in by the Holtzman entourage. However, he saw that this might be to his advantage. Josie could be his route in, his guest list entry. But why wouldn't she look around and catch his eye? If he laughed loud enough, surely she would hear, and recognize his voice. He tried. But nothing. Not one of them looked around. Finally, out of desperation, he decided to walk past her. He planned to pretend he was on his way to the toilet. The trouble was, the nearer he got to Holtzman the more handsome he appeared.

From where Paul stood, Joe looked great. He wasn't topless like most other men, but wore a black short-sleeved shirt with the buttons undone. It fit just right over his arms, which looked strong but not pumped. The fact that the shirt was open allowed a just a suggestion of how he might look naked. The sexiest thing was that it looked like he wasn't trying and that he didn't care about anybody else's opinion of how he dressed. In Trade where everything was extreme, plumage, over the top, excessive, and larger than was necessary in life, Joe's appearance stood out. It was a statement, which spoke clearly. Paul heard; solid, no nonsense, understated, quietly confident and just up to the brim, but no more, I'm enough.

Inside Paul's head the thoughts weren't structured, but he felt that Joe might be the last undamaged tin on the shelf. It was clear he had a long expiration date, so it was unlikely that somebody wouldn't eat him at some future date.

Adversely, Paul saw himself very differently. He thought that naturally his shelf life was overdue and he'd expired. Yet, artificial additives kept him looking fresh. These included; HIV meds, acyclovir, steroids, antidepressants, Botox, diazepam, temazepam, rohypnol, in fact all downers, and of course 'recreational' drugs, which he referred to as meds also. These included hash, opium, heroin, crystal, regular speed, ketamine, coke, crack, acid, magic mushrooms and the mother's-milk-of-all-modern-drugs ecstasy.

Paul believed that Joe wouldn't be interested, because the contrast between them was too extreme. In reality, to an untrained, un-neurotic, non-judgemental eye, there was hardly a difference. Most other men at Trade would have thought them both indiscriminately 'hot'.

In this mental state, he approached Holtzman's crowd, and so understandably, he started to get nervous. Random images flashed through his mind; Joe at the market, having dinner, working out, and naked while in the shower. Within the time it takes to move about two meters in Trade when it's busy, Paul wondered what it would be like to fuck with Holtzman, sleep with him, wake-up with him saying "*I love you Paul.*"

Ryan and Uli sat to Joe's right, in a separate little cluster. Paul wondered who they were. Joe appeared to be interested in them, but why? He thought them cute enough, but a bit young to be any fun in bed. One of them seemed to be making Josie laugh a lot. He was what Paul called a 'city surfer', meaning that he probably never went near an ocean and the only board he probably ever rode was a skateboard.

When near enough to be heard, Paul said, "Josie! You're here."

"Paul! We've been here a while." Josie gave him a hug. She never made kiss noises to the side of your face, squeezed you as though you might crack, or acted-out affection. If she noticed you, and felt you worth acknowledging, she gave you her full attention. Paul always felt lucky that he was someone she liked. As she hugged him, he smelled her perfume. She'd always worn the same subtle Geranium scent she got especially from Paris. Even through the virtually solid soiled air of Trade, it was recognizable as his dear friend, familiar, and reassuring.

"Good to see you," he said earnestly.

"Likewise." He knew she meant this, but didn't stop to show it. She had work to do on his behalf. "Joe, this is Paul, the man I told you about."

Joe looked at Paul and said, "Hey!" Neither his words nor his tone were off-putting, but something wasn't quite right. Paul put it down to micro gestures on Joe's face.

"Hey!" said Paul. He thought *hey* was a dumb thing for Joe to have said, and even more of a dumb response.

"This is Ryan and Uli," said Josie.

"Hey, Ryan," said Paul. Then he turned in an exaggerated way and said, "Hey, Uli." They all found this funny. Paul didn't know why he suddenly adopted the expression *hey*. He'd never used it before.

Neither of them responded as though they were gay. If they weren't, he wondered what their relationship was to Joe. He thought that they might be rent-boys. The one called Ryan looked like one.

From her unique perspective, of just a few feet away, and knowing Paul so well, Josie watched to see his interaction with Joe. In her heart of hearts, she felt Paul was too good for Joe. Judging, compartmentalizing, and evaluating others wasn't usually her way, but she had a vested interest in her Paul. This was her profound love for him and it was because she knew his worth. The way she saw it was this, he had a commitment to life that no other soul bothered to aspire to, let alone attain. Some thought Paul obsessive. For her this was attention to detail. Others found him compulsive but she admired this as relentless determination. What many called his insecurity, she saw as a constant questioning, not just of his internal self, but him in context of everybody and everything. No wonder he was tired. He was worn out. Done. Yet, still he tried, kept on searching for - Josie could barely comprehend - what.

Josie could tell Paul was feeling self-conscious, mainly because he fancied Joe, but also because that he wanted to make a good impression in front of her new friends.

A moment of silence grew, and before it could do any harm, Flora kindly jumped in to stop it. "And I'm Flora. Hi!"

"Yes, quite," said Paul, grateful that he'd finally dropped *hey*. "I'm sorry. You were next on my list. There's just so many of you to get through." As soon as he'd said this, he felt awkward, as though he'd made a dig at them. Quickly he looked at Josie for reassurance, or at least a distraction.

"What have you taken?" asked Josie, hoping to explain his uneasiness to the others.

"Ecstatic, or something. An old gypsy woman sold it to me. She said it would bring me luck."

"Is that the same as get lucky?" said Flora.

"I hope so," said Paul, and unintentionally caught Joe's eye. "Sorry, that wasn't meant to be addressed to you, Joe. I just . . ." Words failed him suddenly.

"Maybe you should quit while you're ahead," offered Josie.

"You call this ahead?" He looked behind him quickly as though somebody had called his name. "If I blamed it on the drugs, would I get away with it?"

"If you said you'd taken something really, really, really, really strong," said Flora.

"Something that gives you clumsy tongue, broken-mouth, and thought-paralysis," said Josie.

"Can I remind you that you're my friend, and you like me?" said Paul.

At this, Josie took hold of him, and sang as though petting a baby. "My lovely damaged thing." Then she sat him down in her chair and sat on his knee. "So, talk, you two," she said to Paul and Joe, who now sat side by side. "No pressure." She paused. "In your own time." She paused again. "Whenever you're ready." Then she sat looking at them both, arms folded, waiting.

"Your name's Snow?" said Paul, improvising. "What's your favourite colour, and what's your birth sign?"

"Funny you should say that. My nickname at school was Snowy Joey." He was genuinely surprised and so paused to give it some thought. "Yellow. And Aquarius."

"Yellow's mine, too," said Paul.

"That's 'cause it's the best." Joe was just being polite for Josie's sake and therefore Flora's. Yet, initially he found Paul amusing in a consumed-with-paranoia-own-worst-enemy kind of way.

"I know that," said Paul. "What's your blah, blah, blah." He turned to Josie. "Look, Mum, we're talking." Then he pretended he'd been telling a joke, and said, "That's how I came to have three ears and live in a giant shoe."

"I want whatever you had," said Flora. "Anybody seen that old gypsy woman?"

Josie felt that Paul wasn't on form, and so close to his ear she said, "Come to the toilet. Let's sort you out." To Flora, she said, "I'll just be a minute." This meant half an hour, or more.

They stood, and Josie held Paul's hand all the way upstairs. Near the top, where the music wasn't so loud she said, "They should rename this place, Homogenize."

"Or Turd!"

"Bitter?"

"Maybe," said Paul as they walked in the toilets, which were surprisingly empty.

"*Maybe* you're just too good for him," said Josie, and then spotted a door beginning to open and headed towards it.

"Nice try, but a bit corny," said Paul.

'So, anyway?"

"He seems okay, but what's with all that fluff on his arm?"

"Ryan is his nephew. Well kind of. But I think he likes the blond." Josie wiped the cistern off with some toilet paper. "I don't know the story there." She handed Paul a wrap. "Let's do a big line and see what we can do about the situation." Josie had a wicked look in her eye. Paul spotted it, and a little excited, chopped two lines. "What are you saving that for? My great-grandmother would turn her nose up at those." He pushed more of the coke into the lines. Josie looked at him as though he'd done something wrong. "All of it!"

"But we'll be flying."

"Yeah, but first class."

Paul emptied the wrap, split the powder in two and said, "I wish I'd brought my extra nostrils."

"Lightweight," said Josie.

"They're not even lines, they're mounds"

"Um. Good."

"At least let me do them in parts."

"However you want, but you're not leaving here till you've finished Hoovering." Paul bent over and did about a quarter of his pile up the one nostril and another quarter up the other. His nose was clear, so it landed somewhere between his sinuses and his throat. It made him cough. Luckily, Josie had brought her drink, so Paul took a swig to clear his throat. "Have I not taught you anything over the years?"

"Probably lots."

"Obviously nothing important. You can't even do your drugs properly."

"Sorry Mum." Josie bent forward. There was nothing left of her line when she came up. "Impressive!"

"Some people are good with children. Some travel the world doing charity work. I do a mean line of Charlie. It takes all sorts." Paul looked at the coke again, and thought twice about doing any more. He shuddered, bent, and snorted. Luckily, his nose had begun to block, so this time the coke settled in mucus. He stood up and rubbed his nose to massage it in. "That's my boy! Now out of here."

"Let me pee first," said Paul.

After a few minutes of standing with his dick out, talking, Josie said, "Shall we call it a day?"

"Sounds good to me."

"So the plan is. I'll take Uli to dance and you work on Joe."

On the way back downstairs, they could see over the dance floor. On it, there were hundreds of arms stabbing into the air, and faces on spin-cycle, which looked as though asking questions, to which the answers usually were, *You're at Trade. You're drug-fucked as hell. And you look like shit.*

None of their crowd had moved away, but they had mutated. Branches went off in different directions, as people tagged on. Josie took hold of Flora's hand, and Uli's, and without explaining led them off. Immediately,

Paul grabbed Uli's seat, next to Joe.

Paul didn't know where to begin, but was coke-confident enough not to care. Usually this worked fine. He generally found that if he showed enough confidence, most men gave in to what he wanted.

"I bring my son here, too," he said, referring to Uli being led away bewildered and amazed.

"Really," said Joe, uninterested, but at the same time offended.

"How would you like a big dick up your arse?" said Paul. In response, Joe initially thought *how* 70s. Then remembered how much David hated come-on lines. Next, he found himself considering that there was probably a time when this mental image would have caused a physical sensation in his groin, but he couldn't recall when. Was it so long ago? This question made him feel a sudden and overwhelming sadness.

In reaction he said, "It's charming of you to ask, but . . ."

Paul cut him off. "Sorry, did I get it wrong? A nice arse around your dick?"

This was definitely preferable to Joe, but still abstract. "I like the concept," he said.

"Excellent! We're making progress."

Joe had noticed that Paul's butt was near perfect, but still this didn't translate into sexual desire. "Only I was planning on it being someone else's."

"Oh! There's a *someone else*."

Yeah, thought Joe, *my friends, Uli, and David*, but with this on his mind, all he could muster was a nod.

"How about that *someone else* and *me* in the middle?" Paul wasn't going to give in that easily.

Enough, thought Joe, but he said, "No. I'm more into one on one."

"So ditch the kid." Although he wasn't aware of it, Paul had crossed a line. Now - even in Trade - he was just being rude.

Joe wondered why Paul was being so pushy. *Surely, he could have any man in the club.* As far as Joe could tell, and along with Paul's unspoken PR, he had all the right attributes physically.

"*Why was he so desperate?*" thought Joe. He suddenly felt for Paul. This wasn't the desired or a particularly sexy response. "I'm going to get a drink." Joe decided to make an effort not to be cruel. "Do you want one?"

"Vodka-Red Bull please." Paul tried to act cheap-sitcom-sexy and added, "By the way, you don't know what you're missing."

I do, thought Joe. *David.* He stood up. "So. A large vodka-Red Bull." He went off into the crowd, leaving Paul feeling weird and kind of annoyed. At least on coke, he didn't feel rejected.

Josie was quickly by Paul's side. She'd been watching. "No joy?" she said.

"I think he's smitten with somebody, but for some reason, I don't think it's the kid."

"That's funny. I haven't heard about anybody else."

"Well, another time," said Paul.

"How do you feel?"

"Coked-up to fuck."

"Me too."

Paul looked around the room and said, "I feel like getting really, really cunted."

"Sounds marvellous."

"Do you know what I fancy?"

"Go on, surprise me."

"Acid."

"God!" said Josie. "I haven't done acid for years."

"That doesn't sound like a *no*."

"You know me and drugs, our relationship."

"Yeah, monogamous right?"

"Married actually. Do you want me to get?"

"No, let's go together."

Under the stairs, in his usual place, they found a dealer. It was somebody who hoped to get Paul into bed, so although he'd only been asked for two, he gave them a small plastic bag full.

"Don't forget," said the dealer. "Later, if you think you're losing it, just give me a shout and I'll look after you. I mean real good." Then as incentive he added, "I've got some wicked stuff. Anything you want." With this, he winked at Paul, and then quickly returned to the growing line of people waiting to get served.

On the way back to where they'd been sitting, they bumped into Ryan. They asked him if he liked acid. On seeing his enthusiastic response, they gave him two tabs. Acid was Ryan's favorite drug, so he didn't think twice about taking the whole tab in one go. After just a short time, when it didn't seem to be working, assuming it was weak, he took the other. Like generations before him, this is when the first one started to work, and it felt strong. Realizing what he'd done, he thought it wise to get home before the second kicked in. With some difficulty, he found Joe, told him what had happened, excused himself, swore he'd be fine, and said goodbye. It was all a bit arduous, so he was quite glad to have to leave. Joe and Uli walked him to the door, and put him in a cab that was sitting there. They were careful to make sure the cab driver knew exactly where he was going. It was a licensed black cab, so they felt assured that Ryan would get home safe. They went back inside with nothing to worry about but what the next stage of their high would be like, and of course, every tragic person in the club.

29

When tripping on acid it's best not to do anything practical, especially if it *needs* doing. So, even without his faculties in order Ryan was aware that he couldn't let go and give into the acid. The luxury of enjoying his trip would have to wait. With fundamentals like comfort, security, and safety guaranteed, then he could devour, lush-out, and savor what promised to be the trip of a lifetime. The first step was getting home.

Until then, he had to concentrate on concentrating, focus on the basics of here and now, be careful not to let his mind wander off, get distracted and lost in the images around him; the vibrating angles of the buildings, how the reds and yellows of the McDonald's logo bickered.

The voice of the cabbie brought him back into his context. "Ampstead innit?"

" . . . Right . . ." Ryan's words stammered with hesitation as his present caught up to his speech. ". . . Cheers."

"Daydreamin' mate?"

"Yeah."

"Ome to the missus?"

Ryan didn't feel like chatting, but already it was helping keep his head together. "No," he said picturing Leila. "Not tonight."

"I get ya, mate."

A vague memory rose in Ryan's mind, but the driver's comment diverted his attention.

"Good club?"

"Probably."

"Interestin' crowd," said the cabbie in a bawdy way, clearly using the word *interesting* as a euphemism.

"What's interesting mean?" asked Ryan.

"Lotta the gays go there."

"Quite a lot." Ryan thought this a weird thing to say, but knew he was alone in finding it funny.

"Like 'em do ya?"

This time the implication goaded him, "I don't *not* like them."

The cabbie turned and asked over his shoulder, "Why'd ya go there then?"

Confused, "I don't know . . . Cause my mates do?"

"Don't get me wrong. Ain't got nuffink against 'em. As long as they don't touch the kiddies, they can do what they want."

Jesus, thought Ryan, people still speak this way. Then it dawned on him where he'd seen the cabbie before.

"We had you earlier, didn't we?"

The man gave a freakish disturbed look in his mirror. "Ain't nobody ad me, mate."

"I *mean*, you drove us to the club."

"Could of. Like I said I live 'round 'ere."

Like I said, Ryan repeated in his head, surely that meant he's said it before. Then he remembered. "You picked me up another time, too."

"Don't fink so."

"You *did*. From Trade. I was with a girl. She had purple hair. And she'd been sick."

"No, I'd av remembered. I got one a them photogenic memories."

Photographic, thought Ryan, with knee jerk response, *stupid*! Then he noticed the cabbie eyes in his rear-view mirror, but thought he was probably trying to recognize him.

The streets were quiet at this time of the morning, so the cab sped on. Occasionally they stopped at traffic lights or junctions, which gave Ryan a chance to take in his surroundings. It was only when still could he tell how much he was tripping.

"Yer me las' fare," said the driver.

"How come you were outside Trade?"

"Jus dropped off mate. It's yer lucky night innit."

"Right, those mini cabs really rip you off."

"Yer better off wiv a black cab."

After a few minutes of sitting in silence Ryan said, "Fuck!"

"Whassup?"

Ryan hadn't realised he'd spoken. He was just acknowledging a massive wave of acid. It came on unexpectedly, and was only just able to respond, "Nothing."

The driver talking into his mirror asked, "You all right?"

Ryan managed to muster, "Sweet!" Now he leaned against the window, his eyes beginning to roll and his lids flicker.

"Yer should get to bed mate," said the cabby. "Anyone

at 'ome to look after ya?"

"No . . . I'm cool."

"No one? Ya sure?"

Ryan attempted a nod; sick of talking, wishing the driver would shut up. He closed his eyes and fell into a full-on trip. With his eyes closed he could see the driver talking, could actually see the words. They came out as threatening and dangerous. Now, Leila was with him and they weren't in the cab anymore, but at home on one of the green sofas watching a film. David was there, too, and Joe with Uli. David began to cry, saying Joe didn't love him enough. It was Ryan's job to deal with this, to love him instead. Leila was David now, both just one person, sexual, passionate, and loving. Their breasts were butt cheeks, and their dicks were syringes. Uli merged with them, and Ryan set about loving them all.

"Ere ye go, mate."

Ryan opened his eyes. They were outside the house.

"Shit!" He came around. "That was quick."

"Fink ye nodded off or summink."

"Right." *I must be wasted*, he thought.

With difficulty Ryan managed to pay and get out of the cab.

"Need any 'elp?"

"I'm good," said Ryan, leaning on the cab for balance.

"You okay gettin in the 'ouse?"

"I'm sweet." He moved away from the cab and mustered up the mental energy it took to take steps. A cartoon he'd seen came to mind, in which the character was in a world that had the same toffee-like consistency as the one he tried to walk in now.

The driver watched his slow progression. Next was

the necessary activity of opening the front door. Keys had to be found in challenging and vast pockets. After going through each one methodically several times, he found them in the pocket he'd always kept them in, but wondered why he'd moved them. *Coordination*, he reminded himself. Damn! With difficulty he got the key in the door and turned. As it opened, he fell into the hallway. He picked himself up, feeling not just clumsy but disjointed. He leaned against the wall for support. As he closed the door, he looked back at the cab. It hadn't left yet, and the driver wasn't there. If Ryan wasn't so high, he might have thought it suspicious, but the overriding thought in his head was to get to bed. Once upstairs, as he passed David's and Joe's room on the way to his own room, he suddenly had a strong urge to be near David, so he went into his and Joe's room instead and lay on their bed.

He didn't bother to turn the light on. Laying there in the dark images of a baby came to mind. Comfort. Safe. No, he didn't feel right. He was normally good at navigating his trips, but he'd had too much coke and speed, so his thoughts raced, going from one negative idea to another. Maybe if he undressed and got free of the restraints of his clothes he'd feel better. That sometimes helped. He started to undress, but because he was still lying down, it was too difficult. With his jeans and boxers half way down, he gave up and lay naked from the waist to his knees. *Valium*, he thought. It would soften his trip. The trouble was he just wanted to feel nice, not get sleepy. *Special K* was the next on his list of antidotes. Fortunately, Joe always kept some in his beside drawer. In the dark, Ryan reached into the drawer and found the little brown bottle. He screwed open the little bottle but instead of hooking a scoop with a key, or measuring some on to the back of his hand first, he tipped the bottle and snorted the entire content of the bottle. *Fuck*, was one of the last thoughts he was capable of voicing within his head.

The drug started to take effect quickly, and it did what he'd hoped. No longer did he feel anxiety or anything much at all physically. In less than two minutes, he fell into a K-hole. How perfect. Was this as good as it gets? A womb might as well have been suspending him now. Drug bliss. The acid had already been distorting shape, color and Ryan's sense of reality, but now in addition to this, the K obliterated all his intuition, fucked his instincts, and left him entirely untroubled.

In the reality outside of his head, the cabbie smashed glass on the back door and gained entry. He crept cautiously through the downstairs, stopping, looking around in the half-light, and being spooked the unusual décor. At the bottom of the stairs he paused, straining to see up into the dark. Quietly he took his first few steps, but then the old boards squeaked underfoot. Damn! Instinctively, the cabbie held his breath, in an attempt to be quieter. He paused again, listened, but upstairs nobody stirred. The cabbie continued, getting closer and closer. Despite Ryan's complex internal self, its link to the everyday was tenuous, so to anybody who came upon him, he would appear to be nothing but a kid laying on a bed - with what Flora referred to as his 'smooth muscular thighs, his blond pubic hair, and his thick, brown, uncircumcised boy meat" - on display.

On the landing, after the bathroom, Joe's was the first

door the cabbie came to. It was open slightly. The cabbie stood calculating his next move. First, he listened, but could only hear random groaning noises. Next, he looked around the edge of the door. There was little light. All he could make out was a figure lying on a bed, and assumed it was the kid from his cab. He stepped into the room. The open door let in just enough light so that the cabbie could now see that the kid's eyes were closed, although his lids seemed to be flickering, and he rolled his head from side to side. Still, it was impossible to tell if he was asleep and dreaming, or just fucked up. It was best to be cautious. Again, he held his breath and took another few steps forward. *Shit*! A floorboard squeaked, *fuckin' loud*.

The kid heard and lifted his head with his eyes open wide. Then he slurred the word, "David!"

In the half-light, only the cabbie's outline was visible. "Thas right! David 'ere."

Even though Ryan faced the cabbie, his sight was focused within himself, on his internal world. He wasn't seeing anything actual, because he had no capacity to reason. All that was in his head was noise of various kinds, loads of it.

Now, the cabbie knelt on the bed with the kid beneath, and this is what went through his mind; *All them years of flirtin', teasin', an' tauntin' me, wiv that pritty mouf sayin, "Will ya take me?" I'll take ya. Wantin' me to take 'im. I'll give it to ya. Look at ya. Made yerself up all pritty like a girl, so I'd wanna fuck ya, wiv yer long blond hair, an' yer smoove skin. You bin after this ferevva. Wantin' me in yer cunt. Wha' ya sayin', ye want me to fuck yer 'ole? Legs spread, beggin' me ta fuck 'im, like a real geezer. Want me in yer cunt? I'll finger yer cunt, fuckin' 'ard! Can ya feel that?*

Ryan's eyes tore open. There was severe pain, but because he was in a K-hole, his brain disassociated it from his body and self. Besides this, his mind was busy, crowded with David. In this Ketamine state, he registered things on some level that had nothing to do with actually understanding it.

"Eh . . . pritty boy."

Synaptic sparks fired in Ryan's head, only they didn't turn into rational thought. *I love you, David*, was the nearest thing to anything that formed within Ryan. He actually thought he'd said it out loud, but he couldn't have, because a filthy hand was covering his mouth, almost suffocating him. Ryan had no grasp of what was really going on.

"Yer gonna get me geezer dick in yer cunt."

These words echoed through Ryan's head, crackling like an old radio. It sounded distant and remote. Maybe David was speaking to him from death.

Ryan had to answer *yes*. He'd have given him anything now to prove he loved him.

The man burst out laughing. "Yer said *yeah*. Yer dirty bastard." He laughed again. "Dumb cunt! Yer Cunt Boy." He stuck his finger into Ryan's butt again. "There ya go Cunt Boy. Tha's where ya wannit, innit! Keep yer eyes open, thas if yer wanna see, pretty boy? Yer'll never 'av a man like me in yer cunt again."

Glassy and vacant, Ryan's eyes opened wide. A thread of near-thought came from the fractured blackness, and the nearest thing to words it meant was, *I'm sorry, David*.

Ryan never allowed himself to grieve his uncle's death. He couldn't, because he blamed himself. He felt that David went down into the toilet at the exhibition to avoid him. After replaying their previous night together, so many times in his head, he always asked himself the same question; why didn't he say that he hadn't fucked David? In what way did he need his uncle to love him? He even felt that he'd instigated the whole thing. It was obvious David loved him, so why had he pushed it all towards sex?

Now in bed - underneath everything that was happening - Ryan cried with a lack of understanding, like a small child.

In order to get at Ryan's butt the cabbie hitched Ryan up onto and over the headboard of the bed. He jabbed his finger into the little hole with great force. It made him bleed.

"Don't let yer cunt get all messy on me now."

The words smeared around inside Ryan's head even as he managed to say, "I love you."

"Pretty boy loves *me*," said the cabby and let out a loud greedy laugh.

This noise woke Leila. Not in her own bed at home in her mum's house she was disorientated. In the glow of the nightlight beside the bed, she saw that the walls were painted with coloured disks and there were cascades of fairy lights that fell from the ceiling in each corner of the room. She recognised her surroundings, and this made her smile, filled with love and happiness. It was her baby's room in London. She'd been lying naked, waiting to surprise him. Further more, she'd died her hair white and wore it piled up on top like Marie

Antoinette. Her face was also white with scarlet rouge high on her cheeks. This was all an elaborate attempt to surprise, entertain and seduce Ryan.

Although still not having woken properly, she was excited. Yet something disturbed her. The noise. It was a man's voice, but it sounded strange. It kept repeating things, as though looped. Ryan might be home, and now that she was awake, she didn't want to wait. One of his old t-shirts lay on the floor beside the bed, and she put it on as she got out. Modesty wasn't exactly a character trait of Leila's, but Joe might have guests. Uncharacteristically, she didn't want to shock or embarrass them.

Quietly, she opened the door of her bedroom and crept out into the hallway. The voice was coming from Joe's room next door. Along the landing she snuck, careful to walk close to the wall where the boards creaked less. Her plan was to listen at the door, until she knew what was going on. The voice got louder as she approached. When right beside the doorframe she could hear the vulgar language. *Nobody speaks like that*, she thought. *It must be a joke*. The she realised, Joe must be having sex with somebody. She held her hand over her mouth to stop herself giggling and listened a little longer. No. Joe wouldn't have sex with anybody who spoke to him like that. Then it fell into place. *How silly*, she thought. It was the soundtrack to porn. Obviously nobody was having sex, or even just jerking off, because the door was open. It must just be some kind of joke. Maybe Joe was showing Flora or Ryan something he'd found on the Internet. It did sound completely over the top. Leila thought she should do something silly herself, so she decided to get her gun from her purse and pretend that she thought somebody was attacking Joe. To make it even better she pulled off her t-shirt. This would make it all the more comical, her standing in the doorway with white hair, naked, with a gun in her hand. She could hardly stop herself from laughing.

After fetching her gun, she stood beside the doorframe with legs wide apart, arms stretched out in front of her, and her gun held firmly in both hands. Her mental image was *Charlie's Angels*. Silently she slid around the doorframe, then strode into the doorway and threw on the lights. "Stick 'em up, scum!"

It wasn't Joe. Who the fuck was it! Fear shot through her. Someone was crouching on the bed.

She screamed. It was a stranger. Instantly, he turned his head and froze, his eyes unhinged, yet intensely focused on Leila.

Now that he faced her she recognized the man. Even more shocked, Leila screamed again. Then she saw Ryan folded over the head of the bed, and the man's hands were covered in blood. *Fight*, was her instant reaction. Her only thought, *stop*.

With pure rage, she cried, "Get off him!"

What happened next took place so quickly that she had no time to register it. The full weight of the cabbie smashed Leila back against the wall. The gun fired. She collapsed to the floor. He tore downstairs and out the front door. Fortunately, a neighbour had seen him lurking earlier and called the police. The cabbie ran straight into them.

Leila dragged herself off the floor. Disoriented, she clambered onto her knees. Her heart pounded as she looked into Joe's room. When she saw Ryan slumped lifeless she screamed again.

On hearing this, two officers rushed up the stairs of the house. When at the entrance of the room the first thing they noticed was a pair crumpled on a bed in a heap. The second was the firearm. This had to be dealt with before anything else. A blond officer with heavy acne scars promptly stepped towards it, and nudged it towards the doorway with his foot. The other, taller, red haired officer carefully picked it up.

The blond officer who seemed in charge said, "Miss?" Then when not getting a response he repeated, "Miss!" Again Leila didn't respond. Next, he tried to move her, but she was like deadweight and wouldn't budge. "Give me a hand," he said to the red-haired officer, "First, let's get some light in here." The blond drew back a pair of heavy velvet curtains and then wound-up a blackout blind.

The red haired officer pointed up to the ceiling where the bullet had blasted a hole. The blond followed his line of sight, while at the same time he took hold of Ryan's wrist to see if he had a pulse. Next he listened for breathing, and then he pulled back his eyes lids to check he was responsive to light.

Red picked up the little brown bottle and said, "I think he's taken something."

"Any idea what?"

"It's not cocaine, tastes too salty."

"Miss!" said Blond, "What's he taken?"

Leila could barely speak, but managed, "I don't know!" As the light from the window fell on our pair it made Leila's hair look brittle, and her make-up uneven, plus now she was smeared with blood. All the while, with desperation, she clutched onto Ryan's hand. With a whimper she said, "Is he alive?"

Blond spoke into his radio, calling for an ambulance. Then to Leila he said, "We'll get him to a hospital as soon as we can."

With more of a cry than real words, she said again, "Is he alive?"

"He's breathing. When the ambulance gets here we'll know more."

As the minutes passed, the light from the window crawled further into the room, and now it was at the bedside table. On it, leaning against his lamp was an old photo worn with tattered edges. It was of a little boy - Ryan - and two handsome men - David and Joe. They were all on a water park theme ride. The shot was taken just as they splashed through a trough of water. Ryan was sitting in the middle and had his hands in the air while screeching with joy. He looked as though - at that moment in time - he was the happiest boy in the entire world. At his side was Joe looking proud, content and lucky as fuck. On the other side, and holding tightly to both was David. He looked the happiest, proudest, and luckiest of all.

Adult film legend **Aiden Shaw** is the author of the best-selling memoir, *My Undoing: Love in the Thick of Sex, Drugs, Pornography, and Prostitution* and the series of novels *Brutal, Wasted,* and *Boundaries.* Born in London, Shaw made his way to Hollywood where he was discovered by gay adult film director and industry sensation Chi Chi La Rue. Shaw has appeared in more than 50 films earning him international acclaim, as well as the distinction of serving as the namesake for *Sex and the City*'s own Aiden Shaw character. More recently the author studied at Goldsmiths University of London where he received a Masters Degree in Creative and Life Writing. Shaw divides his time between London and the U.S. Visit him online at www.aidenshaw.com.